Praise for *Firefly Lane*

"Hannah's latest is a moving and realistic portrait of a complex and enduring friendship." —*Booklist*

"A lovely, touching read that examines one of the most important things in our lives: enduring friendship." —Elizabeth Buchan, author of *Revenge of the Middle-Aged Woman*

"Although I look forward to every one of her books, *Firefly Lane* just may be Kristin Hannah's most important work yet. It is a gift you should give to yourself and then share with every other woman in your life." —Rene Kirkpatrick, All for Kids & Grown-ups Too

"A tearjerker that is sure to please the author's many fans." —*Library Journal*

"I can't remember the last time a book haunted me this much. Long after I turned the last page, I shed tears for the love, laughter, heartache, and loyalty tenderly depicted in *Firefly Lane*. A stunner." —Danielle Marshall, Powell's Books

"You will love *Firefly Lane*, Kristin Hannah's poignant, warmhearted valentine to a thirty-year friendship between two fascinating women. Heartbreaking and funny, clear-eyed and sweet, *Firefly Lane* is honest, deeply felt, and addictive. It reminds us why we love to read." —Patricia Gaffney, author of *The Saving Graces*

"This exceptional story will move you and reaffirm the needs of life that only women can fill for each other." —Holly Frakes, Schuler Books & Music

FIREFLY LANE

Kristin Hannah

St. Martin's Paperbacks

Published in the United States by St. Martin's Paperbacks, an imprint of St. Martin's Publishing Group

FIREFLY LANE

For information, address St. Martin's Publishing Group, 120 Broadway, New York, NY 10271.

www.stmartins.com

Library of Congress Catalog Card Number: 2007040442

ISBN: 978-1-250-78798-9

Our books may be purchased in bulk for promotional, educational, or business use. Please contact your local bookseller or the Macmillan Corporate and Premium Sales Department at 1-800-221-7945, ext. 5442, or by email at MacmillanSpecialMarkets@macmillan.com.

Printed in the United States of America

St. Martin's Press hardcover edition / February 2008
St. Martin's Griffin edition / January 2009
St. Martin's Paperbacks edition 2021

10 9 8 7 6 5 4 3

This book is dedicated to "us." The girls.
Friends who see one another through the hard times,
big and small, year in and year out. You know
who you are.
Thanks;

To the people who make up so many of my memories:
my father, Laurence; my brother, Kent; my sister,
Laura; my husband, Benjamin; and my son, Tucker.
Wherever we all go in the world,
you are in my heart;

And to my mom, who inspires so many of my novels;
this one most of all.

ACKNOWLEDGMENTS

Thanks go out to:

Marianne McClary, for helping out on the TV and broadcasting stuff. Your expertise was invaluable. Thanks.

Jennifer Enderlin, Jill Marie Landis, Kim Fisk, Andrea Cirillo, and Megan Chance. Each of you helped me find the path of this story. Thanks.

The fabulous team at St. Martin's Press: Thank you for this opportunity.

The best mirror is an old friend.

—GEORGE HERBERT

CHAPTER ONE

They used to be called the Firefly Lane girls. That was a long time ago—more than three decades—but just now, as she lay in bed listening to a winter storm raging outside, it seemed like yesterday.

In the past week (unquestionably the worst seven days of her life), she'd lost the ability to distance herself from the memories. Too often lately in her dreams it was 1974; she was a teenager again, coming of age in the shadow of a lost war, riding her bike beside her best friend in a darkness so complete it was like being invisible. The place was relevant only as a reference point, but she remembered it in vivid detail: a meandering ribbon of asphalt bordered on either side by gullies of murky water and hillsides of shaggy grass. Before they met, that road seemed to go nowhere at all; it was just a country lane named after an insect no one had ever seen in this rugged blue and green corner of the world.

Then they saw it through each other's eyes. When they stood together on the rise of the hill, instead of towering trees and muddy potholes and distant snowy mountains, they saw all the places they would someday go. At night, they sneaked out of their neighboring houses and met on that road. On the banks of the Pilchuck River they smoked stolen cigarettes, cried to the lyrics of "Billy, Don't Be a Hero," and told each other everything, stitching their lives together until by summer's end no one knew where one girl ended and the other began. They became to everyone who knew them simply TullyandKate, and for more than thirty years that friendship was the bulkhead of their lives: strong, durable, solid. The music might have changed with the decades, but the promises made on Firefly Lane remained.

Best friends forever.

They'd believed it would last, that vow, that someday they'd be old women, sitting in their rocking chairs on a creaking deck, talking about the times of their lives, and laughing.

Now she knew better, of course. For more than a year she'd been telling herself it was okay, that she could go on without a best friend. Sometimes she even believed it.

Then she would hear the music. Their music. "Goodbye Yellow Brick Road." "Material Girl." "Bohemian Rhapsody." "Purple Rain." Yesterday, while she'd been shopping, a bad Muzak version of "You've Got a Friend" had made her cry, right there next to the radishes.

She eased the covers back and got out of bed, being careful not to waken the man sleeping beside her. For a moment she stood there, staring down at him in the shadowy darkness. Even in sleep, he wore a troubled expression.

She took the phone off its hook and left the bedroom, walking down the quiet hallway toward the deck. There, she stared out at the storm and gathered her courage. As she punched in the familiar numbers, she wondered what she would say to her once-best friend after all these silent months, how she would start. *I've had a bad week . . . my life is falling apart . . .* or simply: *I need you.*

Across the black and turbulent Sound, the phone rang.

Part One

THE SEVENTIES

Dancing Queen

young and sweet,
only seventeen

CHAPTER TWO

For most of the country, 1970 was a year of upheaval and change, but in the house on Magnolia Drive, everything was orderly and quiet. Inside, ten-year-old Tully Hart sat on a cold wooden floor, building a Lincoln Log cabin for her Liddle Kiddles, who were asleep on tiny pink Kleenexes. If she were in her bedroom, she would have had a Jackson Five forty-five in her Close 'N Play, but in the living room, there wasn't even a radio.

Her grandma didn't like music much, or television or board games. Mostly—like now—Grandma sat in her rocking chair by the fireplace, doing needlepoint. She made hundreds of samplers, most of which quoted the Bible. At Christmastime she donated them to the church, where they were sold at fundraisers.

And Grandpa . . . well, he couldn't help being quiet. Ever since his stroke, he just stayed in bed. Sometimes he rang his bell, and that was the only time Tully ever saw her grandma hurry. At the first tinkling of the bell, she'd smile and say, "Oh, my," and run for the hallway as fast as her slippered feet would take her.

Tully reached for her yellow-haired Troll. Humming very quietly, she made him dance with Calamity Kiddle to "Daydream Believer." Halfway through the song, there was a knock at the door.

It was such an unexpected sound that Tully paused in her playing and looked up. Except for Sundays, when Mr. and Mrs. Beattle showed up to take them to church, no one ever came to visit.

Gran put her needlework in the pink plastic bag by her chair and got up, crossing the room in that slow, shuffling way that had become normal in the last few years. When she opened the door, there was a long silence, then she said, "Oh, my."

Gran's voice sounded weird. Peering sideways, Tully saw a tall woman with long messy hair and a smile that wouldn't stay in place. She was one of the prettiest women Tully had ever seen: milky skin, a sharp, pointed nose and high cheekbones that slashed above her tiny chin, liquid brown eyes that opened and closed slowly.

"Thass not much of a greeting for your long-lost daughter." The lady pushed past Grandma and walked straight to Tully, then bent down. "Is this my little Tallulah Rose?"

Daughter? That meant—

"Mommy?" she whispered in awe, afraid to believe it. She'd waited so long for this, dreamed of it: her mommy coming back.

"Did you miss me?"

"Oh, *yes,*" Tully said, trying not to laugh. But she was so happy.

Gran closed the door. "Why don't you come into the kitchen for a cup of coffee?"

"I didn't come back for coffee. I came for my daughter."

"You're broke," Grandma said tiredly.

Her mother looked irritated. "So what if I am?"

"Tully needs—"

"I think I can figure out what my daughter needs." Her mother seemed to be trying to stand straight, but it wasn't working. She was kind of wobbly and her eyes looked funny. She twirled a strand of long, wavy hair around her finger.

Gran moved toward them. "Raising a child is a big responsibility, Dorothy. Maybe if you moved in here for a while and got to know Tully, you'd be ready . . ." She paused, then frowned and said quietly, "You're drunk."

Mommy giggled and winked at Tully.

Tully winked back. Drunk wasn't so bad. Her grandpa used to drink lots before he got sick. Even Gran sometimes had a glass of wine.

"Iss my birthday, Mother, or have you forgotten?"

"Your birthday?" Tully shot to her feet. "Wait here," she said, then ran to her room. Her heart was racing as she dug through her vanity drawer, scattering her stuff everywhere, looking for the macaroni and bead necklace she'd made her mom at Bible school last year. Gran had frowned when she saw it, told her not to get her hopes up, but Tully hadn't been able to do that. Her hopes had been up for years. Shoving it in her pocket, she rushed back out, just in time to hear her mommy say,

"I'm not drunk, Mother, dear. I'm with my kid again for the first time in three years. Love is the ultimate high."

"Six years. She was four the last time you dropped her off here."

"That long ago?" Mommy said, looking confused.

"Move back home, Dorothy. I can help you."

"Like you did last time? No, thanks."

Last time? Mommy had come back before?

Gran sighed, then stiffened. "How long are you going to hold all that against me?"

"It's hardly the kind of thing that has an expiration date, is it? Come on, Tallulah." Her mom lurched toward the door.

Tully frowned. This wasn't how it was supposed to happen. Her mommy hadn't hugged her or kissed her or asked how she was. And everyone knew you were supposed to pack a suitcase to leave. She pointed at her bedroom door. "My stuff—"

"You don't need that materialistic shit, Tallulah."

"Huh?" Tully didn't understand.

Gran pulled her into a hug that smelled sweetly familiar, of talcum powder and hair spray. These were the only arms that had ever hugged Tully, this was the only person who'd ever made her feel safe, and suddenly she was afraid. "Gran?" she said, pulling back. "What's happening?"

"You're coming with me," Mommy said, reaching out to the doorframe to steady herself.

Her grandmother clutched her by the shoulders, gave her a little shake. "You know our phone number and address, right? You call us if you get scared or something goes wrong." She was crying; seeing her strong, quiet grandmother cry scared and confused Tully. What was going on? What had she done wrong already?

"I'm sorry, Gran, I—"

Mommy swooped over and grabbed her by the shoulder, shaking her hard. "Don't *ever* say you're sorry. It makes you look pathetic. Come on." She took Tully's hand and pulled her toward the door.

Tully stumbled along behind her mother, out of the house and down the steps and across the street to a rusted VW bus that had plastic flower decals all over it and a giant yellow peace symbol painted on the side.

The door opened; thick gray smoke rolled out. Through the haze she saw three people in the van. A black man with a huge afro and a red headband was in the driver's seat. In the back was a woman in a fringed vest and striped pants, with a brown kerchief over her blond hair; beside her sat a man in bell-bottoms and a ratty T-shirt. Brown shag carpeting covered the van floor; a few pipes lay scattered about, mixed up with empty beer bottles, food wrappers, and eight-track tapes.

"This is my kid, Tallulah," Mom said.

Tully didn't say anything, but she hated to be called Tallulah. She'd tell her mommy that later, when they were alone.

"Far out," someone said.

"She looks just like you, Dot. It blows my mind."

"Get in," the driver said gruffly. "We're gonna be late."

The man in the dirty T-shirt reached for Tully, grabbed her around the waist, and swung her into the van, where she positioned herself carefully on her knees.

Mom climbed inside and slammed the door shut. Strange music pulsed through the van. All she could make out were a few words: *some-thin' happenin' here* . . . Smoke made everything look soft and vaguely out of focus.

Tully edged closer to the metal side to make room beside her, but Mom sat next to the lady in the kerchief. They immediately started talking about pigs and marches and a man named Kent. None of it made sense to Tully and the smoke was making her dizzy. When the man beside her lit up his pipe, she couldn't help the little sigh of disappointment that leaked from her mouth.

The man heard it and turned to her. Exhaling a cloud of gray smoke right into her face, he smiled. "Jus' go with the flow, li'l girl."

"Look at the way my mother has her dressed," Mommy said bitterly. "Like she's some little doll. How's she s'posed to be *real* if she can't get dirty?"

"Right on, Dot," the guy said, blowing smoke out of his mouth and leaning back.

Mommy looked at Tully for the first time; really *looked* at her. "You remember that, kiddo. Life isn't about cooking and cleaning and havin' babies. It's about bein' free. Doin' your own thing. You can be the fucking president of the United States if you want."

"We could use a new president, thass for sure," the driver said.

The woman in the headband patted Mom's thigh. "Thass tellin' it like it is. Pass me that bong, Tom." She giggled. "Hey, that's almost a rhyme."

Tully frowned, feeling a new kind of shame in the pit of her stomach. She thought she looked pretty in this dress. And she didn't want to be the president. She wanted to be a ballerina.

Mostly, though, she wanted her mommy to love her. She edged sideways until she was actually close enough to her mother to touch her. "Happy birthday," she said quietly, reaching into her pocket. She pulled out the necklace she'd worked so hard on, agonized over, really, still gluing glitter on long after the other kids had gone out to play. "I made this for you."

Mom snagged the necklace and closed her fingers around it. Tully waited and waited for her mom to say thank you and put the necklace on, but she didn't; she just sat there, swaying to the music, talking to her friends.

Tully finally closed her eyes. The smoke was making her sleepy. For most of her life she'd missed her mommy, and not like you missed a toy you couldn't find or a friend who stopped coming over to play because you wouldn't share. She *missed* her mommy. It was always inside her, an empty space that ached in the daytime and turned into a sharp pain at night. She'd promised herself that if her mommy ever came back, she'd be good. Perfect. Whatever she'd done or said that was so wrong, she'd fix or change. More than anything she wanted to make her mommy proud.

But now she didn't know what to do. In her dreams, they'd always gone off together alone, just the two of them, holding hands.

"Here we are," her dream mommy always said as they walked up the hill to their house. "Home sweet home." Then she'd kiss Tully's cheek and whisper, "I missed you so much. I was gone because—"

"Tallulah. Wake up."

Tully came awake with a jolt. Her head was pounding and her throat hurt. When she tried to say, *Where are we?* all that came out was a croak.

Everyone laughed at that and kept laughing as they bundled out of the van.

On this busy downtown Seattle street, there were people everywhere, chanting and yelling and holding up signs that read MAKE LOVE NOT WAR, and HELL NO, WE WON'T GO. Tully had never seen so many people in one place.

Mommy took hold of her hand, pulled her close.

The rest of the day was a blur of people chanting slogans and singing songs. Tully spent every moment terrified that she'd somehow let go of her mother's hand and be swept away by the crowd. She didn't feel any safer when the policemen showed up because they had guns on their belts and sticks in their hands and plastic shields that protected their faces.

But all the crowd did was march and all the police did was watch.

By the time it got dark, she was tired and hungry and her head ached, but they just kept walking, up one street and down another. The crowd was different now; they'd put away their signs and started drinking. Sometimes she heard whole sentences or pieces of conversation, but none of it made sense.

"Did you see those pigs? They were *dyin'* to knock our teeth out, but we were peaceful, man. Couldn't touch us. Hey, Dot, you're bogarting the joint."

Everyone around them laughed, Mommy most of all. Tully couldn't figure out what was going on and she had a terrible headache. People swelled around them, dancing and laughing. From somewhere, music spilled into the street.

And then, suddenly, she was holding on to nothing.

"Mommy!" she screamed.

No one answered or turned to her, even though there were people everywhere. She pushed through the bodies, screaming for her mommy until her voice failed her. Finally, she went back to where she'd last seen her mommy and waited at the curb.

She'll be back.

Tears stung her eyes and leaked down her face as she sat there waiting, trying to be brave.

But her mommy never came back.

For years afterward, she tried to remember what had happened next, what she did, but all those people were like a cloud that obscured her memories. All she ever remembered was waking up on a dirty cement stoop along a street that was totally empty, seeing a policeman on horseback.

From his perch high above her, he frowned down at her and said, "Hey, little one, are you all alone?"

"I am," was all she could say without crying.

He took her back to the house on Queen Anne Hill, where her grandma held her tightly and kissed her cheek and told her it wasn't her fault.

But Tully knew better. Somehow today she'd done

something wrong, been bad. Next time her mommy came back, she'd try harder. She'd promise to be the president and she'd never, ever say she was sorry again.

Tully got a chart of the presidents of the United States and memorized every name in order. For months afterward, she told anyone who asked that she would be the first woman president; she even quit taking ballet classes. On her eleventh birthday, while Grandma lit the candles on her cake and sang a thin, watery version of "Happy Birthday," Tully glanced repeatedly at the door, thinking, *This is it,* but no one ever knocked and the phone didn't ring. Later, with the opened boxes of her gifts around her, she tried to keep smiling. In front of her, on the coffee table, was an empty scrapbook. As a present, it sort of sucked, but her grandma always gave her stuff like this—projects to keep her busy and quiet.

"She didn't even call," Tully said, looking up.

Gran sighed tiredly. "Your mom has . . . problems, Tully. She's weak and confused. You've got to quit pretending things are different. What matters is that you're strong."

She'd heard this advice a bazillion times. "I know."

Gran sat down on the worn floral sofa beside Tully and pulled her onto her lap.

Tully loved it when Gran held her. She snuggled in close, rested her cheek on Gran's soft chest.

"I wish things were different with your mama, Tully, and that's the God's honest truth, but she's a lost soul. Has been for a long time."

"Is that why she doesn't love me?"

Gran looked down at her. The black horn-rimmed glasses magnified her pale gray eyes. "She loves you, in her way. That's why she keeps coming back."

"It doesn't feel like love."

"I know."

"I don't think she even likes me."

"It's me she doesn't like. Something happened a long time ago and I didn't . . . Well, it doesn't matter now." Gran tightened her hold on Tully. "Someday she'll be sorry she missed these years with you. I'm certain of that."

"I could show her my scrapbook."

Gran didn't look at her. "That would be nice." After a long silence, she said, "Happy birthday, Tully," and kissed her forehead. "Now I'd best go sit with your grandfather. He's feeling poorly today."

After her grandmother left the room, Tully sat there, staring down at the blank first page of her new scrapbook. It would be the perfect thing to give her mother one day, to show her what she'd missed. But how would Tully fill it? She had a few photographs of herself, taken mostly by her friends' moms at parties and on field trips, but not many. Her gran's eyes weren't good enough for those tiny viewfinders. And she had only the one picture of her mom.

She picked up a pen and very carefully wrote the date in the upper right-hand corner; then she frowned. What else? *Dear Mommy. Today was my eleventh birthday . . .*

After that day, she collected artifacts from her life. School pictures, sports pictures, movie ticket stubs. For years whenever she had a good day, she hurried home and wrote about it, pasting down whatever receipt or ticket proved where she had been or what she'd done. Somewhere along the way she started adding little embellishments to make herself look better. They weren't lies, really, just exaggerations. Anything that would make her mom someday say she was proud of her. She filled that scrapbook and then another and another. On every birthday, she received a brand-new book, until she moved into the teen years.

Something happened to her then. She wasn't sure what it was, maybe the breasts that grew faster than anyone else's, or maybe it was just that she got tired of putting her life down on pieces of paper no one ever asked to see. By fourteen, she was done. She put all her little-girl books in a big cardboard box and shoved them to the back of her closet, and she asked Gran not to buy her any more.

"Are you sure, honey?"

"Yeah," had been her answer. She didn't care about her mother anymore and tried never to think about her. In fact, at school, she told everyone that her mom had died in a boating accident.

The lie freed her. She quit buying her clothes in the little-girls departments and spent her time in the juniors area. She bought tight, midriff-baring shirts that showed off her new boobs and low-rise bellbottoms that made her butt look good. She had to hide these clothes from Gran, but it was easy to do; a puffy down vest and a quick wave could get her out of the house in whatever she wanted to wear.

She learned that if she dressed carefully and acted a certain way, the cool kids wanted to hang out with her. On Friday and Saturday nights, she told Gran she was staying at a friend's house and went roller-skating at Lake Hills, where no one ever asked about her family or looked at her as if she were "poor Tully." She learned to smoke cigarettes without coughing and to chew gum to camouflage the smell on her breath.

By eighth grade, she was one of the most popular girl in junior high, and it helped, having all those friends. When she was busy enough, she didn't think about the woman who didn't want her.

On rare days she still felt . . . not quite lonely . . . but something. Adrift, maybe. As if all the people she hung around with were place-holders.

Today was one of those days. She sat in her regular seat on the school bus, hearing the buzz of gossip go on around her. Everyone seemed to be talking about family things; she had nothing to add to the conversations. She knew nothing about fighting with your little brother or being grounded for talking back to your parents or going to the mall with your mom. Thankfully, when the bus pulled up to her stop, she hurried off, making a big show of saying goodbye to her friends, laughing loudly and waving. Pretending; she did a lot of that lately.

After the bus drove away, she repositioned her backpack over her shoulder and started the long walk home. She had just turned the corner when she saw it.

There, parked across the street, in front of Gran's house, was a beat-up red VW bus. The flower decals were still on the side.

CHAPTER THREE

It was still dark when Kate Mularkey's alarm clock rang. She groaned and lay there, staring up at the peaked ceiling. The thought of going to school made her sick.

Eighth grade blew chips as far as she was concerned; 1974 had turned out to be a totally sucky year, a social desert. Thank God there was a month left of school. Not that the summer promised to be any better.

In sixth grade she'd had two best friends; they'd done everything together—showed their horses in 4-H, gone to youth group, and ridden their bikes from one house to the next. The summer they turned twelve, all that ended. Her friends went wild; there was no other way to put it. They smoked pot before school and skipped classes and never missed a party. When she wouldn't join in, they cut her loose. Period. And the "good" kids wouldn't come near her because she'd been part of the stoners' club. So now books were her only friends. She'd read *Lord of the Rings* so often she could recite whole scenes by memory.

It was not a skill that aided one in becoming popular.

With a sigh, she got out of bed. In the tiny upstairs closet that had recently been turned into a bathroom, she took a quick shower and braided her straight blond hair, then put on her spazo horn-rimmed glasses. They were hopelessly out of date now—round and rimless were what the cool kids wore—but her dad said they couldn't afford new glasses yet.

Downstairs, she went to the back door, folded her belled pant leg around each calf, and stepped into the huge black rubber boots they kept on the concrete steps. Moving like Neil Armstrong, she made her way through the deep mud to the shed out back. Their old quarterhorse mare limped up to the fence, whinnied a greeting. "Heya, Sweetpea," Kate said, throwing a flake of hay onto the ground, and then scratching the horse's velvety ear.

"I miss you, too," she said, and it was true. Two years ago they'd been inseparable; Kate had ridden this mare all that summer, and won plenty of ribbons at the Snohomish County Fair.

But things changed fast. She knew that now. A horse could get old overnight and go lame. A friend could become a stranger just as quickly.

"'Bye." She clomped back up the dark, muddy driveway and left her dirty boots on the porch.

When she opened the back door, she stepped into pandemonium. Mom stood at the stove, dressed in her faded floral housedress and fuzzy pink slippers, smoking an Eve menthol cigarette and pouring batter into an oblong electric frying pan. Her shoulder-length brown hair was divided into two scrawny pigtails; each one was held in place by a strand of hot-pink ribbon. "Set the table, Katie," she said without glancing up. "Sean! Get down here."

Kate did as she was told. Almost before she was finished, her mother was behind her, pouring milk into the glasses.

"Sean—breakfast," Mom yelled up the stairs again. This time she added the magic words: "I've poured the milk."

Within seconds eight-year-old Sean came running down the stairs and rushed toward the beige speckled Formica table, giggling as he tripped over the Labrador puppy who'd recently joined the family.

Kate was just about to sit down at her regular place when she happened to glance across the kitchen and into the living room. Through the large window above the sofa, she saw something that surprised her: A moving van was turning into the driveway across the street.

"Wow." She carried her plate through the two rooms and stood at the window, staring out over their three acres and down on the house across the street. It had been vacant for as long as anyone could remember.

She heard her mother's footsteps coming up behind her; hard on the fake brick linoleum of the kitchen floor, quiet in the moss-green carpeting of the living room.

"Someone's moving in across the street," Kate said.

"Really?"

No. I'm lying.

"Maybe they'll have a girl your age. It would be nice for you to have a friend."

Kate bit back an irritated retort. Only mothers thought it was easy to make friends in junior high. "Whatever." She turned away abruptly, taking her plate into the hallway, where she finished her breakfast in peace beneath the portrait of Jesus.

As expected, Mom followed her. She stood by the tapestry wall hanging of *The Last Supper,* saying nothing.

"What?" Kate snapped when she couldn't take it anymore.

Mom's sigh was so quiet it could hardly be heard. "Why are we always bickering lately?"

"You're the one who starts it."

"By saying hello and asking how you're doing? Yeah, I'm a real witch."

"You said it, not me."

"It's not my fault, you know."

"What isn't?"

"That you don't have any friends. If you'd—"

Kate walked away. Honest to St. Jude, one more if-you'd-only-try-harder speech and she might puke.

Thankfully—for once—Mom didn't follow her. Instead, she went back into the kitchen, calling out, "Hurry up, Sean. The Mularkey school bus leaves in ten minutes."

Her brother giggled. Kate rolled her eyes and went upstairs. It was so lame. How could her brother laugh at the same stupid joke every day?

The answer came as quickly as the question had: because he had friends. Life with friends made everything easier.

She hid in her bedroom until she heard the old Ford station wagon start up. The last thing she wanted was to get driven to school by her mom, who yelled good-bye and waved like a contestant on *The Price Is Right* when Kate got out of the car. Everyone knew it was social suicide to be driven to school by your parents. When she heard tires crunching slowly across gravel, she went back downstairs, washed the dishes, gathered her stuff, and left the house. Outside, the sun was shining, but last night's rain had studded the driveway with inner-tube-sized potholes. No doubt the old-timers down at the hardware store were already starting to talk about the flooding. Mud sucked at the soles of her fake Earth shoes, making her progress slow. So intent was she on saving her only rainbow socks that she was at the bottom of the driveway before she noticed the girl standing across the street.

She was gorgeous. Tall and big-boobed, she had long, curly auburn hair and a face like Caroline of Monaco: pale skin and full lips and long lashes. And her *clothes*: low-rise, three-button jeans with huge, tie-dyed wedges of fabric in the seams to make elephant bells; cork-bottomed platform shoes with four-inch heels; and an angel-sleeved pink peasant blouse that revealed at least two inches of stomach.

Kate clutched her books against her chest, wishing she hadn't picked her pimples last night. Or that her jeans weren't Sears Rough Riders. "H-hi," she said, stopping on her side of the road. "The bus stops on this side."

Chocolate-brown eyes, rimmed heavily with black mascara and shiny blue eye shadow, stared at her, revealing nothing.

Just then, the school bus arrived. Wheezing and squeaking, it came to a shuddering stop on the road. A boy she used to have a crush on stuck his head out the window and yelled, "Hey, Kootie, the flood's over," and then laughed.

Kate put her head down and boarded the bus. Collapsing into her usual front-row seat—by herself—she kept her head bowed, waiting for the new girl to walk past her, but no one else got on. When the doors thumped shut and the bus lurched forward, she dared to look back at the road.

The coolest-looking girl in the world wasn't there.

Already Tully didn't fit in. It had taken two hours to choose her clothes this morning—an outfit right out of the pages of *Seventeen* magazine—and every bit of it was wrong.

When the school bus drove up, she made a split-second

decision. She wasn't going to go to school in this hick backwater. Snohomish might be less than an hour from downtown Seattle, but as far as she was concerned, she might as well be on the moon. That was how alien this place felt.

No.

Hell, no.

She marched down the gravel driveway and shoved the front door open so hard it cracked against the wall.

Drama, she'd learned, was like good punctuation: it underscored your point.

"You must be high," she said loudly, realizing a second too late that the only people in the living room were the moving men.

One of them paused and looked wearily her way. "Huh?"

She pushed past them, grazing the armoire so hard they swore under their breath. Not that she cared. She hated it when she felt like this, all puffed up with anger.

She wouldn't let her so-called mother make her feel twisted up inside, not after all the times that woman had abandoned her.

In the master bedroom, her mom was sitting on the floor, cutting pictures out of *Cosmo*. As usual, her long hair was a wavy, fuzzy nightmare held in check by a grossly out-of-date beaded leather headband. Without looking up, she flipped to the next page, where a naked, grinning Burt Reynolds covered his penis with one hand.

"I'm *not* going to this backwater school. They're a bunch of hicks."

"Oh." Mom flipped to the next page, then reached for her scissors and began cutting out a spray of flowers from a Breck ad. "Okay."

Tully wanted to scream. "Okay? *Okay?* I'm fourteen years old."

"My job is to love and support you, baby, not to get in your face."

Tully closed her eyes, counted to ten, and said again, "I don't have any friends here."

"Make new ones. I heard you were Miss Popular at your old school."

"Come on, Mom, I—"

"Cloud."

"I'm not calling you Cloud."

"Fine, Tallulah." Mom looked up to make sure her point had been made. It had.

"I don't belong here."

"You know better than that, Tully. You're a child of the earth and sky; you belong everywhere. The Bhaga-vad Gita says . . ."

"That's it." Tully walked away while her mother was still talking. The last thing she wanted to hear was some drug-soaked advice that belonged on a black-light poster. On the way out, she snagged a pack of Virginia Slims from her mom's purse and headed for the road.

For the next week, Kate watched the new girl from a distance.

Tully Hart was boldly, coolly different; brighter, somehow, than everyone else in the faded green hall-ways. She had no curfew and didn't care if she got caught smoking in the woods behind the school. Every-one talked about it. Kate heard the whispered awe in their voices. For a group of kids who'd grown up in the dairy farms and paper mill workers' homes of the Sno-homish Valley, Tully Hart was exotic. Everyone wanted to be friends with her.

Her neighbor's instant popularity made Kate's alien-ation more unbearable. She wasn't sure why it wounded her so much. All she knew was that every morning, as they stood at the bus stop beside each other and yet worlds apart, separated by yawning silence, Kate felt a desperate desire to be acknowledged by Tully.

Not that it would ever happen.

". . . before *The Carol Burnett Show* starts. It's ready now. Kate? Katie?"

Kate lifted her head from the table. She'd fallen asleep on her open social studies textbook at the kitchen table. "Huh? What did you say?" she asked, pushing her heavy glasses back up into place.

"I made Hamburger Helper for our new neighbors. I want you to take it across the street."

"But . . ." Kate tried to think of an excuse, anything that would get her out of this. "They've been here a week."

"So I'm late. Things have been crazy lately."

"I've got too much homework. Send Sean."

"Sean's not likely to make friends over there, now, is he?"

"Neither am I," Kate said miserably.

Mom faced her. The brown hair she'd curled and teased so carefully this morning had fallen during the day and her makeup had faded. Now her round, apple-cheeked face looked pale and washed out. Her purple and yellow crocheted vest—a Christmas present from last year—was buttoned wrong. Staring at Kate, she crossed the room and sat down at the table. "Can I say something without you jumping all over me?"

"Probably not."

"I'm sorry about you and Joannie."

Of all the things Kate might have expected, that was not even on the list. "It doesn't matter."

"It matters. I hear she's running with a pretty fast crowd these days."

Kate wanted to say she couldn't have cared less, but

to her horror, tears stung her eyes. Memories rushed at her—Joannie and her on the Octopus ride at the fair, sitting outside their stalls at the barn, talking about how much fun high school would be. She shrugged. "Yeah."

"Life is hard sometimes. Especially at fourteen."

Kate rolled her eyes. If there was one thing she knew, it was that her mother knew nothing about how hard life could be for a teenager. "No shit."

"I'm going to pretend I didn't hear that word from you. It'll be easy because I'll never hear it again. Right?"

Kate couldn't help wishing she was like Tully. *She'd* never back down so easily. She'd probably light up a cigarette right now and dare her mom to say something.

Mom dug through the baggy pocket of her skirt and found her cigarettes. Lighting up, she studied Kate. "You know I love you and I support you and I would never let anyone hurt you. But Katie, I have to ask you: What is it you're waiting for?"

"What do you mean?"

"You spend all your time reading and doing homework. How are people supposed to get to know you when you act like that?"

"They don't want to know me."

Mom touched her hand gently. "It's never good to sit around and wait for someone or something to change your life. That's why women like Gloria Steinem are burning their bras and marching on Washington."

"So that I can make friends?"

"So that you know you can be whatever you want to be. Your generation is so lucky. You can be anything you want. But you have to take a risk sometimes. Reach out. One thing I can tell you for sure is this: we only regret what we don't do in life."

Kate heard an odd sound in her mom's voice, a sadness that tinted the word *regret*. But what could her mother possibly know about the battlefield of junior high popularity? She hadn't been a teenager in decades. "Yeah, right."

"It's true, Kathleen. Someday you'll see how smart I am." Her mom smiled and patted her hand. "If you're like the rest of us, it'll happen at about the same time you want me to babysit for the first time."

"What are you talking about?"

Mom laughed at some joke Kate didn't even get. "I'm glad we had this talk. Now go. Make friends with your new neighbor."

Yeah. That would happen.

"Wear oven mitts. It's still hot," Mom said.

Perfect. The mitts.

Kate went over to the counter and stared down at the red-brown glop of a casserole. Dully, she fitted a sheet of foil across the top, curled the edges down, and then put on the puffy, quilted blue oven mitts her Aunt Georgia had made. At the back door, she slipped her stockinged feet into the fake Earth shoes on the porch and headed down the spongy driveway.

The house across the street was long and low to the ground, a rambler-style in an L shape that faced away from the road. Moss furred the shingled roof. The ivory sides were in need of paint, and the gutters were overflowing with leaves and sticks. Giant rhododendron bushes hid most of the windows, runaway junipers created a green spiky barrier that ran the length of the house. No one had tended to the landscaping in years.

At the front door Kate paused, drawing in a deep breath.

Balancing the casserole in one hand, she pulled off one oven mitt and knocked.

Please let no one be home.

Almost instantly she heard footsteps from inside.

The door swung open to reveal a tall woman dressed

in a billowy caftan. An Indian-beaded headband circled her forehead. Two mismatched earrings hung from her ears. There was a strange dullness in her eyes, as if she needed glasses and didn't have them, but even so, she was pretty in a sharp, brittle kind of way. "Yeah?"

Weird, pulsing music seemed to come from several places at once; though the lights were turned off, several lava lamps burped and bubbled in eerie green and red canisters.

"H-hello," Kate stammered. "My mom made you guys this casserole."

"Right on," the lady said, stumbling back, almost falling.

And suddenly Tully was coming through the doorway, sweeping through, actually, moving with a grace and confidence that was more movie star than teenager. In a bright blue minidress and white go-go boots, she looked old enough to be driving a car. Without saying anything, she grabbed Kate's arm, pulled her through the living room, and into a kitchen in which everything was pink: walls, cabinets, curtains, tile counters, table. When Tully looked at her, Kate thought she saw a flash of something that looked like embarrassment in those dark eyes.

"Was that your mom?" Kate asked, uncertain of what to say.

"She has cancer."

"Oh." Kate didn't know what to say except, "I'm sorry." Quiet pressed into the room. Instead of making eye contact with Tully, Kate studied the table. Never in her life had she seen so much junk food in one place. Pop-Tarts, Cap'n Crunch and Quisp boxes, Fritos, Funyuns, Twinkies, Zingers, and Screaming Yellow Zonkers. "Wow. I wish my mom would let me eat all this stuff." Kate immediately wished she'd kept her mouth shut. Now she sounded hopelessly uncool. To give herself something to do—and somewhere to look besides Tully's unreadable face—she put the casserole on the counter. "It's still hot," she said, stupidly, considering that she was wearing oven mitts that looked like killer whales.

Tully lit up a cigarette and leaned against the pink wall, eyeing her.

Kate glanced back at the door to the living room. "She doesn't care if you smoke?"

"She's too sick to care."

"Oh."

"You want a drag?"

"Uh . . . no. Thanks."

"Yeah. That's what I thought."

On the wall, the black Kit-Kat Klock swished its tail.

"Well, you probably have to get home for dinner," Tully said.

"Oh," Kate said again, sounding even more nerdy than she had before. "Right."

Tully led the way back through the living room, where her mother was now sprawled on the sofa. "'Bye, girl from across the street with the cool neighbor attitude."

Tully yanked the door open. Beyond it, the falling night was a blurry purple rectangle that seemed too vivid to be real. "Thanks for the food," she said. "I don't know how to cook, and Cloud is cooked, if you know what I mean."

"Cloud?"

"That's my mom's current name."

"Oh."

"It'd be cool if I *did* know how to cook. Or if we had a chef or something. With my mom having cancer and all." Tully looked at her.

Tell her you'll teach her.

Take a risk.

But she couldn't do it. The potential for humiliation was sky-high. "Well . . .'bye."

"Later."

Kate stepped past her and into the night.

She was halfway to the road when Tully called out to her, "Hey, wait up."

Kate slowly turned around.

"What's your name?"

She felt a flash of hope. "Kate. Kate Mularkey."

Tully laughed. "Mularkey? Like bullshit?"

It was hardly funny anymore, that joke about her last name. She sighed and turned back around.

"I didn't mean to laugh," Tully said, but she didn't stop.

"Yeah. Whatever."

"Fine. Be a bitch, why don't you?"

Kate kept walking.

CHAPTER
FOUR

Tully watched the girl walk away.

"I shouldn't have said that," she said, noticing how small her voice sounded beneath the enormous star-spangled sky.

She wasn't even sure why she'd said it, why she'd suddenly felt the need to make fun of the next-door neighbor. With a sigh, she went back into the house. The moment she stepped into the room, the smell of pot overwhelmed her, stung her eyes. On the sofa, her mom lay spread-eagled, one leg on the coffee table, one on the back cushions. Her mouth hung open; drool sparkled the corners of her lips.

And the girl next door had seen this. Tully felt a hot wave of shame. No doubt rumors would be all over school by Monday. *Tully Hart has a pothead mom.*

This was why she never invited anyone over to her house. When you were keeping secrets, you needed to do it alone, in the dark.

She would have given anything to have the kind of mom who made dinner for strangers. Maybe that was why she'd made fun of the girl's name. The thought pissed her off and she slammed the door shut behind her. "Cloud. Wake up."

Mom drew in a sharp, snorting breath and sat up. "Whass the matter?"

"It's dinnertime."

Mom pushed the gob of hair out of her eyes and worked to focus on the wall clock. "What are we—in a nursing home? Iss five o'clock."

Tully was surprised her mom could still tell time. She went into the kitchen, served the casserole onto two white CorningWare plates, and returned to the living room. "Here." She handed her mother a plate and fork.

"Where'd we get this? Did you cook?"

"Hardly. The neighbor brought it over."

Cloud looked blearily around. "We have neighbors?"

Tully didn't bother answering. Her mother always forgot what they were talking about anyway. It made any real conversation impossible, and usually Tully didn't care—she wanted to talk to Cloud like she wanted to watch black and white movies—but now, since that girl's visit, Tully felt her differentness keenly. If she had a real family—a mom who made casseroles and sent them as gifts to new neighbors—she wouldn't feel so alone. She sat down in one of the mustard-colored beanbag chairs that flanked the sofa and said cautiously, "I wonder what Gran's doing right now."

"Pro'ly making one of those god-awful PRAISE JESUS samplers. As if that'll save her soul. Ha. How's school?"

Tully's head snapped up. She couldn't believe her mom had just asked about her life. "Lots of kids hang around with me, but . . ." She frowned. How could she put her dissatisfaction into words? All she really knew was that she was lonely here, even among her new friends. "I keep waiting for . . ."

"Do we have ketchup?" her mother said, frowning down at her heap of Hamburger Helper, poking at it with her fork. She was swaying to the music.

Tully hated the disappointment she felt. She knew better than to expect anything from her mother. "I'm going to my room," she said, climbing out of the bean-bag chair.

The last thing she heard before she slammed her bedroom door was her mother saying, "Maybe it needs cheese."

Late that night, long after everyone else had gone to bed, Kate crept down the stairs, put on her dad's huge rubber boots, and went outside. It was becoming a habit lately, going outside when she couldn't sleep. Overhead, the huge black sky was splattered with stars. It made her feel small and unimportant, that sky. A lonely girl looking down at an empty street that went nowhere.

Sweetpea nickered and trotted toward her.

She climbed up onto the top rail of the fence. "Hey there, girl," she said, pulling a carrot out of her parka's pocket.

She glanced over at the house across the street. The lights were still on at midnight. No doubt Tully was having a party with all the popular kids. They were probably laughing and dancing and talking about how cool they were.

Kate would give everything she owned to be invited to just one party like that.

Sweetpea nudged her knee, snorted.

"I know. I'm dreaming." Sighing, she slid off the

fence, petted Sweetpea one last time, and then went
back to bed.

A few nights later, after a dinner of Pop-Tarts and
Alpha-Bits cereal, Tully took a long, hot shower, shaved
her legs and underarms carefully, and dried her hair
until it fell straight from her center part without a single
crease or curl. Then she went to her closet and stood
there, trying to figure out what to wear. This was her
first high school party. She needed to look just right.
None of the other girls from the junior high had been
invited. She was The One. Pat Richmond, the best-
looking guy on the football team, had chosen Tully for
his date. They'd been at the local hamburger hangout
last Wednesday night, his group of friends and hers.
All it had taken was one look between them. Pat had
broken free of the crowd of huge guys and walked right
over to Tully.

She'd seen him heading her way and practically
fainted. On the jukebox, "Stairway to Heaven" had been
playing. Talk about romantic.

"I could get in trouble just for talking to you," he said.

She tried to look mature and worldly as she said, "I
like trouble."

The smile he gave her was like nothing she'd ever
seen before. For the first time in her life, she felt as beautiful as people always said she was.

"You wanna come to the party with me on Friday?"

"I could make that work," she said. It was a phrase
she'd heard Erica Kane use on *All My Children*.

"I'll pick you up at ten." He leaned closer. "Unless
that's past your curfew, little girl?"

"Seventeen Firefly Lane. And I don't have a curfew."

He smiled again. "I'm Pat, by the way."

"I'm Tully."

"Well, Tully, I'll see you at ten."

Tully still couldn't believe it. For the past forty-eight hours she'd obsessed over this first real date. All the other times she'd gone out with boys it was in a group or to a school dance. This was totally different, and Pat was practically a man.

They could fall in love; she knew it. And then, with him holding her hand, she'd stop feeling so alone.

She finally made her clothes choice.

Low-rise, three-button bell-bottom jeans, a pink scoop-necked knit top that showed off her cleavage, and her favorite cork platforms. She spent almost an hour on her makeup, layering more and more on until she looked foxy. She couldn't wait to show Pat how pretty she could be.

She grabbed a pack of her mom's cigarettes and left her bedroom.

In the living room, Mom looked up blearily from her magazine. "Hey, iss almos' ten o'clock. Where are you going?"

"This guy invited me to a party."

"Is he here?"

Right. Like Tully would invite anyone to come in. "I'm meeting him on the road."

"Oh. Cool. Don't wake me up when you get home."

"I won't."

Outside, it was dark and cold. The Milky Way stretched across the sky in a path of starlight.

She waited by her mailbox on the main road, moving from foot to foot to keep warm. Goose bumps pebbled her bare arms. The mood ring on her middle finger changed from green to purple. She tried to remember what that meant.

Across the street and up the hill, the pretty little farmhouse glowed against the darkness. Each window was like a pat of warm, melting butter. They were prob-ably all at home, clustered around a big table, playing Risk. She wondered what they'd do if she just visited one day, showed up on the porch and said hey.

She heard Pat's car before she saw the headlights. At the roar of the engine, she forgot all about the family across the street and stepped into the road, waving.

His green Dodge Charger came to a stop beside her; the car seemed to pulse with sound, vibrate. She slid into the passenger seat. The music was so loud she knew he couldn't hear what she said.

Grinning at her, Pat hit the gas and they were off like a rocket, blasting down the quiet country lane.

As they turned onto a gravel road, she could see the party going on below. Dozens of cars were parked in a huge circle in a pasture, with their headlights on. Bachman-Turner Overdrive's "Taking Care of Business" blared from someone's car radio. Pat parked over in the stand of trees along the fence line.

There were kids everywhere, gathered around the flames of the bonfire, standing beside the kegs of beer set up in the grass. Clear plastic cups littered the ground. Down by the barn, a group of guys were playing touch football. It was late in May, and summer was still a ways away, so most people were wearing coats. She wished she hadn't forgotten hers.

Pat held her hand tightly, leading her through the crowd of couples toward the keg, where he poured two cups full.

Taking hers, she let him lead her down to a quiet spot just beyond the perimeter of cars. There, he spread his letterman's jacket down on the ground and motioned for her to sit down.

"I couldn't believe it when I first saw you," Pat said, sitting close to her, sipping his beer. "You're the prettiest girl ever to live in this town. All the guys want you."

"But you got me," she said, smiling at him. It felt as if she were falling into his dark eyes.

He took a big drink of his beer, practically finishing it, then he set it down and kissed her.

Other guys had kissed her before; mostly they were fumbling, nervous attempts made during a slow dance. This was different. Pat's mouth was like magic. She sighed happily, whispering his name. When he drew back, he was staring at her with pure, sunshiny love in his eyes. "I'm glad you're here."

"Me, too."

He finished off his beer and got up. "I need more brew."

They were in line at the keg when he frowned at her. "Hey, you aren't drinking. I thought you were cool with partying."

"I am." She smiled nervously. She'd never really drank before, but he wouldn't like her if she acted like a nerd, and she was desperate for him to want her. "Bottoms up," she said, tilting the plastic tumbler to her lips and drinking the whole amount without stopping. When she finished, she couldn't help burping and giggling.

"Far out," he said, nodding, pouring two more beers.

The second one wasn't so bad, and by the third beer Tully had completely lost her sense of taste. When Pat brought out a bottle of Annie Green Springs wine, she guzzled some of that, too. For almost an hour, they sat on his jacket, tucked close together, drinking and talking. She didn't know any of the people he talked about, but that didn't matter. What mattered was the way he looked at her, the way he held her hand.

"Come on," he whispered, "let's dance."

She felt woozy when she stood up. Her balance was off and she kept stumbling during their dance. Finally, she fell down altogether. Pat laughed, took her hand to pull her up, and led her to a dark, romantic spot in the trees. Giggling, she hobbled awkwardly behind him, gasping when he took her in his arms and kissed her.

It felt so good; made her blood feel tingly and hot. She pressed up against him like a cat, loving the way he was making her feel. Any minute he was going to draw back and look down at her and say, *I love you,* just like Ryan O'Neal in *Love Story.*

Maybe Tully would even call him preppie when she said it back to him. Their song would be "Stairway to Heaven." They'd tell people they met while—

His tongue slipped into her mouth, pressing hard, sweeping around like some kind of alien probe. Suddenly it didn't feel good anymore, didn't feel right. She tried to say, *Stop,* but her voice had no sound; he was sucking up all her air.

His hands were everywhere: up her back, around her side, plucking at her bra, trying to undo it. She felt it come free with a sickening little pop. And then he was touching her boob.

"No . . ." she whimpered, trying to push his hands away. This wasn't what she wanted. She wanted love, romance, magic. Someone to love her. Not . . . this. "No, Pat, don't—"

"Come on, Tully. You know you want it." He pushed her back and she stumbled, fell to the ground hard, hitting her head. For a second, her vision blurred. When it cleared, he was on his knees, between her legs. He held both her hands in one of his, pinning her to the ground.

"That's what I like," he said, pushing her legs apart.

Shoving her top up, he stared down at her naked chest. "Oh, yeah . . ." He cupped one breast, tweaked her nipple hard. His other hand slipped into her pants, beneath her underwear.

"Stop. Please . . ." Tully tried desperately to get free, but her wriggling only seemed to excite him.

Between her legs, his fingers probed her hard, moving inside her. "Come on, baby, let yourself like it."

She felt herself starting to cry. "Don't—"

"Oh, yeah . . ." He covered her body with his, pressed her into the wet grass.

She was crying so hard now she could taste her own tears, but he didn't seem to care. His kisses were something else now—slobbering, sucking, biting; it hurt, but not as much as his belt, hitting her stomach when he pulled it off, or his penis, ramming—

She squeezed her eyes shut as pain ripped between her legs, scraped her insides.

Then, suddenly, it was over. He rolled off her, lay beside her, holding her close, kissing her cheek as if what he'd just done to her had been love.

"Hey, you're crying." He gently smoothed the hair away from her face. "What's the matter? I thought you wanted it."

She didn't know what to say. Like every girl, she'd imagined losing her virginity, but it had never felt like this in her dreams. She stared at him in disbelief. "Wanted *that*?"

An irritated frown creased his forehead. "Come on, Tully, let's dance."

The way he said it, so quietly, as if he were actually confused by her reaction, only made it worse. She'd done something wrong, obviously, been a prick tease, and this was what happened to girls who played at it.

He stared at her for a minute longer, then stood up and pulled his pants up. "Whatever. I need another drink. Let's go."

She rolled onto her side. "Go away."

She felt him beside her, knew he was staring down at her. "You acted like you wanted it, damn it. You can't lead a guy on and then just go cold. Grow up, little girl. This is your fault."

She closed her eyes and ignored him, thankful when he finally left her. For once she was glad to be alone.

She lay there, feeling broken and hurt and, worst of all, stupid. After an hour or so, she heard the party break up, heard the car engines start, and the tires pealing through loose gravel as they drove away.

And still she lay there, unable to make herself move. This was all her fault; he was right about that. She was stupid and young. All she'd wanted was someone to love her.

"Stupid," she hissed, finally sitting up.

Moving slowly, she got dressed and tried to stand. At the movement, she felt sick to her stomach and immediately puked all over her favorite shoes. When it was over, she bent down for her purse, clutched it to her chest, and made her long, painful way back up to the road.

There were no cars out this late at night, and she was glad for that. She didn't want to have to explain to anyone why her hair was full of pine needles and her shoes were stained with vomit.

All the way home she relived what had happened— the way Pat had smiled at her when he asked her to the party; the gentle first kiss he'd given her; the way he talked to her as if she mattered; then the other Pat, with his harsh hands and his probing tongue and fingers, with his hard cock and how roughly he'd stuck it up inside her.

The more she replayed it in her mind, the lonelier and more desolate she felt.

If only she had someone she trusted to talk to. Maybe that would ease a little of this pain. But, of course, there was no one.

This was another secret she'd have to keep, like her

weirdo mother and unknown father. People would say she had it coming, a junior high girl at a high school party.

As she neared her driveway, she walked a little more slowly. The thought of going home, of feeling alone in a place that should be a refuge for her, with a woman who was supposed to love her, was suddenly unbearable.

The neighbors' old gray horse trotted up to the fence line and nickered at her.

Tully crossed the street and walked up the hill. At the fence, she yanked up a handful of grass and held it out to him. "Hey there, boy."

The horse sniffed the handful of grass, snorted wetly, and trotted away.

"She likes carrots."

Tully looked up sharply and saw her neighbor sitting on the top rail of the fence.

Long minutes passed in silence between them; the only noise was the horse's quiet nickering.

"It's late," the neighbor girl said.

"Yeah."

"I love it out here at night. The stars are so bright. Sometimes, if you stare up at the sky long enough, you'll swear tiny white dots are falling all around you, like fireflies. Maybe that's how this street got its name. You probably think I'm a nerd for even saying that."

Tully wanted to answer but couldn't. Deep, deep inside she'd started to shake and it took all her concentration just to stand still.

The girl—Kate, Tully remembered—slipped down from her perch. She was wearing an oversized T-shirt with a Partridge Family decal on the front that was peeling off. As she moved forward, her boots made a sucking noise in the mud. "Hey, you don't look so good." A retainer drew the *s* into a long lisp. "And you reek like puke."

"I'm fine," she said, stiffening as Kate drew close.

"Are you okay? Really?"

To Tully's complete horror, she started to cry.

Kate stood there a moment, staring at her from behind those dork-o-rama glasses. Then, without saying anything, she hugged Tully.

Tully flinched at the contact; it was foreign and unexpected. She started to pull away, but found that she couldn't move. She couldn't remember the last time someone had held her like this, and suddenly she was clinging to this weirdo girl, afraid to let go, afraid that without Kate, she'd float away like the S.S. *Minnow* and be lost at sea.

"I'm sure she'll get better," Kate said when Tully's tears subsided.

Tully drew back, frowning. It took her a second to understand.

The cancer. Kate thought she was worried about her mom.

"Do you want to talk about it?" Kate said, taking out her retainer, putting it on the mossy top of a fence post.

Tully stared at her. In the silvery light from a full moon, she saw nothing but compassion in Kate's magnified green eyes, and she wanted to talk, wanted it with a fierceness that made her feel sick. But she didn't know how to start.

Kate said, "Come on," and led her up the hill to the slanted front porch of the farmhouse. There, she sat down, pulling her threadbare T-shirt over her bent knees. "My Aunt Georgia had cancer," she said. "It was grody. Lost all her hair. But she's fine now."

Tully sat down beside her, put her purse on the

ground. The smell of vomit was strong. She pulled out a cigarette and lit up to cover the stench. Before she knew it, she'd said, "I went to a party down by the river tonight."

"A high school party?" Kate sounded impressed.

"Pat Richmond asked me out."

"The quarterback? Wow. My mom wouldn't let me stand in the same checkout line as a high school senior. She's so lame."

"She's not lame."

"She thinks eighteen-year-old boys are dangerous. She calls them penises with hands and feet. Tell me that isn't lame."

Tully glanced out over the field and took a deep, steadying breath. She couldn't believe she was going to tell this girl what happened tonight, but the truth was a fire inside her. If she didn't get rid of it, she'd burn up. "He raped me."

Kate turned to her. Tully felt those green eyes boring into her profile, but she didn't move, didn't turn. Her shame was so overwhelming that she couldn't stand to see it reflected in Kate's eyes. She waited for Kate to say something, to call her an idiot, but the silence just went on and on. Finally, she couldn't take it anymore. She looked sideways.

"Are you okay?" Kate asked quietly.

Tully relived it all in those few words. Tears stung her eyes, blurred her vision.

Once again, Kate hugged her. Tully let herself be comforted for the first time since she was little. When she finally drew back, she tried to smile. "I'm drowning you."

"We should tell someone."

"No way. They'd say it was my fault. This is our secret, okay?"

"Okay." Kate frowned as she said it.

Tully wiped her eyes and took another drag on her cigarette. "Why are you being so nice to me?"

"You looked lonely. Believe me, I know how that feels."

"You do? But you have a family."

"They *have* to like me." Kate sighed. "The kids at school treat me like I've got an infectious disease. I used to have friends, but . . . you probably don't know what in the heck I'm talking about. You're so popular."

"Popular just means lots of people think they know you."

"I'd take that."

Silence fell between them. Tully finished her cigarette and put it out. They were so different, she and Kate, as full of contrasts as this dark field bathed in moonlight, but it felt so completely easy to talk to her. Tully found herself almost smiling, and on this, the worst night of her life. That was something.

For the next hour, they sat there, talking now and then and sometimes just sitting in silence. They didn't say anything really important or share any more secrets, they just talked.

Finally, Kate yawned and Tully stood up. "I better book."

They got up and walked down to the road. At the mailboxes, Kate stopped. "Well. 'Bye."

"'Bye." Tully stood there a moment, feeling awkward. She wanted to hug Kate, maybe even cling to her and tell her how much this night had been helped by her, but she didn't dare. She'd learned a thing or two about vulnerability from her mother, and she felt too fragile now to risk humiliation. Turning, she headed down to her house. Once inside, she went straight to the shower. There, with the hot water beating down on her, she thought about what had happened to her tonight—what she'd let happen because she wanted to be cool—and she cried. When she was done and the tears had turned into a hard little knot in her throat, she took the memory of this night and boxed it up. She shelved it in the back alongside memories of the times Cloud had abandoned her and immediately began working on forgetting it was there.

CHAPTER FIVE

Kate lay awake long after Tully had left. Finally, she threw back the covers and got out of bed.

Downstairs, she found what she needed: a small statue of the Virgin Mary, a votive candle in a red glass holder, a book of matches, and her grandmother's old rosary beads. Taking everything back up to her room, she created an altar on top of her dresser, and lit the candle.

"Heavenly Father," she prayed, head bowed and hands clasped, "please watch out for Tully Hart and help her through this hard time. Also, please heal her mother's cancer. I know You can help them. Amen." She said a few Hail Marys, and then went back to bed.

But all night she tossed and turned, dreaming about the encounter with Tully, wondering what would happen in the morning. Should she talk to Tully today at school, smile at her? Or was she expected to pretend it had never happened? There were rules to popularity, secret codes written in invisible ink that only girls like Tully could read. All Kate knew was that she didn't want to make a mistake and embarrass herself. She knew that sometimes the popular girls were "secret friends" with nerds; like, they smiled and said hi when they weren't in school or when their parents were friends. Maybe that was how it would be with her and Tully.

Finally, she quit trying to sleep and got up. Putting on her robe, she went downstairs. In the living room, her dad looked up from the newspaper and smiled. "Top of the mornin' to you, Katie Scarlett. Come give your old man a hug."

She plopped into his lap, rested her cheek against the rough wool of his shirt.

He tucked a strand of hair around her ear. She could see how tired he looked; he was working so hard, doing double shifts at Boeing so they could afford their yearly family camping trip. "How's school going?"

It was the same question he always asked. Once, a long time ago, she'd actually answered, said, "Not so good, Dad," and then waited for his advice or comfort or something, but no such words had come. He'd heard what he wanted to hear, not what she'd said. Her mom had said it was because he worked so many hours at the plant.

Kate could have been upset by his distraction, but somehow it had made her love him even more. He never yelled at her or told her to pay attention or reminded her that she was responsible for her own happiness. Those were her mother's words; her dad just quietly went on loving her no matter what.

"Great," she answered, smiling to reinforce the lie.

"How could it not be?" he said, kissing her temple. "You're the prettiest girl in town, eh? And your mum named you after one of the great literary heroines of all time."

"Yeah, Scarlett O'Hara and I have a ton in common."

"You'll see," he said, chuckling. "There's a fair bit of life still ahead of you, missy."

She looked at him. "Do you think I'll be pretty when I grow up?"

"Ah, Katie," he said. "You're a rare beauty already."

She took those words and tucked them in her pocket like worry stones; every now and again as she got ready for school she felt them, turned them around in her fingers.

By the time she was dressed and ready to go, the house was empty. The Mularkey family bus had left the station.

She was so nervous she arrived at the bus stop early. Every minute that passed seemed to last an eternity, but there was still no sign of Tully when the school bus drove up and came to a shuddering stop.

Kate dropped her chin and took a seat in the first row.

All through morning classes, she looked for Tully, but didn't see her. At lunch she hurried past the crowd of popular kids, who were busy cutting to the front of the food line whenever they felt like it, and sat down at one of the long tables at the very end of the cafeteria. On the other side of the room, kids were laughing and talking and shoving each other; these tables in social Siberia were sadly quiet, though. Kate, like the others seated around her, rarely looked up.

It was a survival skill the unpopular kids learned early: junior high was like the jungles of Vietnam; it was best to crouch low and keep quiet. So intent was she on her lunch that when someone came up to her and said, "Hey," she practically jumped out of her seat.

Tully.

Even on this cool May day, she wore a cut-to-there miniskirt, white go-go boots, shiny black panty hose, and a tube top. Several peace-symbol necklaces bounced against her cleavage. Her hair glinted with copper streaks in the light. A huge macramé-knot purse hung against her thigh. "Have you told anyone about last night?"

"No. Of course not."

"So, we're friends, right?"

Kate didn't know which surprised her more: the question or the vulnerability in Tully's eyes. "We're friends."

"Excellent." Tully pulled a package of Twinkies out of her purse, then sat down beside Kate. "Now let's talk about makeup. You need help, and I'm not being a bitch. Really. I just know about fashion. It's a gift. Can I drink your milk? Good. Thanks. Are you gonna eat that banana? I could come to your house after school . . ."

Kate stood outside the drugstore looking up and down the street for someone who might know her mom. "Are you sure about this?"

"Absolutely."

The answer was slim comfort, actually. In the day they'd officially been friends, Kate had learned one thing about Tully: she was a girl who made Plans.

And today's plan was to make Kate beautiful.

"Don't you trust me?"

There it was, the big question. It was like rolling a Yahtzee: once Tully said it, Kate lost the game. She had to trust her new friend. "Of course I do. It's just that I'm not allowed to wear makeup."

"Believe me, I'm such an expert your mom will never know. Come on."

Tully walked boldly through the drugstore, choosing eye shadow and blush colors that were "right" for Kate, and then—amazingly—she paid for everything. When

Kate said something, Tully said airily, "We're friends, aren't we?"

On the way out of the store, Tully bumped her, shoulder to shoulder.

Kate giggled and bumped her back. They made their way through town and followed the river toward home. All the while, they talked about clothes and music and school. Finally, they turned off the old road and went down Tully's driveway.

"My gran would freak if she saw this place," Tully said, looking embarrassed. Rhodies the size of hot-air balloons covered the side of the house. "She owns this house, you know."

"Does she visit you?"

"Nah. It's easier to wait."

"For what?"

"My mom to forget about me again." Tully stepped over a mound of newspapers and around a trio of garbage cans, then opened the door. Inside, the smoke in the room was thick.

Tully's mom was in the living room, lying on the sofa, with her eyes half opened.

"H-hello, Mrs. Hart," Kate said. "I'm Kate from next door."

Mrs. Hart tried to sit up, but obviously she was too weak to manage it. "Hello, girl from nex' door."

Tully grabbed Kate's hand and pulled her through the living room and into her bedroom, then slammed the door shut. She immediately went to her stack of records, pulled out *Goodbye Yellow Brick Road,* and put it on the turntable. When the music started up, she tossed Kate a *Tiger Beat* and dragged a chair over to the vanity. "You ready?"

Kate's nervousness came swooping back. She knew she'd get in trouble for this, but how would she ever make friends or become popular if she didn't take a few risks? "I'm ready."

"Good. Sit down. We'll do your hair first. It needs some highlights. This is exactly what Maureen McCormick uses."

Kate looked at Tully in the mirror. "How do you know that?"

"I read it in last month's *Teen* magazine."

"I'm guessing she goes to professionals." Kate opened the *Tiger Beat* and tried to concentrate on the article ("Jack Wild's Dream Date—It Could Be You!").

"Take that back. I read the instructions twice."

"Is there any chance I'm going to end up bald?"

"Hardly any. Now be quiet. I'm reading the instructions again."

Tully separated Kate's hair into strips and began spraying Sun-In onto the pieces. It took almost an hour to get it done to her satisfaction. "You are going to look like Marcia Brady when I'm done."

"What's it like, being popular?" Kate hadn't meant to ask the question; it just slipped out.

"You'll see. But you'll stay my friend, won't you?"

Kate laughed at that. "Very funny. Hey, that sort of burns."

"Really? That can't be good. And some of your hair is falling out."

Kate managed not to make a face. If going bald was the price of being Tully's friend, she'd pay it.

Tully reached for the blow dryer and turned it on, blasting Kate's hair with heat.

"I got my period," Tully yelled. "So at least assface didn't knock me up."

Kate heard the bravado in her friend's voice and saw it in her eyes. "I prayed for you."

"You did?" Tully asked. "Wow. Thanks."

Kate didn't know what to say to that. To her, praying was like brushing your teeth before bed, just something you did.

Tully clicked off the dryer and smiled, but she looked worried again. Maybe it was the smell of burning hair. "Okay. Take a shower and rinse it out."

Kate did as she was told. A few minutes later, she got out of the shower, dried off, and got dressed again.

Tully immediately grabbed her hand and led her back to the chair. "Is your hair falling out?"

"Some is," she admitted.

"If you're bald, I'll shave my head. Promise." Tully combed and dried Kate's hair.

Kate couldn't look. She closed her eyes and let Tully's voice meld into the whine of the dryer.

"Open your eyes."

Kate looked up slowly. At this distance, she didn't need her glasses, but force of habit made her lean forward. The girl in the mirror had straight streaked blond hair, parted with precision and dried perfectly. For once it looked soft and pretty instead of thin and lank. The white highlights showed off her leaf-green eyes and the hint of pink on her lips. She looked almost pretty. "Wow," she said, too choked up with gratitude to say more.

"Wait till you see what mascara and blush can do," Tully said, "and concealer for those zits on your forehead."

"I'll always be your friend," Kate said, thinking she'd whispered the promise, but when Tully grinned, she knew she'd been heard.

"Good. Now let's go on the makeup. Have you seen my razor?"

"What do you need a razor for?"

"Your eyebrows, silly. Oh, there it is. Close your eyes."

Kate didn't think twice. "Okay."

Kate didn't even bother to hide her face when she came into the house. That was how confident she felt. For the first time ever, she knew she was beautiful.

Her dad was in the living room, sitting in his La-Z-Boy. At Kate's entrance, he looked up. "Good Lord," he said, clanking his drink down on the French provincial end table. "Margie!"

Mom came out of the kitchen, wiping her hands on her apron. She wore her school-day uniform: striped rust and olive polyester blouse, brown corduroy bell-bottoms, and a wrinkled apron that read: A WOMAN'S PLACE IS IN THE HOUSE . . . AND THE SENATE. When she saw Kate, she stopped. Slowly, she untied her apron and tossed it on the table.

The sudden quiet brought Sean and the dog running into the room, tripping over each other. "Katie looks like a skunk," Sean said. "Pee-ew."

"Go wash your hands for dinner," Mom said sharply. "Now," she added when he didn't leave.

Sean grumbled and went upstairs.

"Did you give her permission to do that to her hair, Margie?" Dad said from the living room.

"I'll handle this, Bud," Mom said, frowning at Kate as she crossed the room. "The girl across the street do this to you?"

Kate nodded, trying to hold on to the memory of feeling pretty.

"Do you like it?"

"Yes."

"Well. Me, too, then. I remember when your Aunt Georgia dyed my hair red. Grandma Peet was livid." She smiled. "But you should have asked. You're still young, Kathleen, no matter what you girls want to be true. Now, what have you done to your eyebrows?"

"Tully shaved them. Just to give them shape."

Mom tried not to smile. "I see. Well, plucking is really the way to go. I should have taught you how already, but I thought you were too young." She looked around for her cigarettes. Finding them on the table, she flipped one out and lit up. "After dinner, I'll show you how. And I suppose a little lip gloss and mascara would be all right for school. I'll show you how to make it look more natural."

Kate hugged her mom. "I love you."

"I love you, too. Now get started on the cornbread. And Katie, I'm glad you made a friend, but no more breaking the rules, okay? That's how young girls get into trouble."

Kate couldn't help thinking of the high school party Tully had gone to. "Okay, Mom."

Within a week, Kate became cool by association. Kids raved over her new look and didn't turn away from her in the halls. Being a friend of Tully Hart's meant she was okay.

Even her parents noticed the difference. At dinner, Kate wasn't her usual quiet self. Instead, she couldn't shut up. Story after story spilled out of her. Who was dating whom, who won at tetherball, who got detention for wearing a MAKE LOVE, NOT WAR T-shirt to school, where Tully got her hair cut (in Seattle by a guy named Gene Juarez—how cool was that?), and what movie was playing at the drive-in this weekend. She was still talking about Tully after dinner, while she and Mom did the dishes.

"I can't wait for you to meet her. She's super cool. Everyone likes her, even the heads."

"Heads?"

"Druggies? Stoners?"

"Oh." Mom took the glass meatloaf pan from her and dried it. "I've . . . asked around about this girl, Katie. She tries to buy cigarettes from Alma at the drugstore."

"She's probably buying them for her mom."

Mom set the dry pan down on the speckled Formica counter. "Just do me a favor, Katie. You think for yourself around Tully Hart. I wouldn't want you to follow her into trouble."

Kate threw the crocheted dishrag in the soapy water. "I can't *believe* you. What about all your take-a-risk speeches? For years you tell me to make friends, and the second I find someone, you call her a slut."

"I hardly called her a—"

Kate stormed out of the kitchen. With each step she expected her mother to call her back and ground her, but silence followed her dramatic exit.

Upstairs, she went into her room and slammed the door for effect. Then she sat down on her bed and waited. When Mom came in she'd be sorry; for once Kate had been the strong one.

But Mom didn't show, and by ten o'clock, Kate was starting to feel sort of bad. Had she hurt her mom's feelings? She got up, paced the small room.

There was a knock at the door.

She raced over to the bed and climbed in, trying to look bored. "Yeah?"

The door opened slowly. Mom stood there, wearing the floor-length red velour robe they'd gotten her for Christmas last year. "May I come in?"

"Like I could stop you."

"You could," Mom said quietly. "May I come in?"

Kate shrugged, but scooted to the left to make room for her mom.

"You know, Katie, life is—"

Kate couldn't help groaning. Not another life-is speech.

Mom surprised her by laughing. "Okay, no more speeches. Maybe you're too old for that." She paused at the altar on the dresser. "You haven't made one of these since Georgia was in chemo. Who needs our prayers?"

"Tully's mom has cancer and she was ra—" She snapped her mouth shut, horrified by what she'd nearly revealed. For most of her life she'd told her mother everything; now she had a best friend, though, so she'd need to be careful.

Mom sat down on the bed beside Kate, just as they did after every fight. "Cancer? That's quite a load for a girl your age to carry."

"Tully seems cool with it."

"Does she?"

"She seems cool with everything," Kate said, unable to keep the pride out of her voice.

"How so?"

"You wouldn't understand."

"I'm too old, huh?"

"I didn't say that."

Mom smoothed the hair off Kate's forehead in a touch that was as familiar as breathing. Kate always felt five years old when her mom did that. "I'm sorry you thought I was judging your friend."

"You should be."

"And you're sorry for being so mean to me, right?"

Kate couldn't help smiling. "Yeah."

"I'll tell you what: Why don't you invite Tully over for dinner Friday night?"

"You'll love her. I know you will."

"I'm sure I will," Mom said, kissing her forehead. "'Night."

"'Night, Mom."

Long after her mother had left and the house had

gone quiet for the night, Kate lay there, too wound up to sleep. She couldn't wait to invite Tully for dinner. Afterward, they could watch *I Dream of Jeannie,* or play Operation, or practice putting on makeup. Maybe Tully would even want to spend the night. They could—

Tap.

—talk about boys and kissing and—

Tap.

Kate sat up. That wasn't a bird on the roof or a mouse in the walls.

Tap.

It was a small rock, hitting the glass!

She threw the covers back and hurried to the window, shoving it open.

Tully was in her backyard, holding a bike beside her. "Come on down," she said, much too loudly, making a hurry gesture with her hand.

"You want me to sneak out?"

"Uh. Duh."

Kate had never done anything like this, but she couldn't act like a nerd now. Cool kids broke the rules and sneaked out of the house. Everyone knew that. Everyone knew, too, that trouble could follow. And this was exactly what her mom had been talking about.

You think for yourself around Tully Hart.

Kate didn't care about that. What mattered was Tully.

"I'm on my way." Closing the window, she looked around for clothes. Fortunately, her overalls were in the corner, folded neatly beneath a black sweatshirt. She slipped out of her old Scooby-Doo jammies and dressed quickly, then crept down the hall. As she passed her parents' bedroom, her heart was pounding so fast she felt light-headed. The stairs creaked ominously with every footfall, but finally she made it.

At the back door she paused just long enough to

think, *I could get in trouble for this,* and then she opened the door.

Tully was there, waiting. Beside her was the most amazing bike Kate had ever seen. It had curly handlebars, a tiny kidney-shaped seat on a platform, and a bunch of cables and wires. "Wow," she said. It would take a lot of berry-picking money to get a bike like that.

"It's a ten-speed," Tully said. "My grandma gave it to me last Christmas. You want to ride it?"

"No way." Kate closed the door quietly behind her. In the carport she found her old pink bicycle with the U-shaped handlebars, flower-decaled banana seat, and white wicker basket. It was hopelessly uncool; a little girl's bike.

Tully didn't even seem to notice. They mounted up and rode down the wet, bumpy driveway to the paved road. There, they veered left and kept going. At Summer Hill, Tully said, "Watch this. Do what I do."

They crested the hill as if they were flying. Kate's hair whipped back from her head; tears stung her eyes. All around them black trees whispered in the breeze. Stars glittered in the velvet black sky.

Tully leaned back and put her arms out. Laughing, she glanced at Kate. "Try it."

"I can't. We're going too fast."

"That's the point."

"It's dangerous."

"Come on. Let go, Katie. God hates a coward." Then, quietly, she added, "Trust me."

Now Kate had no choice. Trust was part of being friends, and Tully wouldn't hang out with a chicken. "Come on," she said to herself, trying to sound stern.

Taking a deep breath, she said a prayer and eased her arms out.

She was flying, sailing through the night sky, down

the hill. The air smelled of the riding stable nearby, of horses and sweet hay. She heard Tully laughing beside her, but before she could even smile, something went wrong. Her front tire hit a rock; the bike bucked like a Brahman bull and twisted sideways, catching Tully's tire in its arc.

She screamed, reached for the handlebars, but it was too late. She was in the air, really flying this time. The pavement rushed up, smacked her hard, and she skidded across it, landing in a heap in a muddy ditch.

Tully rolled across the asphalt and slammed into her. The bikes clattered to the ground.

Dazed, Kate stared up at the night sky. Every part of her hurt. Her left ankle might be broken. It felt swollen, tender. She could feel where the road had ripped off her skin in patches.

"That was *incredible*," Tully said, laughing.

"Are you kidding? We could have been killed."

"Exactly."

Kate winced in pain as she tried to get up. "We should get out of this ditch. A car could come along—"

"But wasn't that cool? Wait till we tell the kids about this."

The kids at school. This would be a *story*, and Kate would be one of the stars in it. People would listen raptly, ooh and aah, say things like, *You sneaked out? Summer Hill without hands? It's gotta be a lie . . .*

And suddenly Kate was laughing, too.

They helped each other to their feet and retrieved their bikes. By the time they were across the road, Kate barely noticed where she was hurt. She felt like a different girl suddenly—bolder, braver, willing to try anything. So what if trouble followed a night like this? What was a sprained ankle or a bloody knee next to an adventure? For the past two years she'd followed all the rules and stayed home on weekend nights. No more.

They left their bikes by the side of the road and limped toward the river. In the moonlight, everything looked milky and beautiful—the silvery waves, the jagged rocks along the shore.

Tully sat down by a decaying, moss-covered nurse log in a place where the grass was as thick as shag carpeting.

Kate sat down beside her, so close their knees were almost touching. Together they stared up at the star-spangled sky. The song of the river floated toward them, sounded like a young girl's laugh. Just now, with the world so still and silent, it was as if the breeze had drawn in its cool breath and left them all alone in this place that until right now had been just another bend in a river that flooded every autumn.

"I wonder who named our street," Tully said. "I haven't seen any fireflies."

Kate shrugged. "Over by the old bridge is Missouri Street. Maybe some pioneer was homesick. Or lost."

"Or maybe it's *magic*. This could be a magical street." Tully turned toward her. "That could mean we were meant to be friends."

Kate shivered at the power of that. "Before you moved here, I thought it was just a road that went nowhere."

"Now it's our road."

"We can go all kinds of places when we grow up."

"Places don't matter," Tully said.

Kate heard something in her friend's voice, a sadness she didn't understand. She turned sideways. Tully was staring up at the sky.

"Are you thinking about your mom?" Kate asked tentatively.

"I try not to think about her." There was a long pause, then she dug into her pocket for a Virginia Slims cigarette and lit up.

Kate was careful not to make a face about the smoking.

"You want a drag?"

Kate knew she had no choice. "Uh. Sure."

"If my mom were normal—not sick, I mean—I could have told her about what happened to me at the party."

Kate took a tiny drag, coughed hard, and said, "Do you think about it a lot?"

Tully leaned back against the log, taking the cigarette again. After a long pause, she said, "I have nightmares about it."

Kate wished she knew what to say. "What about your dad? Can you talk to him?"

Tully wouldn't look at her. "I don't think she even knows who he is." Her voice fell. "Or he heard about me and ran."

"That's harsh."

"Life is harsh. Besides, I don't need them. I've got you, Katie. You're the one that helped me through it."

Kate smiled. The sharp tang of smoke filled the air between them, stung her eyes, but she didn't care. What mattered was being here, with her new best friend. "That's what friends are for."

That next night Tully was on the last chapter of *The Outsiders* when she heard her mother yelling through the house. "Tully! Answer the damn door."

She slammed the book down and went out into the living room, where her mother sat sprawled on the sofa, taking a bong hit as she watched *Happy Days*.

"You're right by the door."

Her mother shrugged. "So?"

"Hide your bong."

Sighing dramatically, Cloud leaned over and put her bong beneath the end table beside the couch. Only a blind person would miss it, but that was as good as Cloud was likely to do.

Tully smoothed the hair away from her face and opened the door.

A small, dark-haired woman stood there, holding a foil-covered casserole dish. Electric-blue eye shadow accentuated her brown eyes, and rose-hued blush—applied with too heavy a hand—created the illusion of sharp cheekbones in her round face. "You must be Tully," the woman said in a voice that was higher somehow than expected. It was a girl's voice, full of enthusiasm, and it matched the sparkle in her eyes. "I'm Kate's mom. Sorry to come without calling, but your line has been busy."

Tully pictured the phone by her mother's bed off the hook. "Oh."

"I brought you and your mom a tuna casserole for dinner. I imagine she doesn't feel much like cooking. My sister had cancer a few years ago, so I know the drill." She smiled and stood there. Finally, her smile faded. "Are you going to invite me in?"

Tully froze. *This is going to be bad,* she thought. "Um . . . sure."

"Thank you." Mrs. Mularkey moved past her and went into the house.

Cloud lay on the sofa, sort of spread-eagled; she had a pile of marijuana on her stomach. Smiling blearily, she tried to sit up and failed. The failure made her shoot out a few swear words and then laugh. The whole house reeked of pot.

Mrs. Mularkey came to a stop. Confusion pleated her forehead. "I'm Margie from next door," she said.

"I'm Cloud," Tully's mother said, trying again to sit up. "It's cool to meet you."

"And you."

For a terrible, awkward moment, they just stared at

each other. Tully had no doubt at all that Mrs. Mularkey's sharp eyes saw everything—the bong under the end table, the bag of Maui-wowie on the floor, the overturned, empty wineglass, and the pizza boxes on the table. "Also, I wanted to let you know that I'm home most days, and I'd be happy to drive you to the doctor's office or run errands. I know how chemo can make you feel."

Cloud frowned blearily. "Who's got cancer?"

Mrs. Mularkey turned to look at Tully, who wanted to curl up and die.

"Tully, show our cool neighbor with the food where the kitchen is."

Tully practically ran for the kitchen. In that pink hell, junk food wrappers covered the table, dirty dishes clogged the sink, and overflowing ashtrays were everywhere; more evidence of her pathetic life for her best friend's mother to see.

Mrs. Mularkey walked past her, bent over the oven, put the casserole onto the rack, then shut the door with her hip and then turned to study Tully. "My Katie is a good girl," she said at last.

Here it comes. "Yes, ma'am."

"She's been praying for your mother to recover from her cancer. She even has a little altar set up in her room."

Tully looked at the floor, too ashamed to answer. How could she explain why she'd lied? No answer would be good enough, not for a mother like Mrs. Mularkey, who loved her kids. At that, a wave of jealousy joined the shame running through her. Maybe if Tully had had a mother who loved her, she wouldn't find it so easy—so necessary—to lie in the first place. And now she'd lose the one thing that mattered to her: Katie.

"Do you think lying to your friends is okay?"

"No, ma'am." So intently was she staring at the floor that she was startled by a gentle touch on her chin that forced her to look up.

"Are you going to be a good friend to Kate? Or the kind that leads her to trouble?"

"I'd never hurt Katie." Tully wanted to say more, maybe fall to her knees and swear to be a good person, but she was so close to tears she didn't dare move. She stared into Mrs. Mularkey's dark eyes and saw something she never expected: understanding.

In the living room, Cloud stumbled over to the television and changed the channel. Tully could see the screen through the rubble of the messy room: Jean Enersen was reporting on the day's top story.

"You do it, don't you?" Mrs. Mularkey said quietly, as if she worried that Cloud might be eavesdropping. "Pay the bills, grocery-shop, clean the house. Who pays for everything?"

Tully swallowed hard. No one had ever seen through her life so clearly before. "My grandmother sends a check every week."

"My dad was a fall-down drunk and the whole town knew it," Mrs. Mularkey said in a soft voice that matched the look in her eyes. "He was mean, too. Friday and Saturday nights, my sister, Georgia, would have to go to the tavern and drag him home. All the way out of the bar he'd be smacking her and calling her names. She was like one of those rodeo clowns, always stepping between the bull and the cowboy. By the end of my junior year I figured out why she ran with the fast crowd and drank too much."

"She didn't want people to look at her like she was pitiful."

Mrs. Mularkey nodded. "She hated that look. What matters, though, isn't other people. That's what

I learned. Who your mom is and how she lives her life isn't a reflection of *you*. You can make your own choices. And there's nothing for you to be ashamed of. But you'll have to dream big, Tully." She glanced through the open door to the living room. "Like that Jean Enersen on the TV there. A woman who gets to a place like that in her life knows how to go after what she wants."

"How do I know what I want?"

"You keep your eyes open and do the right thing. Go to college. And trust your friends."

"I do trust Kate."

"So you'll tell her the truth?"

"What if I just promise——"

"One of us is going to tell her, Tully. It should be you."

Tully took a deep breath and released it. Though telling the truth went against every instinct she had, she had no choice, really. She wanted Mrs. Mularkey to be proud of her. "Okay."

"Good. So I'll see you for dinner tomorrow night. Five o'clock. It'll be your chance to start over."

The next night, Tully changed her clothes at least four times, trying to find exactly the right outfit. By the time she was actually ready, she was so late that she had to run all the way across the street and up the hill.

Kate's mom opened the door. She wore a pair of purple gabardine bell-bottoms and a striped V-neck sweater with angel sleeves. Smiling, she said, "I warn you, it's loud and crazy in here."

"I love loud and crazy," Tully said.

"Then you'll fit right in." Mrs. Mularkey put an arm around Tully's shoulder and led her toward the beige-walled living room with its moss-green shag carpeting, bright red sofa, and black recliner. A small gold-framed photo of Jesus and another of Elvis were the only decorations on the walls, but dozens of family pictures cluttered the top of the console TV. Tully couldn't help thinking of the TV in her house; its top was covered with overflowing ashtrays and empty cigarette packs, but no family photos.

"Bud?" Mrs. Mularkey said to the beefy, dark-haired man sitting in the recliner. "This is Tully Hart from next door."

Mr. Mularkey smiled at her and put down his drink. "Well, well. So you're the one we've been hearin' about. It's nice to have you here, Tully."

"It's nice to be here."

Mrs. Mularkey patted her shoulder. "Dinner's not till six. Katie's upstairs in her room. It's the one at the very top of the stairs. I'm sure you girls have plenty to talk about."

Tully got the message and nodded, unable to rouse her voice. Now that she was here, in this warm house that smelled of home-cooked meals, standing shoulder to shoulder with the world's most perfect mom, she couldn't imagine losing it all, becoming unwelcome. "I'll never lie to her again," she promised.

"Good. Now go." With a last smile, Mrs. Mularkey walked into the living room.

Mr. Mularkey put an arm around his wife and drew her into the La-Z-Boy with him. Immediately they bent their heads together.

Tully felt a longing so sharp and unexpected, she couldn't move. Everything would have been different for her if she'd had a family like this. She didn't want to turn away from it just yet. "Are you watching the news?"

Mr. Mularkey looked up. "We never miss it."

Mrs. Mularkey smiled. "Jean Enersen is changing

the world. She's one of the first women to anchor a nightly news program."

"I'm going to be a reporter," Tully said suddenly.

"That's wonderful," Mr. Mularkey said.

"There you are," Kate said suddenly, coming up beside her. "Nice of everyone to tell me you were here," she said loudly.

"I was just telling your mom and dad that I'm going to be a news reporter," Tully said.

Mrs. Mularkey beamed at that. In her smile, Tully saw everything that had been missing in her life. "Isn't that a grand dream, Katie?"

Kate looked confused for a moment. Then she hooked her arm through Tully's and pulled her away from the living room and up the stairs. In her small attic bedroom, Kate went to the record player and flipped through a small stack of records. By the time she'd chosen one—Carole King's *Tapestry*—and put it on, Tully was at the window, staring out at the lavender evening.

The surge of adrenaline she'd gotten from her announcement faded, leaving a quiet kind of sadness behind. She knew what she had to do now, but the thought of it made her sick.

Tell her the truth.

If you don't, Mrs. Mularkey will.

"I got the new *Seventeen* and *Tiger Beat,*" Kate said, stretching out on the blue shag carpeting. "You want to read 'em? We can take the 'Can You Be Tony DeFranco's Girlfriend?' quiz."

Tully lay down beside her. "Sure."

"Jan-Michael Vincent is so foxy," Kate said, flipping to a picture of the actor.

"I heard he lied to his girlfriend," Tully said, daring a sideways glance.

"I hate liars." Kate turned the page. "Are you really going to be a news reporter? You never told me that."

"Yeah," Tully said, really imagining it for the first time. Maybe she could be famous. Then everyone would admire her. "You'll have to be one, too, though. 'Cause we do everything together."

"Me?"

"We'll be a team like Woodward and Bernstein, only with better clothes. And prettier."

"I don't know—"

Tully bumped her. "Yes, you do. Mrs. Ramsdale told the whole class that you're an excellent writer."

Kate laughed. "That's true. Okay. I'll be a reporter, too."

"When we get famous, we'll tell Mike Wallace we couldn't have done it without each other."

After that, they fell silent, flipping through the magazines. Tully tried twice to bring up the subject of her mother, but both times Kate interrupted her, and then someone was yelling, "Dinner," and her chance for coming clean had slipped away.

All through the best meal of her life, she felt the weight of her lie. By the time they'd cleared the table and washed and dried the dishes, she was stretched to the breaking point. Even dreaming about fame on television couldn't ease her nerves.

"Hey, Mom," Kate said, putting away the last white CorningWare plate, "Tully and me are going to ride our bikes down to the park, okay?"

"Tully and I," her mother answered, reaching down into the magazine pouch of the La-Z-Boy's arm for the TV guide. "And be back by eight."

"Aww, Mom—"

"Eight," her father said from the living room.

Kate looked at Tully. "They treat me like I'm a baby."

"You don't know how lucky you are. Come on, let's get our bikes."

They rode at a breakneck speed down the bumpy

county road, laughing all the way. At Summer Hill, Tully flung her arms out and Kate followed.

When they got to the river park, they ditched their bikes in the trees and lay on the grass, side by side, staring up at the sky, listening to the river gurgling against the rocks.

"I have something to tell you," Tully said in a rush.

"What?"

"My mom doesn't have cancer. She's a pothead."

"Your mom smokes dope. Yeah, right."

"It's true. She's always high."

Kate turned to her. "Really?"

"Really."

"You *lied* to me?"

Tully could barely maintain eye contact, she was so ashamed. "I didn't mean to."

"People don't lie accidentally. It's not like tripping over a crack in the sidewalk."

"You don't know how it feels to be embarrassed by your mom."

"Are you kidding? You should have seen what my mom wore out to dinner last—"

"No," Tully said. "You don't know."

"Tell me."

Tully knew what Kate was asking of her; she wanted the truth that had spawned the lie, but Tully didn't know if she could do it, turn all her pain into words and pass them out like cards. All her life she'd kept these secrets close. If she told Kate the reality and then lost her as a friend, it would be unbearable.

Then again, if she didn't tell the truth, she'd lose the friendship for sure.

"I was two years old," she finally said, "when my mom first dumped me at my grandparents' house. She went to town for milk and came back when I was four. When I was ten, she showed up again and I thought it meant she loved me. That time she let go of me in a crowd. The next time I saw her I was fourteen. My gran's letting us live in this house and sending us money every week. That'll last until my mom bails again— which she will do."

"I don't understand."

"Of course you don't. My mom isn't like yours. This is the longest amount of time I've ever spent with her. Sooner or later she'll get bored and move on without me."

"How can a mother do that?"

Tully shrugged. "I think there's something wrong with me."

"There's nothing wrong with you. She's the loser. But I still don't get why you lied to me."

Tully finally looked at her. "I wanted you to like me."

"*You* were worried about *me*?" Kate burst out laughing. Tully was just about to ask her what was so funny when she sobered and said, "No more lies, right?"

"Absolutely."

"We'll be best friends forever," Kate said earnestly. "Okay?"

"You mean you'll always be there for me?"

"Always," Kate answered. "No matter what."

Tully felt an emotion open up inside her like some exotic flower. She could practically smell its honeyed scent in the air. For the first time in her life, she felt totally safe with someone. "Forever," she promised. "No matter what."

Kate would always remember the summer after eighth grade as one of the best times of her life. Every weekday, she rushed through her morning chores without complaint and babysat her brother until three o'clock, when her mom came home from running errands and volunteering on the 4-H council. After that, Kate was free. Weekends were, for the most part, her own.

She and Tully rode their bikes all over the valley and spent hours inner-tubing down the Pilchuck River. In the late afternoons, they stretched out on tiny towels, wearing neon-colored crocheted bikinis, their skin slick with a mixture of baby oil and iodine, listening to Top 40 music on the transistor radio they never left behind. They talked about everything: fashion, music, boys, the war and what was still going on over there, what it would be like to be a reporting duo, movies. Nothing was off-limits; no question couldn't be volleyed over the net. Now it was late August and they were in Kate's bedroom, packing makeup for their trip to the fair. As usual, Kate had to change clothes and put on makeup after she left the house. If she wanted to look cool, anyway. Her mom still thought she was too young for everything. "You got your tube top?" Tully asked.

"Got it."

Grinning at their own brilliant plan, they headed downstairs, where Dad was sitting on the sofa, watching television.

"We're going to the fair now," Kate said, thankful that her mother wasn't here. Mom would notice the bag that was too big for the county fair. Her X-ray vision would probably see through the macramé exterior to the clothes, shoes, and makeup within.

"Be careful, you two," he said without looking up.

It was what he always said now, ever since girls had started disappearing in Seattle. The news was calling the killer "Ted" these days because some girl at Lake Sammamish State Park had actually gotten away and given a description and his first name to the police. Girls all across the state were terrified. You couldn't see a yellow VW bug without worrying that it was Ted's car.

"We'll be super careful," Tully said, smiling. She loved it when Kate's parents worried about them.

Kate crossed the room to kiss her dad goodbye. He curled an arm around her and handed her a ten-dollar bill. "Have fun."

"Thanks, Daddy."

She and Tully headed down the driveway, swinging their bags beside them.

"Do you think Kenny Markson will be at the fair?" Kate asked.

"You worry too much about boys."

Kate bumped her friend, hip to hip. "He has a crush on you."

"Big whoop. I'm taller."

Suddenly Tully stopped.

"Jeez, Tully, be a spaz, why don'tcha? I almost fell over—"

"Oh, no," Tully whispered.

"What's the matter?"

Then she noticed the police car parked in Tully's driveway.

Tully grabbed Kate's hand and practically dragged her down the driveway, across the street, and to the front door, which stood open.

A policeman was waiting for them in the living room. When he saw them, his fleshy face pleated into clownlike folds. "Hello, girls. I'm Officer Dan Myers."

"What did she do this time?" Tully asked.

"There was a spotted owl protest up by Lake Quinault that got out of hand yesterday. Your mother and several others staged a sit-in that cost Weyerhaeuser a full day's work. Worse, someone dropped a cigarette in the woods." He paused. "They just got the fire under control."

"Let me guess: she's going to jail."

"Her lawyer is seeking voluntary treatment for drug

addiction. If she's lucky, she'll be in the hospital for a while. If not . . ." He let the sentence trail off.

"Has someone called my grandmother?"

The officer nodded. "She's expecting you. Do you need help packing?"

Kate didn't understand what was happening. She turned to her friend. "Tully?"

There was a terrible blankness in Tully's brown eyes, and Kate knew that this was big, whatever it was. "I have to go back to my grandma's," Tully said, then she walked past Kate and went into her bedroom.

Kate ran after her. "You *can't* go!"

Tully pulled a suitcase out of the closet and flipped it open. "I don't have any choice."

"I'll *make* your mother come back. I'll tell her—"

Tully paused in her packing and looked at Kate. "You can't fix this," she said softly, sounding like a grown-up, tired and broken. For the first time, Kate understood the stories about Tully's loser mom. They'd laughed about Cloud, made jokes about her drug use and her fashion sense and her various stories, but it wasn't funny. And Tully had known this would happen.

"Promise me," Tully said, her voice cracking, "that we'll always be best friends."

"Always," was all Kate could say.

Tully finished packing and locked up her suitcase. Saying nothing, she headed back to the living room. On the radio "American Pie" was playing, and Kate wondered if she'd ever be able to listen to that song again without remembering this moment. *The day the music died.* She followed Tully out to the driveway. There, they clung to each other until Officer Dan gently pulled Tully away.

Kate couldn't even wave goodbye. She just stood there in the driveway, numb, with tears streaming down her cheeks, watching her best friend leave.

CHAPTER
SIX

For the next three years, they wrote letters faithfully back and forth. It became more than a tradition and something of a lifeline. Every Sunday evening, Tully sat down at the white desk in her lavender and pink little-girl's room and spilled her thoughts and dreams and worries and frustrations onto a sheet of notebook paper. Sometimes she wrote about things that didn't matter—the Farrah Fawcett haircut she'd gotten that made her look foxy or the Gunny Sax dress she wore to the junior prom—but every now and then she went deeper and told Katie about the times she couldn't sleep or the way she dreamed of her mother coming back and saying she was proud of her. When her grandfather died, it was Kate to whom Tully turned. She hadn't cried for him until she got the phone call from her best friend that began with, "Oh, Tul, I'm so sorry." For the first time in her life, Tully didn't lie or embellish (well, not too much); she was mostly just herself, and that was good enough for Kate.

Now it was the summer of 1977. In a few short months they'd be seniors, ruling their separate schools.

And today was the day Tully had been working toward for months. Finally, she was going to actually step onto the road Mrs. Mularkey had shown her all those years ago.

The next Jean Enersen.

The words had become her mantra, a secret code that housed the enormity of her dream and made it sound possible. The seeds of it, planted so long ago in the kitchen of the Snohomish house, had sprouted wildly and sent roots deep into her heart. She hadn't realized how much she'd needed a dream, but it had transformed her, changed her from poor motherless and abandoned Tully to a girl poised to take on the world. The goal made her life story unimportant, gave her something to reach for, to hang on to. And it made Mrs. Mularkey proud; she knew that from their letters. She knew, too, that Kate shared this dream. They would be reporters together, tracking down stories and writing them up. A team.

She stood on the sidewalk, staring at the building in front of her, feeling like a bank robber staring at Fort Knox.

Surprisingly, the ABC affiliate, despite its clout and glory, was in a small building in the Denny Regrade section of town. There was no view to speak of, no impressive wall of windows or expensive art-filled lobby. Rather, there was an L-shaped desk, a pretty-enough receptionist, and a trio of mustard-yellow molded plastic lobby chairs.

Tully took a deep breath, squared her shoulders, and went inside. At the receptionist's desk, she gave her name, and then took a seat along the wall. She made sure not to fidget or tap her feet during the long wait for her interview.

You never knew who was watching.

"Ms. Hart?" the receptionist finally said, looking up. "He'll see you now."

Tully gave her a poised, camera-ready smile and stood up. "Thank you." She followed the receptionist through the doors to another waiting area.

There, she came face to face with the man to whom she'd been writing weekly for almost a year.

"Hello, Mr. Rorbach." She shook his hand. "It's excellent to finally meet you."

He looked tired; older than she'd expected, too. There were only a handful of reddish gray hairs growing on his shiny head, and none of them were where they should be. The pale blue leisure suit he wore was decorated with white topstitching. "Come into my office, Miss Hart."

"Ms. Hart," she said. It was always better to start off on the right foot. Gloria Steinem said you'd never get respect if you didn't demand it.

Mr. Rorbach blinked at her. "Excuse me?"

"I'll answer to Ms. Hart, if you don't mind, which I'm sure you don't. How could anyone with a degree in English literature from Georgetown be resistant to change? I'm certain you're on the cutting edge of social consciousness. I can see it in your eyes. I like your glasses, by the way."

He stared at her, his mouth hanging open the slightest bit before he seemed to remember where he was. "Follow me, Ms. Hart." He led her down the bland white hallway to the last fake wood door on the left, which he opened.

His office was a small corner space, with a window that looked directly at the monorail's elevated cement track. The walls were completely bare.

Tully sat on the black fold-up chair positioned in front of his desk.

Mr. Rorbach took his seat and stared at her. "One hundred and twelve letters, Ms. Hart." He patted the thick manila file folder on his desk.

He'd saved all the letters she'd sent. That must mean something. She pulled her newest résumé out of the briefcase and set it on his desk. "As I'm sure you'll notice, the high school paper has repeatedly put my work on its front page. Additionally I've included an in-depth piece on the Guatemalan earthquake, an update on Karen Ann Quinlan, and a heart-wrenching look at Freddie Prinze's last days. They'll surely showcase my ability."

"You're seventeen years old."

"Yes."

"Next month you'll start your senior year of high school."

All those letters had worked. He knew everything about her. "Exactly. I think that's an interesting story angle, by the way. Going in to senior year; watching the class of '78. Maybe we could do monthly features about what really goes on behind the doors of a local high school. I'm sure your viewers—"

"Ms. Hart." He steepled his fingers and rested his chin on the tips, looking at her. She got the impression he was trying not to smile.

"Yes, Mr. Rorbach?"

"This is the ABC affiliate, for gosh sakes. We don't hire high school kids."

"But you have interns."

"From UW and other colleges. Our interns know their way around a TV station. Most of them have already worked on their campus broadcasts. I'm sorry, but you're just not ready."

"Oh."

They stared at each other.

"I've been at this job a long time, Ms. Hart, and I've rarely seen anyone as full of ambition as you." He patted the folder of her letters again. "I'll tell you what, you keep sending me your writing. I'll keep an eye out for you."

"So when I'm ready to be a reporter, you'll hire me?"

He laughed. "You just send me the articles. And get good grades and go to college, okay? Then we'll see."

Tully felt energized again. "I'll send you an update once a month. You'll hire me someday, Mr. Rorbach. You'll see."

"I wouldn't bet against you, Ms. Hart."

They talked for a few more moments, and then Mr. Rorbach showed her out of his office. On the way to the stairs, he stopped at the trophy case, where dozens of Emmys and other news awards glinted golden in the light.

"I'll win an Emmy someday," she said, touching the glass with her fingertips. She refused to let herself be wounded by this setback, and that was all it was: a setback.

"You know what, Tallulah Hart, I believe you. Now go off to high school and enjoy your senior year. Real life comes fast enough."

Outside, it looked like a postcard of Seattle; the kind of blue-skied, cloudless, picture-perfect day that lured out-of-towners into selling their homes in duller, less spectacular places and moving here. If only they knew how rare these days were. Like a rocket blaster, summer burned fast and bright in this part of the world and went out with equal speed.

Holding her grandfather's thick black briefcase against her chest, she walked up the street toward the bus stop. On an elevated track above her head, the monorail thundered past, making the ground quake.

All the way home, she told herself it was really an opportunity; now she'd be able to prove her worth in college and get an even better job.

But no matter how she tried to recast it, the sense of having failed wouldn't release its hold. When she got home she felt smaller somehow, her shoulders weighted down.

She unlocked the front door and went inside, tossing the briefcase on the kitchen table.

Gran was in the living room, sitting on the tattered old sofa, with her stockinged feet on the crushed velvet ottoman and an unfinished sampler in her lap. Asleep, she snored lightly.

At the sight of her grandmother, Tully had to force a smile. "Hey, Gran," she said softly, moving into the living room, bending down to touch her grandmother's knobby hand. She sat down beside her.

Gran came awake slowly. Behind the thick old-fashioned glasses, her confused gaze cleared. "How did it go?"

"The assistant news director thought I was too qualified, can you believe it? He said the position was a dead end for someone with my skills."

Gran squeezed her hand. "You're too young, huh?"

The tears she'd been holding back stung her eyes. Embarrassed, she brushed them away. "I know they'll offer me a job as soon as I get into college. You'll see. I'll make you proud."

Gran gave her the poor-Tully look. "I'm already proud. It's Dorothy's attention you want."

Tully leaned against her gran's slim shoulder and let herself be held. In a few moments, she knew this pain would fade again; like a sunburn, it would heal itself and leave her slightly more protected from the glare. "I've got you, Gran, so she doesn't matter."

Gran sighed tiredly. "Why don't you call your

friend Katie now? But don't stay on too long. It's expensive."

Just the thought of that, talking to Kate, lifted Tully's spirits. With the long-distance charges what they were, they rarely got to call each other. "Thanks, Gran. I will."

The next week Tully got a job at the *Queen Anne Bee*, her neighborhood weekly newspaper. Her duties pretty much matched the measly per-hour wage they paid her, but she didn't care. She was in the business. She spent almost every waking hour of the summer of '77 in the small, cramped offices, soaking up every bit of knowledge she could. When she wasn't bird-dogging the reporters or making copies or delivering coffee, she was at home, playing gin rummy with Gran for matchsticks. Every Sunday night, like clockwork, she wrote to Kate and shared the minute details of her week.

Now she sat at her little-girl's desk in her bedroom and reread this week's eight-page letter, then signed it *Best Friends Forever, Tully* ♥, and carefully folded it into thirds.

On her desk was the most recent postcard from Kate, who was away on the Mularkey family's yearly camping trip. Kate called it Hell Week with Bugs, but Tully was jealous of each perfect-sounding moment. She wished that she'd been able to go on the vacation with them; turning down the invitation had been one of the most difficult things she'd done. But between her all-important summer job and Gran's declining health, she'd had no real choice.

She glanced down at her friend's note, rereading the words she'd already memorized. *Playing hearts at night and roasting marshmallows, swimming in the freezing lake . . .*

She forced herself to look away. It didn't do any good in life to pine for what you couldn't have. Cloud had certainly taught her that lesson.

She put her own letter in an envelope, addressed it, then went downstairs to check on Gran, who was already asleep.

Alone, Tully watched her favorite Sunday night television programs—*All in the Family, Alice,* and *Kojak*—and then closed up the house and went to bed. Her last thought as she drifted lazily toward sleep was to wonder what the Mularkeys were doing.

The next morning she woke at her usual time, six o'clock, and dressed for work. Sometimes, if she arrived early enough at the office, one of the reporters would let her help with the day's stories.

She hurried down the hall and tapped on the last door. Though she hated to wake her grandmother, it was the house rule. No leaving without a goodbye. "Gran?"

She tapped again and pushed the door open slowly, calling out, "Gran . . . I'm leaving for work."

Cool lavender shadows lay along the windowsills. The samplers that decorated the walls were boxes without form or substance in the gloom.

Gran lay in bed. Even from here, Tully could see the shape of her, the coil of her white hair, the ruffle of her nightdress . . . and the stillness of her chest.

"Gran?"

She moved forward, touched her grandmother's velvet, wrinkled cheek. The skin was cold as ice. No breath came from her slack lips.

Tully's whole world seemed to tilt, slide off its foundation. It took all her strength to stand there, staring down at her grandmother's lifeless face.

Her tears were slow in forming; it was as if each one were made of blood and too thick to pass through her tear ducts. Memories came at her like a kaleido-scope: Gran braiding her hair for her seventh birthday party, telling her that her mommy might show up if she prayed hard enough, and then years later admitting that sometimes God didn't answer a little girl's prayers, or a grown woman's, either; or playing cards last week, laughing as Tully swept up the discard pile—again—saying, "Tully, you don't have to have every card, all the time . . ."; or kissing her goodnight so gently.

She had no idea how long she stood there, but by the time she leaned over and kissed Gran's papery cheek, sunlight had eased through the sheer curtains, lighting the room. It surprised Tully, that brightness. Without Gran, it seemed this room should be dark.

"Come on, Tully," she said.

There were things she was supposed to do now; she knew that. She and Gran had talked about this, done things to prepare. Tully knew, though, that no words could have really prepared her for this.

She went over to Gran's nightstand, where a pretty rosewood box sat beneath the photo of Grandpa and alongside the battalion of medications.

She lifted the lid, feeling vaguely like a thief, but Gran expected this of her. *When I go Home,* Gran always said, *I'll leave you something in the box Grandpa bought me.*

Inside, lying atop the cluster of inexpensive jew-elry that Tully could rarely remember her grandmother wearing, was a folded piece of pink paper with Tully's name written on it.

Slowly, she reached out, took the letter, and opened it.

My dearest Tully—
    I am so sorry. I know how afraid you are of being alone, of being left behind, but God has His plan for all of us. I would have stayed with

*you longer if I could have. Your grandfather
and I will always be watching out for you from
Heaven. You will never be alone if you believe in
that.*

You were the greatest joy of my life.

Love, Gran

Were.

Gran was gone.

Tully stood outside the church, watching the crowd of
elderly people stream past her. A few of Gran's friends
recognized her and came over to offer their condolences.

I'm so sorry, dear . . .

. . . but she's in a better place . . .

. . . with her beloved Winston.

. . . wouldn't want you to cry.

She took as much of it as she could because she
knew Gran would have wanted that, but by eleven
o'clock, she was ready to scream. Didn't any of the
well-wishers *see,* didn't they realize that Tully was a
seventeen-year-old girl, dressed in black and all alone
in the world?

If only Katie and the Mularkeys were here, but she
had no idea how to reach them in Canada, and since they
wouldn't be home for two days, she had to endure this
alone. With them beside her, a pretend family, maybe
she would have made it through the service.

Without them, she simply couldn't do it. Instead of
sitting through the terrible, heart-wrenching memories
of Gran, she got up in the middle of the funeral and
walked out.

Outside, in the hot August sunlight, she could
breathe again, even though the tears were always near

to the surface, as was the pointless query, *How could you leave me like this?*

Surrounded by dusty old-model land yachts, she tried not to cry. Mostly, she tried not to remember, or to worry about what would happen to her.

Nearby, a twig snapped and Tully looked up. At first all she saw were the haphazardly parked cars.

Then she saw her.

Over by the property's edge, where a row of towering maple trees delineated the start of the city park, Cloud stood in the shade, smoking a long slim cigarette. Dressed in tattered corduroy bell-bottoms and a dirty peasant blouse, parenthesized by a wall of frizzy brown hair, she looked rail-thin.

Tully couldn't help the tiny leap of joy her heart took. Finally, she wasn't alone. Cloud might be a little nuts, but when the chips were down, she came back. Tully ran toward her, smiling. She would forgive her mother for all the missing years, all the abandonments. What mattered was that she was here now, when Tully needed her most. "Thank God you're here," she said, coming to a breathless stop. "You knew I'd need you."

Her mother lurched toward her, laughing when she almost fell. "You're a beautiful spirit, Tully. All you need is air and to be free."

Tully's stomach seemed to drop. "Not again," she said, pleading for help with her eyes. "Please . . ."

"Always." There was an edge to Cloud's voice now, a sharpness that belied the glassy look in her eyes.

"I'm your flesh and blood and I need you now. Otherwise I'll be alone." Tully knew she was whispering, but she couldn't seem to find any volume for her voice.

Cloud took a stumbling step forward. The sadness in her eyes was unmistakable, but Tully didn't care. Her mother's pseudo-emotions came and went like the sun in Seattle. "Look at me, Tully."

"I'm looking."

"No. *Look*. I can't help you."

"But I need you."

"That's the fucking tragedy of it," her mother said, taking a long drag on the cigarette and blowing smoke out a few seconds later.

"Why?" Tully asked. She was going to add, *Don't you love me*? but before she could form the pain into words, the funeral let out and black-clad people swarmed into the parking lot. Tully glanced sideways, just long enough to dry her tears. When she turned back, her mother was gone.

The woman from social services was as dry as a twig. She tried to say the right things, but Tully noticed that she kept glancing at her watch as she stood in the hallway outside Tully's bedroom.

"I still don't see why I need to pack my stuff. I'm almost eighteen. Gran has no mortgage on this house—I know 'cause I paid the bills this year. I'm old enough to live alone."

"The lawyer is expecting us," was the woman's only answer. "Are you nearly ready?"

She placed the stack of Kate's letters in her suitcase, closed the lid, and snapped it shut. Since she couldn't actually form the words *I'm ready,* she simply grabbed the suitcase, then slung her macramé purse over her shoulder. "I guess so."

"Good," the woman said, spinning briskly around and heading for the stairs.

Tully took one last, lingering look around her bedroom, noticing as if for the first time things she'd overlooked for years: the lavender ruffled bed linens and white twin bed, the row of plastic horses—dusty now—that lined the windowsill, the Mrs. Beasley doll on the top of the dresser, and the Miss America jewelry box with the pink ballerina on top.

Gran had decorated this room for the little girl who'd been dumped here all those years ago. Every item had been chosen with care, but now they'd all be boxed up and stored in the dark, along with the memories they elicited. Tully wondered how long it would be before she could think of Gran without crying.

She closed the door behind her and followed the woman through the now-quiet house, down the steps outside, to the street in front of the house, where a battered yellow Ford Pinto was parked.

"Put your suitcase in the back."

Tully did as she was told and got into the passenger seat.

When the lady started up the car, the stereo came on at an ear-shattering level. It was David Soul's "Don't Give Up on Us." She immediately turned it down, mumbling, "Sorry about that."

Tully figured it was as good a song to apologize for as any, so she just shrugged and looked out the window.

"I'm sorry about your grandmother, if I haven't said that already."

Tully stared at her weird reflection in the window. It was like looking at a negative version of her face, colorless and insubstantial. The way she felt inside, actually.

"By all accounts she was an exceptional woman."

Tully didn't answer that. She couldn't have found much of a voice anyway. Ever since the encounter with her mother, she'd been dry inside. Empty.

"Well. Here we are."

They parked in front of a well-kept Victorian home in downtown Ballard. A hand-painted sign out front read: BAKER AND MONTGOMERY, ATTORNEYS AT LAW.

It took Tully a moment to get out of the car. By the time she did, the woman was giving her a soft, understanding smile.

"You don't need to bring your suitcase."

"I'd like to, thanks." If there was one thing Tully understood, it was the importance of a packed bag.

The woman nodded and led the way up the grass-veined concrete walkway to the white front door. Inside the overly quaint space, Tully took a seat in the lobby, close to the empty receptionist's desk. Cutesy drawings of big-eyed kids lined the ornately papered walls. At precisely four o'clock, a pudgy man with a balding head and horn-rimmed glasses came to get them.

"Hello, Tallulah. I'm Elmer Baker, your Grand-mother Hart's attorney."

Tully followed him to a small upstairs room with two overstuffed chairs and an antique mahogany desk littered with yellow legal pads. In the corner, a standing fan buzzed and thumped and sent warm air spinning toward the door. The social worker took a seat by the window.

"Here. Here. Sit down, please," he said, moving to his own chair behind the elegant desk.

"Now, Tallulah—"

"Tully," she said quietly.

"Quite right. I recall Ima saying you preferred Tully." He put his elbows on the desk and leaned forward. His buglike eyes blinked behind the thick magnifying lenses of his glasses. "As you know, your mother has re-fused to take custody of you."

It took all her strength to nod, even though last night she'd practiced a whole monologue about how she should be allowed to live alone. Now, here, she felt small and much too young.

"I'm sorry," he said in a gentle voice, and Tully actually flinched at the words. She'd come to truly loathe the stupid, useless sentiment.

"Yeah," she said, fisting her hands at her sides.

"Ms. Gulligan here has found a lovely family for you. You'll be one of several displaced teens in their care. The excellent news is that you'll be able to continue in your current school placement. I'm sure that makes you happy."

"Ecstatic."

Mr. Baker looked momentarily nonplussed by her response. "Of course. Now. As to your inheritance. Ima left all her assets—both homes, the car, the bank accounts, and stocks—to you. She has left instructions for you to continue with the monthly payments to her daughter, Dorothy. Your grandmother believed it was the best and only way to keep track of her. Dorothy has proven to be very reliable at keeping in touch when there's money coming." He cleared his throat. "Now . . . if we sell both homes, you won't have to worry about finances for quite some time. We can take care—"

"But then I won't have a home at all."

"I'm sorry about that, but Ima was very specific in her request. She wanted you to be able to go to any college." He looked up. "You're going to win the Pulitzer someday. Or that's what she told me."

Tully couldn't believe she was going to cry again, and in front of these people. She popped to her feet. "I need to go to the restroom."

A frown pleated Mr. Baker's pale forehead. "Oh. Certainly. Downstairs. First door to the left of the front door."

Tully got up from her chair, grabbed her suitcase, and

made her halting way to the door. Once in the hallway, she shut the door behind her and leaned against the wall, trying not to cry.

Foster care could *not* be her future.

She glanced down at the date on her Bicentennial wristwatch.

The Mularkeys would be home tomorrow.

CHAPTER
SEVEN

The drive home from British Columbia seemed to take forever. The air conditioner in the station wagon was broken, so warm air tumbled from the useless vents. Everyone was hot and tired and dirty. And still Mom and Dad wanted to sing songs. They kept bugging the kids to sing along.

Kate couldn't stand how lame it was. "Mom, will you *please* tell Sean to quit touching my shoulder?"

Her brother burped and started laughing. The dog barked wildly.

In the front seat, Dad leaned forward and turned on the radio. John Denver's voice floated through the speakers with "Thank God I'm a Country Boy." "That's all I'm singing, Margie. If they don't want to join in . . . fine."

Kate returned to her book. The car bounced so much the words danced on the page, but that didn't matter; not with as many times as she'd read *The Lord of the Rings*.

I am glad you are here with me. Here at the end of all things.

"Katie. Kathleen."

She looked up. "Yeah?"

"We're home," her dad said. "Put that dang book down and help us unload the car."

"Can I call Tully first?"

"No. You'll unpack first."

Kate slapped her book shut. For seven days she'd been waiting to make that call. But unloading the car was more important. "Fine. But Sean better help."

Her mother sighed. "You just worry about yourself, Kathleen."

They piled out of the smelly station wagon and began the end-of-vacation ritual. By the time they finished, it was dark. Kate put the last of her clothes into the pile on the laundry room floor, started the first load, then went to find her mom, who was sitting on the sofa with Dad. They were leaning against each other, looking dazed.

"Can I call Tully now?"

Dad consulted his watch. "At nine-thirty? I'm sure her grandmother would really appreciate that."

"But—"

"Goodnight, Katie," her dad said firmly, looping his arm around Mom and pulling her close.

"This is so not fair."

Mom laughed. "Whoever told you life would be fair? Now go to bed."

For almost four hours Tully stood at the corner of her house, watching the Mularkeys unload their car. She'd thought about running up the hill a dozen times, just showing up, but she wasn't ready for the boisterousness of the whole family just yet. She wanted to be alone with Kate, someplace quiet where they could talk.

So she waited until the lights went out and then

crossed the street. In the grass beneath Kate's window, she waited another thirty minutes, just to be sure.

Off to her left somewhere, she could hear Sweetpea nickering at her and pawing at the ground. No doubt the old mare was looking for company, too. During the camping trip a neighbor had fed the horse, but that wasn't the same as being loved.

"I know, girl," Tully said, sitting down. She wrapped her arms around her bent legs, hugging herself. Maybe she should have called instead of stalking them like this. But Mrs. Mularkey might have told her to come by tomorrow, that they were tired from their long drive, and Tully couldn't wait anymore. This loneliness was more than she could handle by herself.

Finally, at eleven o'clock, she stood up, brushed the grass off her jeans, and threw a piece of gravel at Kate's window.

It took four tosses before her friend stuck her head out the window. "Tully!" Kate ducked back into her room and slammed the window shut. It took less than a minute for her to appear at the side of the house. Wearing a Bionic Woman nightshirt, her old black-rimmed glasses, and her retainer, Kate ran for Tully, arms outstretched.

Tully felt Kate's arms wrap around her and for the first time in days, she felt safe.

"I missed you so much," Kate said, tightening her hold.

Tully couldn't answer. It was all she could do not to cry. She wondered if Kate knew, really knew, how important their friendship was to her. "I got our bikes," she said, stepping back, looking away so Kate wouldn't see her moist eyes.

"Cool."

Within minutes they were on their way, flying down Summer Hill, their hands outstretched to catch the wind.

At the bottom of the hill, they ditched their bikes in the trees and walked down the long and winding road to the river. All around them trees chattered among themselves; the wind sighed, and leaves fluttered down from branches in an early sign of the coming autumn.

Kate flopped down in their old spot, her back rested against the mossy log, her feet stretched out in the grass that had grown tall in their absence.

Tully felt an unexpected pinch of nostalgia for their youth. They'd spent most of one summer here, taking their separate, lonely lives and braiding them into a rope of friendship. She lay down beside Kate, scooting close enough that their shoulders were touching. After the last few days, she needed to know that her best friend was finally beside her. She positioned her transistor radio nearby and turned up the volume.

"Hell Week with Bugs was even worse than usual," Kate said. "I did talk Sean into eating a slug, though. It was worth the week's allowance I lost." She giggled. "You should have seen his face when I started laughing. Aunt Georgia tried to talk to me about birth control. Can you believe it? She said I should—"

"Do you even know how lucky you are?" The words were out before Tully could stop them, spilling like jelly beans from a machine.

Kate shifted her weight and turned, until she was lying sideways in the grass, looking at Tully. "You usually want to hear everything about the camping trip."

"Yeah, well. I've had a bad week."

"Did you get fired?"

"That's your idea of a bad week? I want your perfect life, just for a day."

Kate drew back, frowning. "You sound pissed at me."

"Not at you." Tully sighed. "You're my best friend."

"So, who are you mad at?"

"Cloud. Gran. God. Take your pick." She took a deep breath and said, "Gran died while you were gone."

"Oh, Tully."

And there it was, what Tully had been waiting for all week. Someone who loved her and was truly sorry for her. Tears stung her eyes; before she knew it, she was crying. Big, gulping sobs that wracked her body and made it impossible to breathe, and all the while, Kate held her, letting her cry, saying nothing.

When there were no tears left inside, Tully smiled shakily. "Thanks for not saying you felt sorry for me."

"I am, though."

"I know." Tully lay back against the log and stared up at the night sky. She wanted to admit that she was scared and that as alone as she'd sometimes felt in life, she knew now what real loneliness was, but she couldn't say the words, not even to Kate. Thoughts—even fears—were airy things, formless until you made them solid with your voice, and once given that weight, they could crush you.

Kate waited a moment, then said, "So what will happen?"

Tully wiped her eyes and reached into her pocket, pulling out a pack of cigarettes. Lighting one up, she took a drag and coughed. It had been years since she'd smoked. "I have to go into foster care. It's only for a while, though. When I'm eighteen I can live alone."

"You're not going to live with strangers," Kate said fiercely. "I'll find Cloud and make her do the right thing."

Tully didn't bother answering. She loved her friend for saying it, but they lived in two different worlds, she and Kate. In Tully's world, moms weren't there to help you out. What mattered was making your own way.

What mattered was not caring.

And the best way not to care was to surround your-self with noise and people. She'd learned that lesson a long time ago. She didn't have long here in Snohomish. In no time at all, the authorities would find her and drag her back to her lovely new family, full of displaced teens and the people paid to house them. "We should go to that party tomorrow night. The one you wrote about in your last letter."

"At Karen's house? The summer's-end bash-o-rama?"

"Exactly."

Kate frowned. "My folks would have a cow if they found out I went to a kegger."

"We'll tell them you're staying at my house across the street. Your mom will believe Cloud is back for a day."

"If I get caught—"

"You won't." Tully saw how worried her friend was, and she knew she should stop this plan right now. It was reckless, maybe even dangerous. But she couldn't stop the train. If she didn't do something drastic, she'd sink into the gooey darkness of her own fears. She'd think about the mother who'd so often and so repeatedly abandoned her, and the strangers with whom she'd soon live, and the grandmother who was gone. "We won't get caught. I promise." She turned to Kate. "You trust me, don't you?"

"Sure," Kate said slowly.

"Great. Then we're going to the party."

"Kids! Breakfast is ready."

Kate was the first one to sit down.

Mom had just put a plate of pancakes down on the table when there was a knock at the door.

Kate jumped up. "I'll get it." She ran for the door

and yanked it open, feigning surprise. "Mom, look. It's Tully. Gosh, I haven't seen you in *forever*."

Mom stood near the table, wearing her zip-up, floor-length red velour robe and pink fuzzy slippers. "Hey, Tully, it's good to see you again. We missed you on the camping trip this year, but I know how important your job is."

Tully lurched forward. Looking up, she started to say something, but no sound came out of her mouth. She just stood there, staring at Kate's mom.

"What is it?" her mother said, moving toward Tully. "What's going on?"

"My gran died," Tully said softly.

"Oh, honey . . ." Mom pulled Tully into a fierce hug, holding her for a long time. Finally, Mom drew back, put an arm around Tully, and led her to the sofa in the living room.

"Turn off the griddle, Katie," Mom said without even looking back.

Kate turned off the griddle and then followed them to the living room. She hung back, standing in the curl of the archway that separated the two rooms. Neither of them seemed to care that she was there.

"Did we miss the funeral?" Mom asked gently, holding Tully's hand.

Tully nodded. "Everyone said they were sorry. I officially hate those words now."

"People don't know what to say, that's all."

"My favorite part was the ever popular 'she's in a better place.' As if dead is better than being with me."

"And your mom?"

"Let's just say she doesn't call herself Cloud for nothing. She came and went." Tully glanced at Kate and added quickly, "But she's here for now. We're staying across the street."

"Of course she is," Mom said. "She knows you need her."

"Can I spend the night there tonight, Mom?" Kate asked; her heart was beating so hard and fast, she was sure her mom could hear it. She tried to look completely trustworthy, but since she was lying, she expected her mother to see through it.

Mom didn't even look at Kate. "Of course. You girls need to be together. And you remember this, Tully Hart: You're the next Jessica Savitch. You will survive this. I promise."

"You really think so?" Tully asked.

"I know so. You have a rare gift, Tully. And you can be certain that your gran is in Heaven watching out for you."

Kate felt a sudden urge to butt in, to step forward and ask her mother if she believed *she* could change the world. She even went so far as to move forward and open her mouth, but before she could form the question, she heard Tully say,

"I'll make you proud, Mrs. M. I promise I will."

Kate paused. She had no idea how she could make her mother proud; she wasn't like Tully. Kate had no rare gift.

The thing was, though, her own mother should think she did and should point it out. Instead, her mother—like everyone else—was caught in the gravitational pull of Tully's sun.

"We're both going to be reporters," Kate said, more harshly than she intended. At their startled looks, she felt like an idiot. "Come on," she said, forcing a smile this time. "We should eat before everything is ruined."

The party was a bad idea. Taunting-Carrie-at-the-prom bad.

Tully knew it but couldn't turn back. In the days since Gran's funeral and Cloud's encore abandonment, her grief had been slowly replaced by anger. It darted through her blood like a predator, puffing her up with emotions that couldn't be tamped down or contained. She knew she was being reckless, but she couldn't change her course. If she slowed down, even for a moment, her fear would catch up with her and the plan was in motion now. They were in her mother's old bedroom, supposedly getting ready.

"Ohmigod," Kate said in an awed voice. "You gotta read this."

Tully marched over to the poorly decoupaged water bed, grabbed the paperback novel out of Kate's hands, and threw it across the room. "I can't believe you brought a book."

"Hey!" Kate tried to sit up; waves rolled around her. "Wulfgar was tying her to the end of the bed. I have to find out—"

"We're going to a party, Kate. Enough with the romance novels. And just for the record, tying a woman to a bed is S-I-C-K."

"Yeah," Kate said slowly, frowning. "I know, but—"

"No buts. Get dressed."

"Okay, okay." She shuffled over to the pile of clothes Tully had laid out for her earlier—a pair of Jordache jeans and a clingy bronze halter top. "My mom would die if she knew I was going out in this."

Tully didn't respond. Truthfully she wished she hadn't heard. Mrs. M. was the last person she wanted to think about right now. She focused instead on getting dressed: jeans, pink tube top, and navy platform lace-up sandals. Bending over, she brushed her hair for maximum Farrah volume, then sprayed it with enough Aqua Net to stop a bug in flight. When she was sure she looked perfect, she turned to Kate. "Are you—"

Kate was dressed for the party and back on the bed reading again.

"You are *so* pathetic."

Kate rolled onto her back and smiled. "It's romantic, Tully. I'm not kidding."

Tully grabbed the book again. She wasn't sure why, but this really pissed her off. Maybe it was Kate's glossy idealism; how could she see Tully's life and still believe in fairy-tale endings? "Let's go."

Without waiting to see if Kate was following, Tully went out to the garage and opened the doors and then slid into the cracked black driver's seat of her grandmother's Queen Victoria, ignoring the way the stuffing poked into her back. She slammed the door shut.

"You have her car?" Kate said, opening the passenger door and poking her head in.

"Technically it's my car now."

Kate slid onto the seat and closed the door.

Tully popped a Kiss tape into the eight-track player and cranked up the volume. Then she put the car in reverse and eased her foot onto the gas.

They sang at the top of their lungs all the way to Karen Abner's house, where at least five cars were already parked. Several of them were tucked into the trees and out of sight. When someone's parents left town, word spread fast; parties sprouted like mushrooms.

Inside, it was a smoke-fest. The sweet smell of pot and incense was almost overpowering. The music was so loud it hurt Tully's ears. She grabbed Kate's hand and led her down the stairs to the rec room in the basement.

The huge room had fake-wood-paneled walls and lime-green indoor-outdoor carpeting. In the center was a cone fireplace surrounded by an orange half-moon-shaped sofa and several brown beanbag chairs. Over to the left, some boys were playing foosball and screaming at every turn of the handle. Kids were dancing wildly, singing to the music. A couple of boys were on the sofa, getting high, and a girl was over by the door, shot-gunning a beer beneath a huge painting of a Spanish matador.

"Tully!"

Before she could respond, her old friends surrounded her, pulled her away from Kate. She went to the keg first and let one of the boys give her a plastic cup full of foamy gold Rainier beer. She stared down at it, jolted by the memory that came with it: *Pat, pushing her to the ground . . .*

She looked around for Kate, but couldn't see her friend in the crowd.

Then everyone began chanting her name. "Tu-lly. Tu-lly."

No one was going to hurt her. Not here; tomorrow, maybe, when the authorities caught up with her, but not now. She chugged the beer and held the cup out for an-other, yelling out Kate's name as she did.

Kate appeared instantly, as if she'd been just out of view, waiting to be called for.

Tully shoved the beer toward her. "Here."

Kate shook her head. It was a slight there-and-gone motion, but Tully saw it and felt ashamed that she'd of-fered the beer, and then angry that her friend was so innocent. Tully had never been innocent; not that she could remember anyway.

"Ka-tie, Ka-tie," Tully yelled, getting the crowd to chant with her. "Come on, Katie," she said quietly. "We're best friends, aren't we?"

Kate glanced nervously at the crowd around her.

Tully felt that shame again and the jealousy. She could stop this right now, protect Katie—

Kate took the beer and chugged it.

More than half of it spilled down her chin and onto her halter top, making the shimmery fabric cling to her breasts, but she didn't seem to notice.

Then the music changed. ABBA's "Dancing Queen" blared through the speakers. *You can dance, you can j-ive . . .*

"I love this song," Kate said.

Tully grabbed Kate's hand and dragged her over to where the kids were dancing. There, Tully let loose and fell into the music and the movement.

By the time the music changed and slowed down, she was breathing hard and laughing easily.

But it was Kate who was the more changed. Maybe it was the one beer, or the pulsing beat of the music; Tully wasn't sure. All she knew was that Kate looked gorgeous, with her blond hair shining in the light from an overhead fixture and her pale, delicate face flushed with exertion.

When Neal Stewart came up to them and asked Kate to dance, Kate was the only one surprised. She turned to Tully. "Neal wants to dance with me," she yelled during a lull in the song. "He must be drunk." Putting her hands in the air, she danced away with Neal, leaving Tully standing alone in the crowd.

Kate pressed her cheek against Neal's soft T-shirt.

It felt so good, the way he had his arms around her, his hands just above her butt. She felt his hips moving against hers. It made her heartbeat speed up, made her breathing quicken. A new feeling overtook her; it was a kind of breathless anticipation. She wanted . . . what?

"Kate?"

She heard the hesitant way he said her name and it struck her suddenly: Did he feel all these things, too?

Slowly, she looked up.

Neal smiled down at her; he was only a little unsteady on his feet. "You're beautiful," he said, and then he kissed her, right there in the middle of the dance floor. Kate drew in a sharp breath and stiffened in his arms. It was so unexpected that she didn't know what she was supposed to do.

His tongue slid into her mouth, forcing her lips to open a little.

"Wow," he said softly when he finally drew back.

Wow what? *Wow, you're a spaz*? or *Wow, what a kiss!*

Behind her, someone yelled, "Cops!"

In an instant, Neal was gone and Tully was beside her again, taking her hand. They made their lurching, desperate way out of the house, up the hill and through the scrub brush, and back down to the trees. By the time they got to the car, Kate was terrified and her stomach was in open revolt. "I'm gonna puke."

"No, you aren't." Tully yanked open the passenger door and shoved Kate inside. "We are *not* gonna get busted."

Tully ran around the front of the car and opened her door. Sliding into the driver's seat, she stabbed the key into the ignition, yanked the gearshift into reverse, and stomped on the gas. They rocketed backward and slammed into something hard. Kate flew forward like a rag doll, cracking her forehead on the dashboard and then slumping back into her seat. Dazed, she opened her eyes, tried to focus.

Tully was beside her, rolling down the driver's-side window.

There, in the darkness, was good old Officer Dan, the man who'd driven Tully away from Snohomish three years ago. "I knew you Firefly Lane girls would be a pain in my ass."

"Fuck," Tully said.

"Nice language, Tallulah. Now, will you please step out of the car?" He bent down, looked at Kate. "You, too, Kate Mularkey. The party's over."

The first thing that happened at the police station was the girls were separated.

"Someone will come talk to you," Officer Dan said, guiding Tully into a room at the end of the hall.

A gunmetal-gray desk and two chairs sat forlornly beneath a bright hanging lightbulb. The walls were a gross green color and the floor was plain bumpy cement. There was a sad, faded stink to the place, a combination of sweat and piss, and old spilled coffee.

The entire left wall was a mirror.

All it took was one episode of *Starsky and Hutch* to know that it was really a window.

She wondered if the social worker was on the other side of it yet, shaking her head in disappointment, saying, *That fine family won't want her now,* or the lawyer, who wouldn't know what to say.

Or the Mularkeys.

At that, she made a little sound of horror. How could she have been so stupid? The Mularkeys had liked her until tonight, and now she'd gone and thrown that all away, and for what? Because she'd been depressed by her mom's rejection? By now she ought to be used to that. When had it ever been any other way?

"I won't be stupid again," she said, looking right at the mirror. "If someone would give me another chance, I'd be good."

After that, she waited for someone to burst in for her, maybe holding handcuffs, but the minutes just ticked by in smelly silence. She moved the black plastic chair to one corner and sat down.

I knew better.

She closed her eyes, thinking the same thing over and over again. Along with that thought, running alongside it like some shadow forming in the twilight was its twin: *Will you be a good friend to Katie?*

"How could I be so stupid?" This time Tully didn't even glance at the mirror. There was no one behind there. Who would be looking at her anyway, the kid no one wanted?

Across the room, the doorknob twisted, turned.

Tully tensed. Her fingers bit into her thighs.

Be good, Tully. Agree with everything they say. Foster care is better than juvenile hall.

The door opened and Mrs. Mularkey walked into the room. In a washed-out floral dress and worn white Keds, she looked tired and poorly put together, as if she'd been wakened in the middle of the night and dressed in whatever she could find in the dark.

Which, of course, was exactly what had happened.

Mrs. Mularkey reached into her dress pocket for her cigarettes. Finding one, she lit up. Through the swirling smoke, she studied Tully. Sadness and disappointment emanated from her, as visible as the smoke.

Shame overwhelmed Tully. Here was one of the very few people who had ever believed in her, and she'd let Mrs. M. down. "How's Kate?"

Mrs. Mularkey exhaled smoke. "Bud took her home. I don't expect she'll leave the house again for a good long while."

"Oh." Tully squirmed uncomfortably. Her every blemish was on view, she was sure of it, from the lies she'd told to the secrets she'd kept to the tears she'd cried. Mrs. M. saw it all.

And she didn't like what she saw.

Tully could hardly blame her. "I know I let you down."

"Yes, you did." Mrs. Mularkey pulled a chair away

from the table and sat down in front of Tully. "They want to send you to juvenile hall."

Tully looked down at her own hands, unable to stand the disappointment she saw on Mrs. M.'s face. "The foster family won't want me now."

"I understand your mother refused to take custody of you."

"Big surprise there." Tully heard the way her voice cracked on that. She knew it revealed how hurt she'd been, but there was no way to hide it. Not from Mrs. M.

"Katie thinks they can find another family for you to live with."

"Yeah, well, Katie lives in a different world than I do."

Mrs. Mularkey leaned back in her chair. Taking a drag on her cigarette, she exhaled smoke and said quietly, "She wants you to live with us."

Just hearing it was like a blow to the heart. She knew she'd spend a long time trying to forget it. "Yeah, right."

It was a moment before Mrs. Mularkey said, "A girl who lived in our house would have to do chores and follow the rules. Mr. Mularkey and I wouldn't stand for any funny business."

Tully looked up sharply. "What are you saying?" She couldn't even put this sudden hope into words.

"And there would definitely be no smoking."

Tully stared at her, feeling tears sting her eyes, but that pain was nothing compared to what was going on deep inside her. It felt suddenly as if she were about to fall. "Are you saying I can live with you?"

Mrs. M. leaned forward and touched Tully's jawline. "I know how hard your life has been up to now, Tully, and I can't stand for you to go back to that."

The falling turned into flying, and suddenly Tully was crying for all of it—Gran, the foster family, Cloud. Her relief was the biggest emotion she'd ever felt. With shaking hands, she pulled the crumpled, half-empty pack of cigarettes out of her purse and handed them over.

"Welcome to our family, Tully," Mrs. M. finally said into the silence, pulling Tully into her arms and letting her cry.

Through all the decades of Tully's life, she would remember that moment as the beginning of something new for her; the becoming of someone new. While she lived with the loud, crazy, loving Mularkey family, she found a whole new person inside her. She didn't keep secrets or tell lies or pretend that she was someone else, and never once did they act as if she were un-wanted or not good enough. No matter where she went in her later years, or what she did or whom she was with, she would always remember this moment and those words: *Welcome to our family, Tully.* Always and forever, she would think of that senior year of high school, when she was inseparable from Kate and a part of the family, as the single best year of her life.

CHAPTER EIGHT

Girls! Quit lollygagging. We're going to hit traffic if we don't leave now."

In the creaky attic bedroom, Kate stood at the edge of her twin bed, staring down at the open suitcase that contained all of her prized belongings. A framed picture of her grandparents lay on top, wedged between her ribbon-wrapped packet of long-ago letters from Tully and a photo of her and Tully taken at graduation.

Although she'd been looking forward to this moment for months (she and Tully had spun endless late-night dreams, all of which began with the words *when we're in college*), now that it was here, she felt reluctant to leave home.

Over the course of their senior year in high school, they'd become a pair. TullyandKate. Everyone at school said their two names as one. When Tully became editor of the school paper, Kate was right beside her, helping her to edit the stories. She lived vicariously through her friend's achievements, rode the wave of her popularity, but all of that had taken place in a world she knew, in a place where she felt safe.

"What if I forgot something?"

Tully crossed the room and came up beside Kate. She closed the suitcase and clamped it shut. "You're ready."

"No. *You're* ready. You're always ready," Kate said, trying not to sound as afraid as she was. It occurred to her suddenly, sharply, how much she'd miss her parents and even her little brother.

Tully stared at her. "We're a team, aren't we? The Firefly Lane girls."

"We have been, but—"

"No buts. We're going to college together, we're pledging the same sorority, and we'll be hired by the same TV station. Period. That's it. We can do it."

Kate knew what was expected of her, by Tully and everyone else: she was supposed to be strong and courageous. If only she felt it more deeply. But since she didn't feel it, she did what she often did lately around Tully. She smiled and faked it. "You're right. Let's go."

The drive from Snohomish to downtown Seattle, which usually took about thirty-five minutes, seemed to pass in a blink. Kate barely spoke, couldn't seem to find her voice, even as Tully and her mom chattered on about the upcoming Rush Week at the sororities. Her mother, it seemed, was more excited about their college adventure than Kate was.

In the towering high-rise of Haggett Hall, they made their way through the loud, crowded corridors to a small, dingy dorm room on the tenth floor. Here was where they'd stay during Rush. When it was over, they'd move into their sorority.

"Well. This is it," Mr. Mularkey said.

Kate went to her parents and threw her arms around them, forming the famous Mularkey family hug.

Tully stood back, looking oddly left out.

"Geez, Tully, get over here," Mom called out.

Tully rushed forward and let them all embrace her.

For the next hour they unpacked and talked and took pictures. Then, finally, Dad said, "Well, Margie, it's time. We don't want to get caught in traffic." There was one last round of hugs.

Kate clung to her mom, battling tears.

"It's going to be okay," Mom said. "Trust in all the dreams you've made. You and Tully are going to become the best reporters this state has ever seen. Your dad and I are so proud of you."

Kate nodded and looked up at her mom through hot tears. "I love you, Mom."

Much too soon, it was over.

"We'll call every Sunday," Tully said behind them. "Right after you get home from church."

And then, suddenly, they were gone.

Tully flopped on the bed. "I wonder what Rush will be like. I bet every house will want us. How could they not?"

"They'll want you," Kate said softly, and for the first time in months she felt like the girl they'd called Kootie all those years ago, the girl in the Coke-bottle glasses and high-water Sears jeans. It didn't matter that she'd gotten contacts and lost her braces and learned how to put on makeup to enhance her features. The sorority girls would see through all that.

Tully sat up. "You know I won't join a sorority unless we're in it together, right?"

"That's not fair to you, though." Kate went to the bed and sat down beside her.

"Remember Firefly Lane?" Tully said, lowering her voice. Over the years those words had become a catch-all phrase, a kind of shorthand for their memories. It was their way of saying that a friendship begun at fourteen, back when David Cassidy was groovy and a song could make you cry, would last forever.

"I haven't forgotten."

"But you don't get it," Tully said.

"Get what?"

"When my mom dumped me, who was there for me? When my gran died, who held my hand and took me in?" She turned to Kate. "You. That's the answer. We're a team, Kate. Forever friends, no matter what. Okay?" She bumped Kate, made her smile.

"You always get your way."

Tully laughed. "Of course I do. It's one of my more endearing traits. Now let's figure out what we're going to wear for the first day . . ."

The University of Washington was everything Tully had hoped it would be and more. Spread out over several miles and comprised of hundreds of gothic buildings, it was a world unto itself. The size daunted Kate, but not Tully; she figured if she could triumph here, she could triumph anywhere. From the moment they moved into their sorority, she began preparing for a reporting job at the networks. In addition to taking the core classes in communications, she made time to read at least four newspapers a day and watch as many newscasts as possible. When her big break came, she was going to be ready.

It had taken her most of the first few weeks of school to get her bearings and figure out what Phase One of the academic plan should be. She'd met with her School of Communications advisor so often that he sometimes avoided her in the hall when he saw her coming, but she didn't care. When she had questions, she wanted answers.

The problem, once again, was her youth. She couldn't get into the upper-level broadcasting or journalism classes; no amount of cajoling or prodding could move the behemoth bureaucracy of this huge state school. She simply had to wait her turn.

Not something she was good at.

She leaned sideways and whispered to Kate, "Why is there a science requirement? I won't need geology to be a reporter."

"Shhh."

Tully frowned and sat back in her chair. They were in Kane Hall, one of the biggest auditoriums on campus. From her chair in the nosebleed section, crammed in among almost five hundred other students, she could barely see the professor, who'd turned out not to be a professor at all, but rather his teaching assistant.

"We can buy lecture notes. Let's go. The newspaper office opens at ten."

Kate didn't even glance at her, just kept scribbling notes on her paper.

Tully groaned and sat back, crossing her arms in disgust, waiting minute by minute for class to end. The second the bell rang, she shot to her feet. "Thank God. Let's go."

Kate finished with her notes and collected her pages, methodically organizing everything in her notebook.

"Are you *making* paper? Come on. I want to meet the editor."

Kate stood up and slung her backpack over one shoulder. "We are not going to get a job at the newspaper, Tully."

"Your mom told you not to be so negative, remember?"

They went downstairs, merging into the loud crowd of students.

Outside, the sun shone brightly on the brick-covered courtyard known as Red Square. Over by Suzzallo Library, a group of long-haired students were gathered beneath a CLEAN UP HANFORD sign.

"Quit complaining to my mom when you don't get your way," Kate said as they headed for the Quad. "We can't even get into journalism classes until we're juniors."

Tully stopped. "Are you really not going to come with me?"

Kate smiled and kept walking. "We aren't going to get the job."

"But you'll come with me, right? We're a team."

"Of course I'm coming."

"I knew it. You were just messing with me."

They kept talking as they walked through the Quad, where the cherry trees were lush and green, as was the grass. Dozens of students in brightly colored shorts and T-shirts played Frisbee and hacky sack.

At the newspaper office, Tully stopped. "I'll do the talking."

"I'm shocked, really."

Laughing, they went into the building, announced themselves to a shaggy-looking kid at the front desk, and were directed to the editor's office.

The entire meeting lasted less than ten minutes.

"Told you we were too young," Kate said as they walked back to the sorority.

"Bite me. Sometimes I think you don't even want to be a reporter with me."

"That's a complete lie: you hardly ever think."

"Bitch."

"Hag."

Kate put an arm around her. "Come on, Barbara Walters, I'll walk you home."

Tully was so depressed over the meeting at the newspaper that Kate spent the rest of the day cajoling her into a good mood.

"Come on," she finally said, hours later, when they were back in their minuscule room in the sorority house. "Let's get ready. You want to look your best for the exchange."

"What do I care about a stupid exchange? Frat boys are hardly my ideal."

Kate struggled not to smile. Everything about Tully was big—she had such high highs and low lows. Their time at UW had only increased her tendencies. The funny thing was that while this huge crowded campus had somehow released Tully's extravagances, it had had an opposite and calming effect on Kate. She felt stronger every day here, more and more ready to become an adult. "You're such a drama queen. I'll let you do my makeup."

Tully looked up. "Really?"

"It's a time-limited offer. You better move your ass."

Tully jumped up, grabbed her hand, and dragged her down the hall to the bathroom, where dozens of girls were already showering and drying off and blowing their hair out.

They waited their turns, took their showers, and went back to the room. Thankfully, their other two roommates weren't there. The tiny space, filled mostly with dressers and desks and a set of bunk beds for the upperclassmen, barely gave the two of them room enough to turn around. Their own twin beds were in the large sleeping porch down the hall.

Tully spent almost an hour on their hair and makeup, then pulled out the fabric they'd bought for their togas—gold for Tully, silver for Kate—and created a pair of magical garments held in place by tight belts and rhinestone pins.

Kate studied her reflection when they were done. The sparkling silver fabric complemented her pale skin and golden hair and brought out the green in her eyes. After all the nerd years, she was still sometimes surprised that she could look good. "You're a genius," she said.

Tully twirled for inspection. "How do I look?"

The gold toga showed off her big boobs and tiny waist, and a riot of curled, teased, sprayed mahogany hair spilled down over her shoulder, à la Jane Fonda in *Barbarella*. Blue eye shadow and heavy liner made her look exotic.

"You look gorgeous," Kate said. "The guys'll be falling all over themselves."

"You care too much about love; must be all those romance novels you read. This is *our* night. Screw the boys."

"I don't want to screw them, but a date would be nice."

Tully grabbed Kate's arm and led her out into the hallway, which was crowded with laughing, talking girls in various stages of dress, running down the busy corridors with curling irons, hair dryers, and bedsheets.

Downstairs in the formal living room, one of the girls was teaching the others to Hustle.

Outside, Kate and Tully merged into the crowd walking down the street. There were people everywhere on this balmy late September night. Most of the fraternities were having an exchange. There were girls in costume, in ordinary clothes, in almost nothing at all, walking in sorority groups toward their various destinations.

The Phi Delt house was big and square, a fairly modern mixture of glass and metal and brick, that was set on a corner. Inside, the walls were worn, the furniture was broken and ripped and ugly, and the décor was prison-era 1950. Not that most of this could be seen through the crowd.

People were packed in like sardines, chugging beer from plastic cups and swaying to the music. "Shout!" blared through the speakers and everyone was singing along, jumping up in time to the music.

A little bit softer now . . .

The crowd crouched, stilled, then raised their hands and rose up again, chanting along.

As always, the minute Tully stepped into a party, she was "on." Gone was the edge of depression, the hesitant smile, the irritation at losing the job. Kate watched in awe; her friend instantly grabbed everyone's attention.

"Shout!" Tully yelled out, laughing. Boys moved in close, drawn to her like moths to a flame, but Tully barely seemed to notice. She surged onto the dance floor, dragging Kate along with her.

It was the most fun Kate had had in years.

By the time she'd group danced to "Brick House," "Twistin' the Night Away," and "Louie Louie," she was hot and sweaty.

"I'll be right back," she yelled to Tully, who nodded, and then she went outside, where she sat on the low brick wall that marked the property's edge. Cool night air breezed across her sweaty face. She closed her eyes and swayed to the music.

"The party's inside, you know."

She looked up.

The guy who'd spoken was tall and broad-shouldered, with wheat-colored hair that fell across the bluest eyes. "Can I sit with you?"

"Sure."

"I'm Brandt Hanover."

"Kate Mularkey."

"Is this your first frat party?"

"Does it show?"

He smiled and went from good-looking to gorgeous. "Just a little. I remember my first year here. It was like being on Mars. I'm from Moses Lake," he said, as if that should explain everything.

"Small town?"

"Speck on the map."

"It *is* kind of overwhelming."

The conversation moved easily on from there. He talked about things she could relate to. He'd grown up on a farm, feeding cows before dawn and driving his dad's hay truck when he was thirteen. He knew about feeling both lost and found in a place as big and sprawling as UW.

Inside, the music changed. Someone turned the volume way up. It was ABBA's "Dancing Queen."

Tully came running out of the house. "Kate!" she yelled, laughing. "There you are."

Brandt immediately stood.

Tully frowned at him. "Who's this?"

"Brandt Hanover."

Kate knew exactly what was going to happen next. Because of what had happened to Tully in the dark woods by the river all those years ago, she didn't trust boys, didn't want anything to do with them, and she was committed to protecting Kate from any kind of harm or heartbreak. Unfortunately, though, Kate wasn't afraid. She *wanted* to date and have fun and even maybe fall in love.

But how could she say that, when Tully was only trying to protect her?

Tully grabbed Kate's arm, pulled her to her feet. "Too bad, Brandt," she said, laughing a little too loudly as she dragged Kate away. "This is our song."

"I saw Brandt at the HUB today. He smiled at me."

Tully fought the urge to roll her eyes. In the six months since that first toga party at the Phi Delts, Kate had found a way to mention Brandt Hanover at least once a day. You'd think they were dating, as often as his name came up. "Let me guess: you pretended not to notice."

"I smiled back."

"Wow. A red-letter day."

"I thought I'd invite him to the spring dance. We could double date."

"I have to write an article on the Ayatollah Khomeini. I figured if I keep sending stuff to the paper, sooner or later they'll publish something. It wouldn't hurt you to try a little harder to—"

Kate turned to her friend. "That's *it*. I renounce our friendship. I know you have no interest in our social life, but I do. If you don't go—"

Tully laughed. "Gotcha."

Kate couldn't help laughing. "Bitch." She slung an arm around Tully. Together they walked along the grass-dotted sidewalk of Twenty-first Street and onto campus.

At the campus security post, Kate said, "I'm headed to Meany. How about you?"

"Drama/TV."

"That's right! Your first broadcast journalism class—and with that famous guy you've been stalking since we got here."

"Chad Wiley."

"How many letters did you have to write to get in?"

"About a thousand. And you should be coming with me. We both need this class."

"I'll get in as a junior. You need me to walk you over?"

Tully loved her friend for that. Somehow Kate knew that despite her show of courage, Tully was nervous about this. Everything she wanted could start today. "No, thanks. How can I make my big entrance with someone else?"

She watched Kate walk away from her. Standing there, alone among the crowd of students moving between the buildings, Tully took a deep, relaxing breath, trying to still herself. She needed to appear calm.

She strolled confidently past the fountain of Frosh Pond and went into the Drama/TV Building, where her first stop was the restroom.

There, she paused in front of the mirrors. Her curled, sprayed hair was perfect, as was her makeup. The skin-tight, flare-legged jeans and shiny white tunic blouse with gold belt and Nehru collar managed to be both sexy and businesslike at the same time.

When the bell rang, she hurried down the hallway, with her backpack bouncing against her ass as she moved. In the auditorium, she walked boldly down to the first row and took a seat.

In the front of the room, the professor sat slumped in a metal chair. "I'm Chad Wiley," he said in a sexy, whiskey-rough voice. "Those of you who recognize my name get an A in the class."

There was a smattering of laughter around the room. Tully's was the loudest. She knew more than his name. She knew his whole life story. He'd come out of college as a kind of wunderkind in broadcasting. He'd moved up the ranks fast, becoming a network anchor before he was thirty. Then, quite simply, he'd lost it. A pair of DWIs, a car crash that broke both of his legs and injured a child, and his star had fallen. There'd been a couple of years with no mention of him at all, and then, finally, he'd surfaced at UW, teaching.

Wiley stood. He was unkempt, with long dark hair and at least three days' growth of gray-black beard, but the intelligence in his dark eyes was undiminished. The stamp of greatness was still on him. No wonder he'd made it.

He handed her a syllabus and started to move on.

"Your coverage of the Karen Silkwood case was inspired," she said, smiling brightly.

He paused, looked down at her. There was something unsettling about the way he stared—intensely, but only for a second; like a laser beam switched on and off—and then he kept walking past her and on to the next student.

He thought she was just another front-row suck-up who wanted to curry favor.

She'd need to be more careful in the future. Nothing mattered more to her right now than impressing Chad Wiley. She intended to learn everything she could from him.

Part Two

THE EIGHTIES

Love Is a Battlefield

heartache to heartache,
we stand

CHAPTER NINE

By the end of her sophomore year, there was no doubt in Tully's mind that Chad Wiley knew who she was. She'd taken two of his classes: Broadcast Journalism I and II. Whatever he taught, she took; whatever he asked of her, she did. Full-bore. Balls to the wall.

The problem was this: he didn't seem to recognize her talent. They'd spent all of last week reading the news from a teleprompter. Each time she finished, she immediately looked at him, but he barely glanced up from his notes. Rather, he spooled off criticism as if he were relaying a recipe to a troublesome neighbor, then called out, "Next."

Day after day, week after week, class after class, Tully waited for him to respond to her obvious talent, to say, *You're ready for KVTS*. Now it was the first week of May. With about six weeks left in her sophomore year, she was still waiting.

Plenty of things had changed in her life the past two years. She'd cut her hair shoulder-length and gone with bangs. Her style icon had gone from Farrah Fawcett-Majors to Jessica Savitch. Nineteen eighty was made for Tully: big hair, bright makeup, glittery fabric, and shoulder pads. No pale colors/sorority-girl styles for her. When she walked into a room these days, people noticed.

Except, of course, for Chad Wiley.

But that was about to change; Tully was sure this time. Last week she'd finally racked enough credits to apply for a summer internship position at KVTS, the local public programming station that was housed on campus. She'd gotten up at six A.M. so that her name appeared first on the sign-up sheet. When she'd been given the audition piece, she'd gone home and practiced it endlessly, trying it at least a dozen different ways until she found the tone of voice that perfectly matched the tone of the story. Yesterday she'd nailed the audition. She was certain of it. Now, finally, it was time to find out what position she'd earned.

"How do I look?"

Kate didn't look up from *The Thorn Birds*. "Awesome."

Tully felt a flash of irritation that was more and more familiar these days. Sometimes she just looked at Kate and felt her blood pressure skyrocket. It was all she could do not to yell.

The problem was love. Kate had spent all of their freshman year mooning over bad-haircut Brandt. By the time they finally dated, it was a letdown that ended fast. Still, Kate didn't seem to care. Through most of sophomore year, she'd dated Ted, who supposedly loved her, and then Eric, who most certainly did not. Kate went to one fraternity dance after another, and though she never fell in love with any of the doofuses she dated—and definitely didn't have sex with them— she talked about them constantly. Every sentence lately seemed to start with some guy's name. Even worse, she hardly ever mentioned the broadcasting plan. She seemed perfectly happy to take classes in other departments. Whenever one of their sorority sisters got engaged, Kate rushed to be a part of the crowd that swooned over the ring.

In truth, Tully was sick of it. She kept writing news stories that the school paper wouldn't publish and hanging around the campus TV station, where no one would give her the time of day, and throughout all of this failure, when she could really use her best friend, Kate just kept yammering on about her latest date. "You totally aren't looking."

"I don't have to."

"You don't know how important this is to me."

Kate finally looked up. "You've been practicing one news story for two weeks. Even when I got up to pee in the middle of the night, I heard you rehearsing. Believe me, I know how psyched you are."

"So how come you're so Joanie about this?"

"I'm no Joanie. I just know you'll get the anchor job." Tully grinned. "I will, won't I?"

"Of course. You're wicked good. You'll be the first junior to actually be on air."

"Professor Wiley will have to admit it this time." Tully grabbed her backpack and slung it over her shoulder. "Want to come with me?"

"Can't. I'm meeting Josh for a study group in Suzzallo."

"That pretty much falls in the blows-chips category of dating, but to each his own." Tully snagged her sunglasses off the dresser and headed out.

The campus was bathed in cool sunlight on this mid-May day. Every plant was in bloom and the grass was so thick and lush it looked like patches of green velvet tucked neatly between strips of cement. She strode confidently through campus to the building that housed KVTS. There, she paused just long enough to smooth her sprayed hair, then went into the quiet, utilitarian-looking hallway. To her left was a bulletin board thick with notices. *Roommate wanted: pot smoker only* was the first one that caught her eye. She noticed that all the phone-number tabs had been ripped off of it, while the ad next to it *(Roommate wanted: Born-again Christian preferred)* looked sadly intact.

Room 214 was shut. No slice of light ran along the floor beneath the door. Beside it, a piece of paper was tacked to the bulletin board.

SUMMER INTERNSHIP POSITIONS/DEPARTMENT

News/Anchor..........................…......Steve Landis
Weather...............................…........Jane Turner
Marketing & Community
Relations...........................….........Gretchen Lauber
Sports.......................................…....Dan Bluto
Afternoon Planning...….............Eileen Hutton
Research Desk/Fact Checking....…....Tully Hart

Tully felt a surge of disappointment, then anger. She yanked open the door and slipped into the dark auditorium where no one could see her, muttering, "Chad Wiley, you sorry-assed loser. You wouldn't know talent if it grabbed your tiny pecker and squeezed—"

"I imagine you're talking about me."

She jumped at the sound of his voice.

He was not twenty feet away from her, standing in the shadows. His dark hair was even messier than usual; it hung in curly disarray to his shoulders.

He moved closer, his fingers trailing on the back of the chair to his right. "Ask me why you aren't an evening news intern and I'll tell you."

"I couldn't care less why."

"Really?" He looked at her for another long minute,

unsmiling, then walked away from her, down the aisle and up onto the stage.

She could either keep her pride or risk her future. By the time she made her decision and hurried after him, he was backstage.

"Okay . . ." The word seemed to catch on something in her throat. "Why?"

He stepped toward her. For the first time she noticed the lines on his face, the creases in his cheeks. The dim overhead lighting accentuated every flaw, every hollow and mark on his skin. "Whenever you come to class, I can tell you've chosen your clothes carefully and spent a lot of time on your hair and makeup."

He was looking at her now, *seeing* her. And she could see him, too. Past the shaggy unkemptness to the sharp bone structure that had once made him so handsome. But it was his eyes that grabbed her; liquid brown and sad, they spoke to the empty places inside of her. "Yeah. So?"

"You know you're beautiful," he said.

No stammering, no desperation. He was cool and steady. Unlike the boys she met at frat parties or on campus or in the taverns playing pool, he wasn't half drunk and desperate for a feel.

"I'm talented, too."

"Maybe someday."

The way he said it pissed her off. She was gathering her wits for a scathing comeback when he closed the distance between them. All she had time for was a bewildered, "What are—" before he kissed her.

At the touch of his lips, gentle yet firm, she felt something exquisite and tender blossom inside her; for no reason at all, she started to cry. He must have tasted her tears, because he drew back, frowned at her. "Are you a woman, Tully Hart, or a girl?"

She knew what he was asking. As hard as she'd

tried to conceal her innocence, he'd sensed it, tasted it. "Woman," she lied, with only the barest wobble on the *w*. She knew now, after just one kiss, that whatever there was to know about sex, her pathetic rape in the woods had taught her none of it. Although she wasn't a virgin, she was something worse somehow, a reservoir of bad and painful memories, and yet, now, with him, for the first time she wanted more.

That was how she'd felt with Pat that night, too.

No. This was different. She was a long way from that desperate, lonely girl who would have gone into any dark woods to be loved.

He kissed her again, murmuring, "Good." This time the kiss went on and on, deepening into something that pulled at her insides and made her ache with need. By the time he began pressing his hips against hers, igniting a fire between her legs, she'd forgotten all about being scared.

"You want more?" he whispered.

"Yes."

He swept her into his arms and carried her to a broken-down sofa tucked against the shadowy back wall. There, he laid her down onto the bumpy, scratchy cushions and slowly, gently began to undress her. As if from far away, she felt her bra unsnap, her underpants peel off. And still his kiss went on and on, stoking this fire inside her.

When they were both naked, he lowered himself to the sofa and took her in his arms. The springs sagged beneath their weight, pinged in protest. "No one has taken time with you, have they, Tully?"

She saw her own desire reflected in his eyes, and for the first time she wasn't afraid in a man's arms. "Is that what you're going to do—take your time?"

He brushed the damp hair away from her face. "I'm

going to teach you things, Tully. Isn't that what you wanted from me?"

It took Tully almost two hours to find Kate. She began her search at the study tables in the basement of the sorority. Next, she spun through the TV room and their bedroom; she even checked on the sleeping porch, although at four o'clock on a sunny May day, it was understandably empty. She tried the undergraduate library and Kate's favorite carrel, then the graduate reading room, where several hippie-looking older students shushed her just for walking through the stacks. She was about ready to give up when she remembered the Annex.

Of course.

She ran through the sprawling campus to the small, two-story, peaked-roof house that they called the Annex. Sixteen lucky upper-class girls got to move out of the main house and into this place every quarter. It was party central. No house mothers, no one to monitor the doors; it was as close to the real world as any of them were likely to get until they left the sorority altogether.

She opened the front door and called out Kate's name. Someone in another room answered.

"I think she's on the roof."

Tully grabbed a pair of TaBs from the fridge and went upstairs. In a back bedroom, the window was open. She leaned through the opening and looked out on the roof of the carport.

There was Kate, all by herself, in a skimpy white crocheted bikini, lying on a beach towel, reading a paperback novel.

Tully climbed out onto the ledge and crossed the

carport roof, which they all called Black Beach. "Hey," she said, offering Kate a TaB. "Let me guess: you're reading a romance novel."

Kate cocked her head and squinted into the sun, smiling. "*The Promise* by Danielle Steel. It's really sad."

"You want to hear about real romance?"

"Like you would know anything about it. You haven't gone on a date since we got here."

"You don't have to go on a date to have sex."

"Most people do."

"I'm not most people. You know that."

"Yeah, right," Kate said. "Like I'm supposed to believe you got laid."

Tully grabbed one of the towels that had been left there and stretched out on it. Trying not to smile, she stared up at the blue sky and said, "Three times, to be exact."

"But you were just going to check on the summer internship . . ." Kate gasped and sat up. "You *didn't*."

"You're going to say we're not supposed to have sex with our professors. I think it's really more of a recommendation. A guideline. Still, you can't tell anyone."

"You had sex with Chad Wiley."

Tully sighed dreamily at the way that sounded. "It was totally cool, Katie. I mean it."

"Wow. What did you do? What did he do? Did it hurt? Were you scared?"

"I was scared," Tully said quietly. "At first all I could think about was . . . you know . . . the night with Pat. I thought I was going to get sick, or maybe run, but then he kissed me."

"And?"

"And . . . I just sort of melted. He had my clothes off before I was even paying attention."

"Did it hurt?"

"Yeah, but not like before." It surprised Tully how

easy it was suddenly to mention the night she was raped. For the first time it was a more distant memory, something bad that had happened to her as a kid. Chad's gentleness had shown her that sex didn't have to hurt, that it could be beautiful. "After a while it felt amazingly good. Now I know what all those *Cosmo* articles are about."

"Did he say he loved you?"

Tully laughed, but deep inside, it wasn't as funny as she wished it were. "No."

"Well, that's good."

"Why? I'm not good enough to fall in love with? That's for nice Catholic girls like you?"

"He's your *prof*, Tully."

"Oh, that. I don't care about stuff like that." She looked at her friend. "I thought you'd go all romance-novel on me and say it was some kind of fairy tale."

"I need to meet him," Kate said firmly.

"It's not like we can double-date."

"Then I guess I'll be the third wheel. Hey, he can probably get the senior rate if we go out to dinner."

Tully laughed. "Bitch."

"Maybe, but I'm a bitch who wants more details. I want to know *everything*. Can I take notes?"

Kate got off the bus and stood on the sidewalk, looking down at the directions in her hand.

This was the address.

All around her, people milled about the sidewalk. Several jostled her as they passed. She squared her shoulders and headed for the door. There was no point in worrying about this meeting—she'd been worrying for more than a month, and for most of that time she'd also been nagging. It had not been easy to get Tully to agree to tonight.

But in the end, Kate had said the magic words—thrown the Yahtzee: *Don't you trust me?* After that, it had only been a matter of scheduling.

So now, on this warm evening, she was moving toward a building that looked like a tavern, on a mission to save her best friend from making the biggest mistake of her life.

Sleeping with a professor.

Really, what good could come of that?

Inside the Last Exit on Brooklyn, Kate found herself in a world unlike anything she'd ever seen before. First off, the place was huge. There had to be seventy-five tables—marble ones along the walls and big, rough wooden ones in the center of the room. An upright piano and stage area seemed to be the centerpiece. On the wall beside the piano, a graying, curling poster of the "Desiderata" poem grabbed her attention. *Go placidly amid the noise and haste, and remember what peace there may be in silence.*

Not that there was peace or silence in here. Or breathable air.

A thick blue-gray haze hung suspended, collecting in the high ceilings. Almost everyone was smoking. Cigarettes zipped up and down throughout the room, caught between fingers that gestured with each word. At first she didn't see any empty tables; every one was full of people playing chess, or reading tarot cards, or arguing politics. Several people sat in chairs around a mic, strumming their guitars.

She made her way through the tables toward the back corner. Through an open door, she could see another area out back filled with picnic tables, where more people sat around talking and smoking.

Tully sat at a table way in the back, tucked in the shadowy corner. When she saw Kate, she stood up and waved.

Kate eased past a woman smoking a clove cigarette and sidled around a post.

That was when she saw him.

Chad Wiley.

He wasn't at all what she'd expected. He sat lazily in the chair, with one leg stretched out. Even in the smoke and shadows, she could see how handsome he was. He didn't *look* old. Tired, maybe, but in a world-weary kind of way. Like an aging gunslinger or a rock star. The smile he gave her started slowly, crinkling up his eyes, and in those eyes, she saw a knowledge that surprised her, made her miss a step.

He knew why she was here: a best friend coming to save a girl making a mistake by dating the wrong man.

"You must be Chad," she said.

"And you must be Katie."

She flinched at the unexpected use of her nickname. It was a forcible reminder that Chad knew Tully, too.

"Sit down," Tully said. "I'll go get a waitress." She was on her feet and gone before Kate could stop her.

Kate looked at Chad; he eyed her back, smiling as if at some secret. "This is an interesting place," she said to make conversation.

"It's like a tavern without beer," he said. "The kind of place where you can change who you are."

"I thought change started from within."

"Sometimes. Sometimes it's forced upon you."

His words caused something to darken his eyes, an emotion of some kind. She was reminded of his back-story suddenly, the bright career he'd lost. "They'd fire you—the university—if they found out about you and Tully, wouldn't they?"

He drew his leg back, sat up straighter. "So that's how you want to play it. Good. I like direct. Yes. I'd lose this career, too."

"Are you some kind of risk junkie?"

"No."

"Have you slept with your students before?"

He laughed. "Hardly."

"So, why?"

He glanced sideways, at Tully, who was at the crowded coffee bar, trying to order. "You, of all people, shouldn't have to ask that. Why is she your best friend?"

"She's special."

"Indeed."

"But what about her career? She'd be ruined if word got out that she was with you. They'd say she slept her way to a degree."

"Good for you, Katie. You should be looking out for her. She needs that. She's . . . fragile, our Tully."

Kate didn't know which upset her more—his description of Tully as fragile or the way he said *our Tully.* "She's a steamroller. I don't call her Tropical Storm Tully for nothing."

"That's on the outside. For show."

Kate sat back, surprised. "You actually care about her."

"More's the pity, I imagine. What will you tell her?"

"About what?"

"You came here to find a way to convince her not to see me anymore, didn't you? You can certainly say I'm too old. Or the prof angle is always a winner. Just so you know, I drink too much, too."

"You want me to tell her those things?"

He looked at her. "No. I don't want you to tell her those things."

Behind them, a young man with wild hair and ratty-looking pants stepped up to the microphone. He introduced himself as Kenny Gorelick, then began playing a saxophone. His music was wildly romantic and jazzy; for a few moments the talk in the place died down. Kate felt swept up in the music, transported by it. Gradually, though, it became background music and she looked at Chad. He was studying her intently. She knew how much it meant to him, this conversation, and how much Tully meant to him. That turned the tables neatly; she was surprised by the suddenness of the switch. Now, sitting here, she was worried that Tully would ruin this man, who frankly looked as if he didn't have the stamina to take another hit like that. Before she could answer the question he'd posed, Tully was back, dragging a purple-haired waitress with her.

"So," she said, frowning and a little breathless, "are you friends yet?"

Chad was the first to look up. "We're friends."

"Excellent," Tully said, sitting on his lap. "Now who wants apple pie?"

Chad dropped them off two blocks from the sorority house, on a dark street lined with aging boarding-houses that were filled with the kind of students who paid no attention to what sorority girls did.

"It was nice to meet you," Kate said as she got out of the car. She stood on the sidewalk, waiting for Tully to quit making out with him.

Finally, Tully got out of the car and waved goodbye as Chad's black Ford Mustang drove away.

"Well?" she demanded suddenly, turning to Kate. "He's handsome, isn't he?"

Kate nodded. "He sure is."

"And cool, right?"

"Definitely cool." She started to walk away, but Tully grabbed her sleeve, stopped her, and spun her around.

"Did you like him?"

"Of course I liked him. He's got a great sense of humor."

"But?"

Kate bit her lip, stalling for time. She didn't want to hurt Tully's feeling or piss her off, but what kind of friend would she be if she lied? The truth was, she *had* liked Chad and she believed he truly cared about Tully; it was also true that she had a bad feeling about their relationship and meeting him had only made it worse.

"Come on, Katie, you're scaring me."

"I wasn't going to say anything, Tully, but since you're forcing me . . . I don't think you should be going out with him." Once her opinion broke through the dam, she couldn't stop. "I mean, he's thirty-one years old. He has an ex-wife and a four-year-old daughter he never sees. You can't be seen publicly with him or he'll get fired. What kind of relationship is that? You're missing your college years."

Tully took a step back. "Missing my college years? You mean going to dances in Tahitian costumes and shotgunning beer? Or dating guys like the nerds you seem to choose—most of them are only slightly smarter than a pet rock."

"Maybe we should just agree to disagree . . ."

"You think I'm with him for my career, don't you? To what—get better grades or a spot at the station?"

"Aren't you? Just a little bit?" Kate knew instantly she shouldn't have said it. "I'm sorry," she said, reaching for her friend. "I didn't mean it."

Tully wrenched free. "Of course you meant it. Miss Perfect with the best family and the flawless grades. I don't even know why you hang around with me: I'm such a slut career hound."

"Wait!" Kate called out, but Tully was already gone, running down the dark street.

CHAPTER
TEN

Tully ran all the way to the bus stop on Forty-fifth.

"Bitch," she muttered, wiping her eyes.

When the bus came, she paid her fare and climbed aboard, muttering, "Bitch," twice more as she found a seat and sat down.

How could Kate have said those things to her?

"Bitch," she said again, but this time the word leaked out, sounding forlorn.

The bus stopped less than a block from Chad's house. She rushed up the sidewalk toward the small Craftsman-style home and knocked on the door.

He answered almost instantly, dressed in a pair of old gray sweats and a Rolling Stones T-shirt. She could tell by the way he smiled at her that he had expected her. "Hey, Tully."

"Take me to bed," she whispered throatily, pushing her hands up underneath his shirt.

They made their fumbling, kissing way through the house and to the small bedroom in the back. She stayed close to him, locked in his arms, kissing him deeply. She didn't look at him, couldn't, but it didn't matter. By the time they fell onto the bed, they were both naked and greedy.

Tully lost herself and her pain in the pleasure of his hands and mouth, and when it was over and they lay there, entwined, she tried not to think of anything except how good he made her feel.

"Do you want to talk about it?"

She stared up at the plain, high-pitched ceiling that had become as familiar to her as her own dreams. "What do you mean?"

"Come on, Tully."

She rolled onto her side and stared at him, propping her head into her hand.

He touched her face in a gentle caress. "You and Kate fought about me, and I know how much her opinion means to you."

The words surprised her, though they shouldn't have. In the time they'd been sleeping together, she'd somehow begun to reveal pieces of herself to him. It had begun accidentally, a comment here or there after sex or while they were drinking, and somehow grown from there. She felt safe in his bed, free from judgment or censure. They were lovers who didn't love each other, and that made talking easier. Still, she saw now that he'd listened to all of her babble and let the words form a picture. The knowledge of that made her feel less lonely all of a sudden, and even though it scared her, she couldn't help being comforted by it.

"She thinks it's wrong."

"It is wrong, Tully. We both know that."

"I don't care," she said fiercely, wiping her eyes. "She's my best friend. She's supposed to support me no matter what." Her voice broke on the last words, the promise they'd made to each other all those years ago.

"She's right, Tully. You should listen to her."

She heard something in his voice, a barely-there

quaver that made her look deeply into his eyes. In them, she saw a sadness that confused her. "How can you say that?"

"I'm falling in love with you, Tully, and I wish I weren't." He smiled sadly. "Don't look so scared. I know you don't believe in it."

The truth of that settled heavily on her, made her feel old suddenly. "Maybe someday I will." She wanted to believe that, at least.

"I hope so." He kissed her gently on the lips. "And now, what are you going to do about Kate?"

"She won't talk to me, Mom." Kate leaned back against the cushioned wall of the tiny cubby known as the phone room. She'd had to wait almost an hour for her turn on this Sunday afternoon.

"I know. I just hung up with her."

Of course Tully would call first. Kate didn't know why that irritated her. She heard the telltale lighting of a cigarette through the phone lines. "What did she tell you?"

"That you don't like her boyfriend."

"That's all?" Kate had to be careful. If Mom found out Chad's age, she'd blow a gasket and Tully would *really* be pissed if she thought Kate had turned Mom against her.

"Is there more?"

"No," she said quickly. "He's all wrong for her, Mom."

"Your vast experience with men tells you this?"

"She didn't go to the last dance because he didn't want to. She's missing out on college life."

"Did you really think Tully would be your average sorority girl? Come on, Katie. She's . . . dramatic. Full of dreams. It wouldn't hurt you to have a little of that fire, by the way."

Kate rolled her eyes. Always there was the subtle—and not so subtle—pressure to be like Tully. "We're not talking about my future. Focus, Mom."

"I'm just saying—"

"I heard you. So what do I do? She is avoiding me completely. I was trying to be a good friend."

"Sometimes being a good friend means saying nothing."

"I'm just supposed to watch her make a mistake?"

"Sometimes, yes. And then you stand by to pick up the pieces. Tully's such a big personality; it's easy to forget her background and how easily she can be hurt."

"So what do I do?"

"Only you can answer that. My days of being your Jiminy Cricket are long past."

"No more life-is speeches, huh? Great. Just when I could have used one."

Through the phone line came the hiss of exhaled smoke. "I do know that she's going to be in the editing room at KVTS at one o'clock."

"You're sure?"

"That's what she said."

"Thanks, Mom. I love you."

"Love you, too."

Kate hung up and hurried back to her room, where she dressed quickly and put on a little makeup: concealer, mostly, to cover the zits that had broken out across her forehead since their fight.

She made her way across campus in record time. It was easy. This late in the quarter people were busy studying for finals. At the door to KVTS, she paused, steeling herself as if for battle, and then went inside.

She found Tully exactly where Mom had predicted: hunched in front of a monitor, logging the raw footage and interviews. At Kate's entrance, she looked up.

"Well, well," Tully said, standing up. "If it isn't the head of the Moral Majority."

"I'm sorry," Kate said.

Tully's face crumpled at that, as if she'd been holding her breath in and suddenly let it go. "You were a real bitch."

"I shouldn't have said all that. It's just . . . we've never held back from each other."

"So that was our mistake." Tully swallowed, tried to smile. Failed.

"I wouldn't hurt you for the world. You're my best friend. I'm sorry."

"Swear it won't happen again. No guy will ever come between us."

"I swear." Kate meant it with every fiber of her being. If she had to staple her tongue down, she'd do it. Their friendship was more important than any relationship. Guys would come and go; girlfriends were forever. They knew that. "Now it's your turn."

"What do you mean?"

"Swear you won't bail on me again without talking. These last three days really sucked."

"I swear it."

Tully wasn't quite sure how it had happened, but somehow this sleeping with her professor had graduated into a full-blown affair. No pun intended. Perhaps Kate had been right and it *had* begun as a kind of career move for her; she no longer remembered. All she knew was that in his arms she felt content, and that was a new emotion for her.

And, of course, he *was* her mentor. In their time together he'd taught her things it would have taken her years to discover by herself.

More importantly, he'd shown her what making love was. His bed had become her port; his arms her life ring. When she kissed him and let him touch her with an unimaginable intimacy, she forgot that she didn't believe in love. Her first time, back in those dark Snohomish woods, faded from her memory a little more each day, until one day she discovered that she no longer carried it around inside of her. It would always be a part of her, a scar on her soul, but like all scars, it faded in time from a bright and burning red to a slim, silvery line that could only sometimes be seen.

But even with all that, with all that he'd shown and given her, it was beginning not to be enough. By fall semester of her senior year, she was growing impatient with the rarefied world of college. CNN had changed the face of broadcasting. Out in the real world, things were happening, things that mattered. John Lennon had been shot and killed outside his New York apartment; a guy named Hinckley had shot President Reagan in a pathetic attempt to impress Jodie Foster; Sandra Day O'Connor had become the first female Supreme Court justice; and Diana Spencer had married Prince Charles in a ceremony so fairy-tale perfect that every girl in America believed in love and happy endings for the entire summer. Kate talked about the wedding so often and in such detail you'd think she'd been invited.

All of it was headline news, made during Tully's life, and yet because she was in school, it was before her time. Oh, sure, she wrote the articles for the school paper and sometimes even got to read a few sentences here and there on air, but it was all make-believe, warm-up exercises for a game she wasn't yet allowed to play.

She yearned to swim in the real waters of local or national news. She'd grown even more tired of sorority dances and frat parties and that most archaic of all rituals—the candle passings. Why all those sorority girls wanted to get engaged was beyond her. Didn't they know what was going on in the world, didn't they see the possibilities?

She'd done everything UW had to offer, taken every broadcast and print journalism class that mattered, and learned what she could from a year's worth of interning at the public affairs station. It was time now to jump into the dog-eat-dog world of TV news. She wanted to surge into the crowd of reporters and elbow her way to the front.

"You're not ready," Chad said, sighing. It was the third time he'd said it in as many minutes.

"You're wrong," she said, leaning toward the mirror above his dresser, applying one more coat of mascara. In the glam early eighties, you couldn't wear too much makeup or have too big a hairdo. "You've made me ready and we both know it. You got me to change my hair to this boring Jane Pauley bob. Every suit I own is black and my shoes look like a suburban housewife's." She put the mascara brush back in the holder and slowly turned around, studying the Lee press-on nails she'd applied this morning. "What more do I need?"

He sat up in bed. From this distance he looked either saddened by their discussion or tired; she wasn't sure which. "You know the answer to that question," he said softly.

She dug through her purse for another color of lipstick. "I'm sick of college. I need to get into the real world."

"You're not ready, Tully. A reporter needs to exhibit a perfect mix of objectivity and compassion. You're too objective, too cold."

This was the one criticism that bugged her. She'd spent years *not* feeling things. Now she was suddenly supposed to be both compassionate and objective at the same time. Empathetic but professional. She couldn't quite pull it off and she and Chad both knew it. "I'm not talking about the networks yet. It's just one interview for a part-time job until graduation." She walked over to the bed. In her black suit and white blouse, she was the picture of conservative chic. She'd even tamed the sexiness of her shoulder-length hair by pulling it back into a banana clip. Sitting on the edge of the mattress, she pushed a long lock of hair away from his eyes. "You're just not ready for me to go out into the world."

He sighed, touched her jawline with his knuckle. "It's true I prefer you in my bed to out of it."

"Admit it: I'm ready." She'd intended to sound sexy and grown-up, but the vulnerable tremble in her voice betrayed her. She needed his approval like she needed air or sunlight. She'd go without it, of course, but less confidently, and today she needed every scrap of confidence she could find.

"Ah, Tully," he said finally. "You were born ready."

Smiling triumphantly, she kissed him—hard—then got up and grabbed her vinyl briefcase. Inside it was a handful of résumés printed on heavy ivory stock; several business cards that read, *Tallulah Hart, TV news reporter*; and a videotape of a story she'd done on-air for KVTS.

"Break a leg," Chad said.

"I will." She caught the bus in front of the Kidd Valley hamburger stand. Even though she was a senior, she hadn't bothered with bringing her car to school. Parking was expensive and hard to find. Besides, the Mularkeys loved having her gran's old land yacht.

All the way through the U District and into the city, she thought about what she knew about the man she was going to meet. At twenty-six, he was already a well-respected former on-air reporter who'd won some big reporting award during a Central American conflict. Something—none of the articles said what—had brought him home, where he'd suddenly changed career tracks. Now he was a producer for the smaller office of one of the local stations. She had practiced endlessly what she would say.

It's nice to meet you, too, Mr. Ryan.

Yes, I have had an impressive amount of experience for a woman of my age.

I'm committed to being a first-rate journalist and hope, no, expect to—

The bus came to a smoking, wheezing stop on the corner of First and Broad.

She hurried off the bus and down the steps. As she stood beneath the bus stop sign, consulting her notes, it started to rain, not hard enough to require an umbrella or a hood, but just enough to ruin her hair and poke her in the eyes. She ducked her head to protect her makeup and ran up the block to her destination.

The small concrete building with curtainless windows sat in the middle of the block with a parking lot beside it. Inside, she consulted the tenant board and found what she was looking for: KCPO—SUITE 201.

She perfected her posture, smiled professionally, and went up to Suite 201.

There, she opened the door and almost walked right into someone.

For a moment Tully was actually taken aback. The man standing in front of her was gorgeous—unruly black hair, electric-blue eyes, shadowy stubble of a beard. Not what she'd expected at all.

"Are you Tallulah Hart?"

She extended her hand. "I am. Are you Mr. Ryan?"

"I am." He shook her hand. "Come in." He led her through a small front room cluttered with papers and cameras and stacks of newspapers everywhere. A couple of open doors revealed other empty offices. Another guy stood in the corner, smoking a cigarette. He was huge, at least six-foot-five, with shaggy blond hair and clothes that looked as if he'd slept in them. A giant marijuana leaf decorated his T-shirt. At their entrance, he looked up.

"This is Tallulah Hart," Mr. Ryan said by way of introduction.

The big guy grunted. "She the one with the letters?"

"That's her." Mr. Ryan smiled at Tully. "He's Mutt. Our cameraman."

"Nice to meet you, Mr. Mutt."

That made them both laugh and the sound of their laughter only cemented her anxiety that she was too young for this.

He led her into a corner office and pointed to a metal chair in front of a wooden desk. "Have a seat," he said, closing the door behind him.

He took a seat behind the desk and looked at her.

She sat up straight, trying to look older.

"So, you're the one who has been clogging my mail with tapes and résumés. I'm sure, with all your ambition, you've researched us. We're the Seattle team for KCPO in Tacoma. We don't have an internship program here."

"That's what your letters said."

"I know. I wrote them." Leaning back in his chair, he wishboned his arms behind his head.

"Did you read my articles and watch my tapes?"

"Actually, that's why you're here. When I realized you weren't going to stop sending me audition tapes, I figured I might as well watch one."

"And?"

"And you'll be good one day. You've got that thing."
One day? Will be?

"But you're a long way from ready."

"That's why I want this internship."

"The nonexistent one, you mean."

"I'll work twenty to thirty hours a week for free, and I don't care if I get college credit or not. I'll write copy, fact-check, do research. Anything. How can you go wrong?"

"Anything?" He was looking at her intently now. "Will you make coffee and vacuum and clean the bathroom?"

"Who does all that now?"

"Mutt and me. And Carol, when she's not following a story."

"Then absolutely I will."

"So you'll do whatever it takes."

"I will."

He sat back, studying her closely. "You understand you'd be a grunt, and an unpaid one at that."

"I understand. I could work Mondays, Wednesdays, and Fridays."

Finally he said, "Okay, Tallulah Hart." He stood up. "Show me what you can do."

"I will." She smiled. "And it's Tully."

He walked her back through the office. "Hey, Mutt, this is our new intern, Tully Hart."

"Cool," Mutt said, not looking up from the camera equipment in his lap.

At the door, Mr. Ryan paused and looked at her. "I hope you intend to take this job seriously, Ms. Hart. Or this is an experiment that will have a shorter shelf life than milk."

"You can count on me, Mr. Ryan."

"Call me Johnny. I'll see you Friday. Say eight A.M.?"

"I'll be here."

She played and replayed the encounter over and over in her head as she walked briskly down the street to the bus stop and caught a ride.

She'd actually made her own internship. Someday, when Phil Donahue interviewed her, she'll tell this story to show her gutsy determination.

Yes, Phil. It was a bold move, but you know broadcasting. It's a dog-eat-dog world, and I was a girl with ambition.

But she'd tell Katie first. Nothing was quite perfect until she shared it with Kate.

This was the start of their dream.

The cherry trees in the Quad marked the passing of time better than any calendar. Pink and full of blossoms in the spring; lush and green in the warm, quiet days of summer; gloriously hued for the start of school; and now, bare on this November day in 1981.

For Kate, life was moving much too quickly. She was light-years away from the shy, quiet girl she'd been on arrival. In her years at UW, she'd learned to direct Rush Week skits, to organize and plan a dance for three hundred people, to chug a glass of beer and shoot a raw oyster, to work the room at a frat party and be comfortable around people she didn't know, to write edgy news stories with a hook and a splash, and to film that same story even if she was moving while it happened. Her journalism professors had graded her highly and told her repeatedly that she had a gift.

The problem, it seemed, was her heart. Unlike Tully, who could barrel forward and ask any question, Kate found it hard to intrude on people's grief. More and more often lately, she held back on her own stories and edited Tully's instead.

She didn't have what it took to be a network news producer or a first-rate reporter. Every day, as she sat in her broadcast and communications classes, she was lying to herself.

She dreamed lately of other things, of going on to law school so that she could fight the injustices she reported on, or writing novels that made people see the world in a better, more positive light . . . or—and this was the most hidden dream of all—falling in love. But how could she tell Tully these things?

Tully, who had taken her hand all those years ago when no one else would, who'd spun the gossamer dream of their lives as partners in TV news. How could she tell her best friend that she no longer shared their dream?

It should be easy to say. They'd been girls all those years ago when they'd chosen to embark on their tandem life. In the years between then and now, the world had changed so much. The war in Vietnam had been lost, Nixon had resigned, Mount St. Helens had blown up, and cocaine had become the Chex mix for a new generation of partygoers. The U.S. hockey team had pulled off a miracle win at the Olympics and a B-rate actor was president. Dreams could hardly remain static in such uncertain times.

She simply had to stand up to Tully, for once, and tell her the truth, say, *Those are your dreams, Tully, and I'm proud of you, but I'm not fourteen anymore and I can't follow you forever.*

"Maybe today," she said aloud, dragging her backpack along beside her as she walked through the gray, foggy campus.

If only she really had a dream of her own, something to replace the twin-TV news stars. Tully might accept that; Kate's vague, *I don't know,* wouldn't hold much water with Tropical Storm Tully.

On the edge of campus, she merged into the stream of kids and crossed the street, smiling and waving at friends as she passed them. At the sorority house, she went right to the living room, where girls sat packed like hot dogs on the sofas and chairs and on every patch of the celery-green carpet.

She tossed her backpack to the floor and found a spot on the floor between Charlotte and Mary Kay. "Has it started?"

About thirty people shushed her as the *General Hospital* theme music started. Laura's face filled the screen. She looked beautiful and dewy-eyed in a gorgeous white headdress. A collective sigh went around the room.

Then Luke appeared in his gray morning suit, smiling at his bride-to-be.

Just then, the sorority door banged open. "Kate!" Tully yelled, walking into the room.

"Ssshhh," everyone said at once.

Tully squatted behind Kate. "We need to talk."

"Shh. Luke and Laura are getting married. You can tell me about your interview—you got it: congratulations—when it's over. Now be quiet."

"But—"

"Shhh."

Tully sank to her knees, mumbling, "How can you all be so gaga over some skinny white guy with a bad perm? And he's a rapist. I think—"

"SHHH."

Tully sighed dramatically and crossed her arms.

As soon as it was over and the music started up again, she popped to her feet. "Come on, Katie. We need to talk." She grabbed Kate's hand and led her away from the publicness of the TV room, through the halls, and down a flight of stairs to the sorority's dirty little secret: the smoking lounge. It was a tiny room, tucked behind the kitchen, with two love seats, a coffee table littered with full ashtrays, and air so thick and blue it hurt your eyes, even when no one was in the room. It was *the* place for after-party gossip and late-night laughter.

Kate hated it down here. The habit that had seemed so cool and defiant at thirteen was gross and stupid now. "So, tell me everything. You got the internship, right?"

Tully grinned. "I did. Mondays, Wednesdays, and Fridays. Some weekends. We're on our way, Katie. I'll nail this job and by the time we graduate, I'll talk them into hiring you. We'll be a team, just like we always said."

Kate took a deep breath. *Do it. Tell her.* "You shouldn't be worrying about me, Tully. This is your day, your start."

"Don't be ridiculous. You still want to be a team, don't you?" Tully paused, stared at Kate, who screwed up her courage and opened her mouth. Then Tully laughed. "Of course you do. I knew it. You were just messing with me. Very funny. I'll talk to Mr. Ryan— he's my new boss—just as soon as he can't live without me. Now I gotta run. Chad will want to hear about the interview, but I had to tell you first." Tully hugged her fiercely and left.

Kate stood there, in the small, ugly room that smelled of stale cigarettes, staring at the open door. "No," she said softly. "I don't want to do that."

There was no one listening.

CHAPTER ELEVEN

Thanksgiving in the Mularkey household was always a spectacle. Aunt Georgia and Uncle Ralph drove over from eastern Washington, bringing enough food with them to feed an entire community. In years past, they'd had their four children with them, but now those kids were adults themselves and sometimes had other families to visit on the holiday. This year, Georgia and Ralph were alone, and looking a little dazed by their situation. Georgia had poured herself a drink before she even bothered saying hello to anyone in the house.

Kate sat on the threadbare arm of the cherry-red sofa that had been the centerpiece of this living room for as long as she could remember. Tully sat cross-legged on the floor at Mom's feet. It was her usual spot on holidays. Tully rarely liked to be too far from the woman she considered the perfect mother. Mom, in Dad's La-Z-Boy, was across from Georgia, who sat on the sofa.

It was the girlfriend hour—a family tradition. Georgia had devised it years ago—before there were any kids to care about, or so family legend had it. Every holiday, for one hour, while the men were watching football, the women gathered in the living room to have cocktails and catch up on the news. They all knew that soon enough there would be a Herculean amount of work to do in the kitchen, but for sixty minutes, no one cared.

This year, for the first time ever, Mom had poured glasses of white wine for Kate and Tully. It made Kate feel very grown up to sit here on the arm of the sofa, sipping her wine. Already the first Christmas album of the year was on the turntable. Elvis, naturally, singing about the little boy in the ghetto.

It was funny how an album, or even just a song, could remind you of so many moments in your life. Kate didn't think there had ever been any family event—Christmas, Thanksgiving, Easter, the yearly camping trip—that had been Elvis-free. It just wasn't a Mularkey family moment without him. Mom and Georgia made sure of that. His death hadn't changed the tradition at all, but sometimes, if they drank enough, they'd hug each other and cry for the loss of him.

"You should see what I got to do this week," Tully said, rising to her knees in her excitement. Kate couldn't help noticing that she looked like a supplicant, waiting for Mom's blessing. "You know the Spokane rapist case? Well," she said dramatically, luring them in, "the guy they arrested? His mother hired someone to kill the judge and prosecutor. Can you believe it? And Johnny—that's my boss—he let me do a first draft of the copy. They even used a sentence I wrote. It was so cool. Next week he's letting me tag along to an interview with a guy who invented some new kind of computer."

"You're really on your way now, Tully," Mom said, smiling down at her.

"Not just me, Mrs. M.," Tully said. "It's going to work out with Kate, too. I'll get her an internship at the station; you'll see. I'm already starting to drop hints. Someday you'll see us both on TV. The first pair of female anchors on a network news show."

"Think of it, Margie," Georgia said dreamily.

"Anchors?" Kate said, straightening. "I thought we were going to be reporters."

Tully grinned. "With our ambition? Are you kidding? We're going straight to the top, Katie."

Kate had to say something now. This was spinning out of control, and honestly, today was a good time to come clean. A round of drinks had softened everyone. "I should tell you—"

"We'll be more famous than Jean Enersen, Mrs. M.," Tully said, laughing. "And definitely richer."

"Imagine being rich," Mom said.

Aunt Georgia patted Kate's thigh. "Everyone in the family is so proud of you, Katie. You'll make a name for all of us."

Kate sighed. Once again she'd lost her chance. Getting up, she walked across the room, past the corner where soon the Christmas tree would be placed, and stood at the window, looking out over the pasture. A blanket of glittery white coated the field, created sparkly mounds on the fence posts. Moonlight turned everything a beautiful frosty blue and white; with the black velvet sky, it looked like a greeting card. As a girl, she'd waited impatiently for this unexpected weather, prayed for it for months, and no wonder. Covered in snow, Firefly Lane looked like something out of a fairy tale. The kind of place where nothing could ever go wrong, where a girl should be able to simply tell her family that she'd changed her mind.

The last few months of their senior year were perfection. Although Tully spent more than twenty-five hours a week at the station where she was interning, and Kate spent an equal number of hours working at Starbucks, the new designer coffee shop in the Pike Place Market, they made sure to spend a lot of their weekend time together, playing pool and drinking beer at Goldies or listening to music at the Blue Moon Tavern. Tully spent a lot of her nights at Chad's, but Kate didn't say much about that. Truthfully, she was having too much fun dating to hassle Tully about her choices.

The only problem in Kate's life—and it was a biggie—was her upcoming graduation. She was going to graduate next month with honors, with a degree in communications/broadcast journalism, and she still hadn't told anyone that it wasn't her dream job.

Now, though, she was going to come clean. She was in one of the third-floor phone rooms, folded up to fit, and she'd just dialed home.

Mom answered on the second ring. "Hello?"

"Hey, Mom."

"Katie! What a great surprise. I can't remember the last time you called in the middle of the week. You must be psychic: Dad and I just got home from the mall. You should see the dress I got for graduation. It's beautiful. Don't let anyone tell you JC Penney doesn't have great clothes."

"What does it look like?" Kate was stalling; with half an ear, she listened to her mom's description. Mom had just said something about shoulder pads and glitter when Kate jumped in. "I just applied for a job at Nordstrom, Mom. In the advertising department."

There was a noticeable pause on the other end, then the telltale sound of a cigarette being lit. "I thought you and Tully were going to be—"

"I know." Kate leaned back against the wall. "A reporting team. World-famous and rich."

"What's really going on, Kathleen?"

Kate tried to put her indecision into words. She just didn't know what she wanted to do with the rest of her life. She believed there had to be something special out there for her, a path that was hers alone and held happiness at its end, but where was the start of it? "I'm not like Tully," she finally said, admitting the truth she'd known for a long time. "I don't eat, sleep, and breathe the news. Sure, I'm good enough to get all A's and my profs love me because I'm never late with an assignment, but journalism—TV or print—is a jungle. I'll be eaten alive by people like Tully who'll do anything for a scoop. It's just not realistic to think I can make it."

"Realistic? Realistic is your dad and me trying to manage our expenses when they keep cutting his hours at the plant. Realistic is me being a smart woman who can't get a job at anything better than minimum wage because I have no education and all I've done is raise kids. Believe me, Katie, you don't want to be realistic at your age. There's plenty of time for that. Now you should dream big and reach high."

"I just want something different."

"What?"

"I wish I knew."

"Oh, Katie . . . I think you're afraid to reach for the brass ring. Don't be."

Before Katie could answer, there was a knock at the door. "I'm in here," she called out.

The door swung open to reveal Tully. "There you are. I've been looking everywhere. Who are you talking to?"

"Mom."

Tully yanked the phone from Kate and said, "Hey, Mrs. M. I'm kidnapping your daughter. We'll call back later. 'Bye." She hung up, then turned to Kate. "You're coming with me."

"Where are we going?"

"You'll see." Tully led her out of the house and down to the parking lot, where her new blue VW bug waited.

All the way into downtown Seattle, Kate asked where they were going and what was up until they pulled up in front of a small office building.

"This is where I work," Tully said when she turned off the engine. "I can't believe you've never been here before. Oh, well, you're here now."

Kate rolled her eyes. Now she knew what was happening: Tully wanted to show off some new triumph—a reel, a tape, a story she'd done that had actually been aired. As usual, Kate followed. "Look, Tully," she said as they made their way down the colorless hallway and into the small, cluttered space that was the Seattle office of KCPO-TV, "I need to tell you something."

Tully opened the door. "Sure. Later. That's Mutt, by the way." She pointed to a huge, long-haired, hunched-over guy standing by the open window, who was blowing his cigarette smoke outside.

"Hey," he said, barely lifting a single finger in greeting.

"Carol Mansour—she's the reporter—is at a city council meeting," Tully said, leading Kate toward a closed door.

As if Kate hadn't been hearing Carol Mansour stories forever.

Tully stopped at the door and knocked. When a male voice answered, Tully opened the door and pulled Kate inside. "Johnny? This is my friend Katie."

A man looked up from behind his desk. "You're Kate Mularkey, huh?"

He was, hands down, the best-looking man Kate had ever seen. He was older than they were, but not by much; maybe five or six years. His long black hair was thick and feathered back, with the barest hint of curl at the ends. Prominent cheekbones and a smallish chin could have made him look pretty, but there was nothing feminine about him. When he smiled at her, she drew in a sharp breath, feeling a jolt of pure physical attraction that was unlike anything she'd ever experienced before.

And here she stood, dressed for work in her preppy Gloria Vanderbilt jeans, penny loafers, and red V-neck sweater. All of last night's curl had fallen out of her hair and she hadn't redone it this morning. She hadn't bothered with makeup, either.

She was going to kill Tully.

"I'll leave you two alone," Tully said, skipping out of the office, closing the door behind her.

"Please. Have a seat," he said, indicating the empty chair across from his desk.

She sat down, perching nervously on the edge of the chair.

"Tully tells me you're a genius."

"Well, she is my best friend."

"You're lucky. She's a special girl."

"Yes, sir, she is."

He laughed at that; it was a rich, contagious sound that made her smile, too. "Please, don't call me sir. It makes me think some old guy is behind me." He leaned forward. "So, Kate, what do you think?"

"About what?"

"The job."

"What job?"

He glanced at the door, said, "Hmmm, that's interesting," then looked at her again. "We have an opening for an office person. Carol used to do all of the phones and filing, but she's going to have a baby, so the cheapass station manager has finally kicked in for a little help."

"But Tully—"

"She wants to stay an intern. Says that thanks to her grandmother she doesn't need the money. Between you and me, she's not great at answering the phones anyway."

This was all coming at Kate too fast. Only an hour ago, she'd finally admitted that she didn't want to go into broadcasting, and now here she was being offered a job every kid in her department at UW would kill for.

"What's the pay?" she asked, stalling.

"Minimum wage, of course."

She did the math in her head. With tips, she made close to double that much at Starbucks.

"Come on," he said, smiling. "How can you turn me down? You can be a receptionist in an ugly office for next to no money. Isn't it every college grad's dream?"

She couldn't help laughing. "When you put it that way, how could I refuse?"

"It's a start in the glamorous world of TV news, right?"

His smile was like some kind of superpower that scrambled her thoughts. "Is it? Glamorous, I mean?"

He looked surprised by the question, and for the first time he really looked at her. His fake smile faded, and the look in his blue eyes turned hard, cynical. "Not in this office."

He got to her. She didn't know why, but it was powerful, this attraction she felt. Nothing like how she'd responded to college boys. It was another reason not to take the job.

Behind her, the door opened. Tully came through, practically bouncing. "Well, did you say yes?"

It was crazy to take a job because you were hot for the boss.

Then again, she was twenty-one years old and he was offering her a start in television.

She didn't look at Tully. If she did, Kate knew she'd

feel as if she were selling out, following again, and for all the wrong reasons.

But how could she say no? Maybe in a real job she'd find that passion and brilliance she needed. The more she thought about it, the more possible it seemed. School wasn't the real world. Perhaps that was why the news business hadn't seized hold of her. Here, the stories would matter.

"Sure," she said at last. "I'll try it, Mr. Ryan."

"Call me Johnny." The smile he gave her was so unsettling she actually had to look away. She was sure somehow that he could see inside her or hear how fast he made her heart beat. "Okay, Johnny."

"All *right,*" Tully said, clapping her hands together.

Kate couldn't help noticing how her friend instantly seized Johnny's full attention. He was sitting at his desk now, staring at Tully.

That was when Kate knew she'd made a mistake.

Kate stared at herself in the small oval mirror above the dresser. Her long, straight, highlighted hair was drawn back from her face and held in place by a black velvet headband. Pale blue eye shadow and two coats of green mascara accentuated the color of her eyes, and pink lip gloss and blush gave her skin some color.

"You'll learn to love the news," she said to her reflection. "And you're not just following Tully."

"Hurry up, Kate," Tully called out, knocking hard on the bedroom door. "You don't want to be late on your first day of work. I'll be down in the parking lot."

"Okay, so maybe you *are* following her." Grabbing her briefcase off the twin bed that was hers, she left her bedroom and headed downstairs.

In this last week of school, the hallways were crazy-busy with girls studying for finals, saying goodbye, and packing up their things. Kate wound through the melee and went out to the small parking lot behind the house, where Tully sat in her brand-new VW Bug, with the engine running.

The second Kate sat down and slammed the door shut, they were off. Prince's *Purple Rain* soundtrack blared from the tiny speakers. Tully had to yell over the music.

"This is so great, isn't it? Us finally going to work together."

Kate nodded. "It sure is." She had to admit she was excited. After all, she was a college graduate—or would be soon—and she'd found an excellent starter position in her major field. It didn't matter that Tully had gotten the job for her, or that she was essentially following her best friend. What mattered was doing this job to the best of her abilities and finding out if broadcast journalism was for her. "Tell me about our boss," she said, turning down the stereo.

"Johnny? He's totally good at what he does. Used to be a war correspondent. In El Salvador or Libya; who the hell knows? I hear he misses combat, but he's a great producer. You can learn a lot from him."

"Have you ever wanted to go out with him?"

Tully laughed. "Just because I slept with my prof doesn't mean every boss is fair game."

Kate was relieved by that; more so than she should be. She wanted to ask if Johnny was married—she'd wanted to ask the question for almost a week—but she couldn't quite form the words. They'd be too revealing.

"Here we are." Tully pulled up to the curb outside the building and parked. All the way up the stairs and down the hall, she talked about how great it was going to be to work together, but once they were in the small, cramped set of offices, she made a beeline for Mutt and huddled with him.

Kate stood there, clutching her fake leather briefcase to her chest, wondering what she should do.

She had just decided to take off her jacket when Johnny appeared, looking both incredibly handsome and profoundly pissed off.

"Mutt! Carol!" he yelled, even though they were all standing right there. "That new company, Microsoft, is announcing something. I don't know what the hell it is. Mike is faxing the info. They want you to go to the company headquarters and see if you can talk to the boss. Bill Gates."

Tully surged forward. "Can I tag along?"

"Who cares? It's a bullshit story," Johnny said, then went back into his office and slammed the door.

The next few moments were a blur of chaotic movement. Carol, Tully, and Mutt gathered up their supplies and rushed out of the office.

Kate stood there after they left, in the now-quiet, vacant office, wondering what in the hell she was supposed to do.

Beside her, the phone rang.

She peeled out of her jacket, hung it over her chair back and sat down, then answered. "KCPO news. This is Kathleen. How may I help you?"

"Hey, honey, it's Mom and Dad. We just wanted to call and say have a great first day at work. We're so proud of you."

Kate was hardly surprised. Some things in life never changed; her family was one of them. She loved them for it. "Thanks, guys."

For the next few hours, she found it remarkably easy to fill her time. The phone rang almost constantly, and the in-box on her desk looked as if it hadn't been touched in years. The files were an absolute mess.

She became so engrossed in her work that the next

time she looked at the clock it was one o'clock and she was starving.

Certainly she was allowed a lunch break? She got up from her desk and crossed the now-clean office. At Johnny's door, she paused, gathered her courage to knock, but before she could do it, she heard yelling from his side of the door. He was on the phone, arguing with someone.

It was better not to interrupt. She set the phone's answering machine on automatic pickup and ran downstairs to the deli. There, she bought herself half a ham and cheese sandwich. On impulse, she bought a cup of clam chowder and a BLT as well. A pair of Cokes finished her order. Bag in hand, she ran upstairs and switched the phones back on.

Then she went to Johnny's door again; silence came from the other side.

She knocked timidly.

"Come in."

She opened the door.

He sat at his desk, looking tired. His long hair was a mess, as if he'd been running his fingers through it constantly, shoving it back from his face. Dozens of newspapers covered his desk, so many that even the phone was hidden. "Mularkey," he said, sighing. "Shit. I forgot you started today."

Kate wanted to make a joke about it, but her voice wouldn't cooperate. She was so keenly aware of him, it was vaguely disturbing that he hadn't even known she was here.

"Come on in. What do you have there?"

"Lunch. I thought you might be hungry."

"You bought me lunch?"

"Was that wrong? I'm sorry, I—"

"Sit down." He pointed at the chair opposite his desk.

"I appreciate it, really. I can't remember the last time I ate."

She moved to the desk, began unpacking their lunch. All the while she felt him watching her, those flame-blue eyes of his intently staring. It made her so nervous she almost spilled the chowder.

"Hot soup," he said, his voice low now, intimate. "So you're one of those."

She sat down, looking at him, unable not to. "One of those?"

"A caretaker." He picked up the spoon. "Let me guess: You grew up in a happy family. Two kids and a dog. No divorce."

She laughed. "Guilty. How about you?"

"No dog. Not so happy."

"Oh." She tried to think of something else to say. "Are you married?" popped out before she could stop it.

"Nope. Never. You?"

She smiled. "No."

"Good for you. This is a job that takes focus."

Kate felt like an imposter. Here she was, sitting across from her boss, trying to focus on saying something that would make him admire her, and she couldn't even make eye contact. It was crazy. He wasn't *that* good-looking. Something about him just hit her so damn hard she couldn't think straight. Finally she said, "You think they'll come up with a good story at Microsoft?"

"Israel invaded Lebanon yesterday. Did you know that? They've driven the Palestinians back to Beirut. That's the real story. And we're in the shit-ass office, dicking around with soft news." He sighed. "I'm sorry. I'm just having a bad day. And it's your first." He smiled, but it didn't reach his eyes. "And you bought me soup. Tomorrow I'll play nice, I promise."

"Tully told me you used to be a war correspondent."

"Yeah."

"I guess you loved that, huh?"

She saw something flash through his eyes then; her first instinct would have been to label it sadness, but how could she know? "It was insane."

"How come you quit?"

"You're too young to understand."

"I'm not that much younger than you. Try me."

He sighed. "Sometimes life kicks the shit out of you; that's all. It's like the Stones said: You can't always get what you want."

"The song says something about getting what you need instead."

He looked at her then, and for a split second, she knew she'd gotten his attention. "Did you find enough to keep yourself busy this morning?"

"The files were a mess. So was the in-box. And I organized and shelved all those tapes that were in the corner."

He laughed. It transformed his face, made him so handsome she drew in a sharp breath. "We've been trying to get Tully to do all that for months."

"I didn't mean—"

"Don't worry. You didn't get your friend in trouble. Believe me, I know what to expect from Tully."

"What's that?"

"Passion," he said simply, packing the empty sandwich wrapper into the Styrofoam soup cup.

Kate almost flinched at the way he said it, and she knew suddenly that she was in trouble. No matter how often she reminded herself that he was her boss, it didn't matter. In the end, what mattered was how she felt when she was near him.

Falling. There was no other word to describe it.

And yet, for the rest of the day, as she answered the phones and filed papers, she replayed in her head that last moment with him and the easy, straightforward way he'd answered her question about Tully: *passion*.

Mostly she remembered the way he'd smiled in admiration when he'd said it.

CHAPTER
TWELVE

The summer after graduation came as close to Heaven as Tully could imagine. She and Kate found a cheap 1960s-style apartment in a great location—above the Pike Place Market. They brought in furniture from Gran's house and filled the kitchen with forty-year-old Revereware pots and Spode china. On the walls, they tacked up favorite posters and put pictures of themselves on all the end tables. Mrs. Mularkey had surprised them one day with bags of groceries and several silk plants, to give the place a homey feel, she said.

The neighborhood created their lifestyle. They were within walking distance of several bars—their favorites were the Athenian inside the Market, and the smoky old Virginia Inn on the corner. At six o'clock in the morning, amid the beeping of delivery trucks and the honking of horns, they walked across the street for lattes from Starbucks and bought croissants from La Panier, a French bakery.

As working single girls, they fell into an easy routine. Each morning they went out for breakfast, sat at ironwork tables on the sidewalk, and read the various papers that they collected. *The New York Times, The Wall Street Journal,* and the *Seattle Times* and *Post-Intelligencer* became their bibles. When they were done, they drove to the office, where every day they learned something new about the business of TV news, and after work, they changed into glittery big shoulder-padded tunics and peg-legged pants and went to one of the many downtown clubs. On any given night they could listen to punk rock, new wave, rock 'n' roll, or pop—whatever they felt like.

And since Tully didn't have to hide Chad's existence anymore, he often took both Katie and her out, and they had a blast.

It was everything she and Kate had dreamed of, all those years ago on the dark banks of the Pilchuck River, and Tully loved every minute of it.

Now they were pulling up to the office. All the way out of the car and into the building, they talked.

But the minute Tully opened the door, she knew something was up. Mutt was near the window, hurriedly packing up his camera gear. Johnny was in his office, yelling at someone on the phone.

"What's going on?" Tully asked, tossing her purse on Kate's neat-as-a-pin desk.

Mutt looked up. "There's a protest going on. It's our story."

"Where's Carol?"

"In the hospital. Labor."

This was Tully's chance. She went straight into Johnny's office, without even bothering to knock. "Let me go on air. I know you think I'm not ready, but I am. And who else is there?"

He hung up the phone and looked at her. "I already told the station you'd do the report. That's what all the yelling was about." He came around the desk and moved toward her. "Don't let me down, Tully."

Tully knew it was unprofessional, but she couldn't help herself: she hugged him. "You're the best. I'll make you proud. You'll see."

She was halfway to the door when he cleared his throat and said her name. She stopped, turned.

"Don't you want to read the background stuff? Or do you want to go in blind?"

Tully felt her cheeks heat up. "Whoops. I'll read it."

He handed her a sheath of slippery fax paper. "It's about some housewife in Yelm who channels ghosts. J. Z. Knight."

Tully frowned.

"Is that a problem?"

"No. I just . . . know someone who lives out there. That's all."

"Well, there won't be time for visiting friends. Now go. I want you back by two to edit."

Without Mutt and Tully, the office was quiet. It was only the second time all summer that Kate had been alone in the office with Johnny. A little unnerved by the silence—as well as by the sight of his open door and the knowledge that he was just on the other side of it—she tended to answer the phone too quickly and even sound a little breathless when she did it.

When Tully was here, there was the noise and commotion. She lived for TV news and no moment of it was beneath her contemplation. All day, every day, she badgered Johnny and Carol and Mutt with questions; she continually sought their collective advice on every topic.

Kate had lost track of the times she'd seen Mutt roll

his eyes as Tully walked away from a conversation. Carol was even less accommodating; the lead reporter barely talked to Tully lately. Not that Tully seemed to care. What mattered to Tully was the news: first, last, and always.

Kate, on the other hand, cared about the people in the office more than she cared about the stories they followed. She had been befriended almost instantly by Carol, who often took her out to lunch to talk about her impending birth, and just as often called upon Kate to edit her copy or research stories. Mutt, too, had chosen Kate as his confidante. He spent long hours talking to her about his family problems and the woman who refused to marry him.

The only person Kate hadn't connected with was Johnny.

She was a nervous wreck around him. All he had to do was look her way and smile, and she'd drop whatever was in her hand. She consistently stuttered when giving him his messages and tripped over the ripped carpet edge in his office.

It was pathetic.

At first, Kate figured it was his looks. He was Irish-Catholic-boy perfect, with his black hair and blue eyes, and when he smiled, his whole face crinkled in a way that made her breath catch in her throat.

She'd assumed her infatuation wouldn't last, that in time, as she got to know him, his looks would be less arresting for her. At the very least, she thought she'd develop an immunity to his smile.

No such luck. Everything he said and did tightened the noose around her heart. Beneath his cynical veneer, she'd glimpsed an idealist, and even more: a wounded one. Something had broken Johnny, left him here, on the fringes of the big story, and the mystery of it tantalized her.

She went over to the corner, where a stack of tapes lay in a heap, waiting to be put away. She'd just picked up an armful when Johnny appeared in the doorway of his office. "Hey," he said. "Are you busy?"

She dropped the stack of tapes. *Idiot.* "No," she said. "Not really."

"Let's grab a real lunch. It's a slow news day and I'm sick of deli sandwiches."

"Uh . . . sure." She concentrated on the tasks in front of her: switching on the answering machine, putting on her sweater, picking up her purse.

He came up beside her. "Ready?"

"Let's go."

She walked alongside him down the block and across the street. Now and then his body brushed against hers, and she was acutely aware of every contact.

When they finally got to the restaurant, he led her over to a table in the corner that overlooked Elliott Bay and the shops at Pier 70. A waitress showed up almost instantly to take their orders.

"Are you old enough to drink, Mularkey?" he asked with a smile.

"Very funny. But I don't drink on the job." At the words, which couldn't have sounded more prim, she winced and thought, *Idiot,* again.

"You're a very responsible girl," he said when the waitress left; he was obviously trying not to smile.

"Woman," she said firmly, hoping she didn't blush.

He smiled at that. "I was trying to compliment you."

"And you chose *responsible*?"

"What would you prefer?"

"Sexy. Brilliant. Beautiful." She laughed nervously, sounding more like a girl than she would have wished. "You know: the words every woman wants to hear." She smiled. This was her chance to make an impression on him, get his attention as he'd gotten hers. She didn't want to blow it.

He leaned back in his chair, hopefully not because he suddenly wanted distance between them. She wished now, fervently, in fact, that she'd slept with one of her college boyfriends. She was certain he could see the stamp of virginity on her. "You've been at the station, what—two months now?"

"Almost three."

"How do you like it?"

"Fine."

"Fine? That's an odd answer. This is a love-it-or-hate-it business." He leaned forward, put his elbows on the table. "Do you have a passion for it?"

That word again: the one that separated her and Tully as cleanly as wheat from chaff.

"Y-yes."

He studied her, then smiled knowingly. She wondered how deeply into her soul that blue gaze had seen. "Tully certainly does."

"Yes."

He tried to sound casual as he asked, "Is she seeing anyone?"

Kate considered it a personal triumph that she didn't flinch or frown. Now, at least, she knew why he'd asked her out for lunch. She should have known. She wanted to say, *Yes; she's been with the same man for years,* but she didn't dare. Tully might not hide Chad anymore, but she didn't flaunt him, either. "What do you think?"

"I think she sees a lot of men."

Thankfully, the waitress returned with their orders and she pretended to be fascinated by her plate. "What about you? I get the feeling you're not exactly passionate about your job."

He looked up sharply. "What makes you say that?"

She shrugged and kept eating, but she was watching him now.

"Maybe not," he said quietly.

She felt herself go still; her fork stayed in midair. For the first time they weren't making idle chitchat. He'd just revealed something important; she was somehow certain of that. "Tell me about El Salvador."

"You know what went on down there? The massacre? It was a bloodbath. Things have been getting worse lately, too. The death squads are killing civilians, priests, nuns."

Kate hadn't known all of that, or any of it, really, but she nodded anyway, watching the play of emotions cross his face. She'd never seen him so animated, so passionate. Again there was an unreadable emotion in his eyes, too. "You sound as if you loved it. Why did you leave?"

"I don't talk about this." He finished his beer and stood up. "We better get back to work."

She looked down at their barely eaten lunches. Obviously she'd gone too far, probed too much. "I got too personal, I'm sorry—"

"Don't be. It's ancient history. Let's go."

All the way back to the office, he said nothing. They walked briskly upstairs and into the quiet office.

There, she couldn't help herself, she touched his arm. "I really am sorry. I didn't mean to upset you."

"Like I said, it's old news."

"It isn't, though, is it?" she said quietly, knowing instantly that she'd overstepped again.

"Get back to work," he said brusquely, and went into his office, slamming the door shut behind him.

Yelm slept in the verdant green valley between Olympia and Tacoma. It had always been the kind of town where people dressed in flannel shirts and faded jeans and waved to one another as they passed.

All that had changed a few years ago, on the day a thirty-five-thousand-year-old warrior from Atlantis supposedly appeared in the kitchen of an otherwise ordinary housewife.

The locals, who believed in the Northwest creed of "live and let live," looked the other way for a long time. They ignored the "weirdos" who came to Yelm (many of them in expensive cars, wearing designer clothes—"Hollywood types") and paid no attention as SOLD signs started appearing on prime pieces of land.

When the whispers began that J. Z. Knight was gearing up to build some kind of compound to house a school for her followers, though, the townsfolk had had enough. According to the South Sound bureau chief at KCPO, people were picketing the Knight property.

The "crowd" protesting the proposed development turned out to be about ten people holding up signs and chatting with one another. It looked more like a coffee klatch than a political gathering—until the news van showed up. Then the crowd started marching and chanting.

"Ah," Mutt said, "the power of the media." He pulled over to the side of the road and turned to Tully.

"Here's what they didn't teach you in college: Get into the middle of it. Wade in. If it looks like there's going to be a fight, I want you there, got it? Just keep asking questions, keep talking. And if I give you the sign, get the hell out of the shot."

Tully's heart was going a mile a minute as she followed his lead.

The protesters surged toward them. Everyone was talking at once, trying to make their point, elbowing each other out of their way.

Mutt shoved Tully, hard. She stumbled forward and came face to chest with a huge, burly guy with a Santa-like beard and a sign that read: JUST SAY NO TO RAMTHA.

"I'm Tallulah Hart from KCPO. What are you out here for today?"

"Get his name," Mutt yelled.

Tully winced. *Shit.*

The man said, "I'm Ben Nettleman. Me and my family's lived in Yelm for nearly eighty years. We don't want to see it turn into some supermarket for new age weirdos."

"They got California for that!" someone yelled.

"Tell me about the Yelm you know," Tully said.

"It's a quiet place, where people look out for each other. We start our day with prayer and mostly we don't care what our neighbors do . . . until they start building shit that don't belong and bringing crazies by the bus-loads."

"And you say crazies because—"

"They are! That lady channels some dead guy who says he lived in Atlantis."

"I can do an Indian accent, too. It don't make me Ramtha," someone yelled.

For the next twenty minutes, Tully did what she did best: she talked to people. Six or seven minutes in, she found her groove and remembered what she'd been taught. She listened and asked the follow-up questions she would have asked anyone on an ordinary day. She had no idea if they were the right questions or if she was always standing in the best place, but she did know that by her third interview, Mutt had stopped directing her and started letting her lead. And she knew that she *felt* good. People really opened up to her, sharing their feelings and concerns and fears.

"Okay, Tully," Mutt said behind her. "That's it. We're done."

The minute the camera was off, the crowd broke up.

"I did it," she whispered. It was all she could do not to actually jump up and down. "What a rush."

"You did good," Mutt said, giving her a smile that she'd never forget.

Mutt packed up his camera gear in record time and climbed into the van.

Tully was on an adrenaline high.

Then she saw the campground sign.

"Turn off here," she said, surprising herself.

"Why?" Mutt asked.

"My mom is . . . on vacation. She's staying at this campground. Give me five minutes to say hi."

"I'll take a smoke break. That'll give you fifteen. But then we gotta boogie."

The van pulled up in front of the campground's reservation desk.

Tully went to the desk and asked about her mother. The man on duty nodded. "Site thirty-six. Tell her she needs to pay when you see her."

Following the path through the trees, Tully almost turned around a dozen times. Honestly, she had no idea why she was here. She hadn't seen or spoken to her mother since Gran's funeral, and although Tully had become the executor of Gran's estate at eighteen, and responsible for the monthly disbursement to Cloud, she'd never once received a thank-you for the money. Just a series of I've-moved-please-send-money-to-this-address postcards. This campground in Yelm was the most recent.

She saw her mother standing by a row of Sani-cans, smoking a cigarette. Wearing a coarse gray Cowichan sweater and pajamalike pants, she looked like an es-

capee from a women's prison. The years had sanded
down some of her beauty and left a network of fine lines
across her hollowed cheeks.

"Hey, Cloud," she said when she got close.

Her mother took a drag of her cigarette and exhaled
slowly, watching her through heavily lidded eyes.

She could see how bad her mother looked, how the
drugs were aging her. Not even forty yet, Cloud looked
fifty, easy. As usual her eyes had the glassy, unfocused
gaze of an addict.

"I'm here on assignment for KCPO news." Tully tried
to keep the pride out of her voice, knowing it was stupid to expect anything from her mother, but it was there
anyway, in her eyes and her voice, the shadowy remnant
of that pathetic little girl who'd filled twelve memory
books so that someday her mother would know her and
be proud. "It was my first on-air report. I told you I'd be
on TV someday."

Cloud's body swayed ever so slightly, as if there were
music in the air that only she could hear. "TV is the opi-
ate of the masses."

"Well, if there's anyone who'd know about drugs, it's
you."

"Speaking of that, I'm kinda short this month. You
got any cash?"

Tully dug in her purse, found the fifty-dollar bill she
kept in her wallet for emergencies, and handed it to her
mother. "Don't give it all to one dealer."

Cloud took a clumsy step forward and palmed the
money.

Tully wished she'd never come here. She knew what
to expect from her mother: nothing. Why couldn't she
seem to remember that? "I'll send money for your next
rehab, Cloud. Every family has its traditions, right?" On
that, she turned and walked back to the van.

Mutt was waiting for her. Dropping his cigarette, he ground it out with his heel and grinned at her. "Mommy proud of her college girl?"

"Are you kidding?" Tully said, grinning brightly and wiping her eyes. "She cried like a baby."

When Tully and Mutt came back, the team clicked into high gear. The four of them crammed into the editing room and turned twenty-six minutes of tape into a sharp, impartial thirty-second story. Kate tried to keep her thoughts focused on the story, just the story, but lunch with Johnny had dulled her senses; or heightened them. She wasn't entirely sure which. All she really knew was that whatever schoolgirl crush she'd had on him before he asked her out to lunch had deepened into something else.

When they finished working, Johnny picked up the phone and called the Tacoma station manager. He talked for a few moments, then hung up and looked at Tully. "They'll air it tonight at ten unless something comes up."

Tully jumped up and clapped her hands. "We did it!"

Kate couldn't help feeling a stab of envy. Just once, she wanted Johnny to look at her the way he looked at Tully.

If only she were like her friend—confident and sexy and willing to make a grab at whatever—and whomever—she wanted. Then she might have a chance, but the thought of Johnny's rejection, of a blank-eyed, *Huh?* kept her standing in the shadows.

Tully's shadow, to be precise. As always, Kate was the backup singer who never stepped into the spotlight.

"Let's go celebrate," Tully said. "Dinner's on me."

"Count me out," Mutt said. "Darla's waiting for me."

"I can't do dinner, but how about drinks at nine?" Johnny said.

"We can do that," Tully said.

Kate knew she should say no. The last thing she wanted to do was sit at the table and watch Johnny watch Tully—but what choice did she have? She was the side-kick. Rhoda Morgenstern. And wherever Mary went, Rhoda had to follow, even if it hurt like hell.

Kate chose her clothes with care: a cap-sleeved white T-shirt, black vintage jacquard vest, and tight jeans tucked into scrunchy ankle boots. After curling her hair, she combed it carefully to one side and anchored it into a ponytail. She thought she looked pretty good until she went out into the living room and saw Tully standing there, dressed in a green jersey dress with a plunging neckline, padded shoulders, and a wide metallic belt, swaying to the music.

"Tully? You ready?"

Tully stopped dancing, flicked off the stereo, and linked arms with Kate. "Come on. We're so outta here."

Down on the street in front of their apartment, they found Johnny leaning against his black El Camino. In faded jeans and an old Aerosmith T-shirt, he looked to-tally sexy in a casual, rumpled kind of way.

"Where are we going?" Tully asked. She immedi-ately linked her other arm with his.

"I've got a plan," Johnny said.

"I love a man with a plan," Tully said. "Don't you, Kate?"

The word *love* paired with his name hit a little close to home, so she didn't look at him when she said, "I do."

Three abreast, they walked down the cobblestone street of the empty market.

At the neon-lit sex shop on the corner, Johnny guided them to turn right.

Kate frowned. There was an invisible line, like the equator, that ran down Pike Street. To the south, it got ugly fast. This was where the tourists didn't go unless they were looking for drugs or hookers. The shops and businesses on both sides of the street were seedy-looking.

They walked past two adult bookstores and an X-rated theater where the *Debbie Does Dallas* sequel was playing on a double feature with *Saturday Night Beaver*.

"This is great," Tully said. "Kate and I never go down here."

Johnny came to a stop beside a ratty-looking wooden door that had obviously once been painted red. "Ready?" he said with a smile.

Tully nodded.

He opened the door. The music was earsplittingly loud.

A huge black man sat on a stool at the entrance. "ID, please," he said, turning on a flashlight to study their driver's licenses. "Go on."

Tully and Kate showed their IDs, then moved on ahead, down the dark narrow hallway that was covered with flyers and posters and bumper stickers.

The hallway opened into a long, rectangular room that was packed with people dressed in metal-enhanced black leather. Kate had never seen so many bizarre hairdos in one room. There were dozens of people with six-inch-long Mohawks gelled to sawblade perfection and dyed in rainbow colors.

Johnny led them through the dance floor, past a few wooden tables, to the bar, where a girl with magenta hair cut into spidery spikes and a safety pin in her cheek took their orders. At the end of the bar, suspended up in the corner, was a good-sized TV that was currently tuned to MTV. No one was paying the slightest attention to it.

When the bartender returned, Johnny gave her a healthy tip and a bright smile, then led Kate and Tully to a table back in the corner, beneath the TV.

Tully immediately lifted her margarita for a toast. "To us. We totally rocked today."

They clinked glasses and drank.

And drank.

By their third round, Tully was drunk. When the right song started—"Call Me," or "Sweet Dreams (Are Made of This)," or "Do You Really Wanna Hurt Me?"—she was on her feet, dancing all by herself right next to the table.

Kate wished she could find that kind of ease in herself, but two drinks weren't enough to undo who she was. Instead, she sat there, watching Johnny watch Tully.

He didn't really look at Kate until Tully went to the bathroom. "She never slows down, does she?"

Kate tried then to think of a response that would steer the conversation away from her best friend, maybe even reveal her own passionate side, but who was she kidding? She had no passionate side. Tully was candy-apple-red silk; Kate was beige cotton. "Yeah."

Tully rushed back from the bathroom, skidded drunkenly into the bar. "Hey, it's ten o'clock. Can we change the channel on the TV? No one is watching it anyway."

"Whatever." The bartender, who looked like an extra from some apocalyptic war movie, climbed up on to a stepladder and changed the channel.

Tully moved toward the TV, looking like a penitent approaching the Pope.

Then her face filled the screen. *"I'm Tallulah Hart in Yelm, Washington. This sleepy town was the site of protest today when followers of J. Z. Knight and the thirty-five-thousand-year-old spirit she calls Ramtha clashed with locals over the proposed building of a compound . . ."*

When it was over, Tully turned to Kate, said, "Well?" in a quiet, nervous voice.

"You were totally bitchin'," Kate said, meaning it. "Excellent."

Tully threw her arms around Kate and held her tightly, then grabbed her hand. "Come on. I want to dance. You, too, Johnny. We can all dance together."

There were men dancing together, and women making out to the beat of the Sex Pistols. The girl beside Kate, wearing a black plastic miniskirt and combat boots with fishnet stockings, was dancing alone.

Tully was the first to start dancing, then Johnny, and finally Kate. At first she felt awkward—literally a third wheel—but by the end of the song, she'd softened. The alcohol was a lubricant, making her body more fluid somehow, and when the music changed and slowed down, she barely hesitated to step into Tully and Johnny's arms. The three of them moved together with a natural ease that was surprisingly sexy. Kate stared up at Johnny, who was gazing at Tully, and she couldn't help wishing just once he'd look at her that way.

"I'll never forget this night," Tully said to both of them.

He leaned down and kissed Tully. Kate was drunk enough that it took her a second to register what she was seeing. Then came the pain.

Tully pulled out of the kiss. "Bad Johnny." She laughed, pushing him away.

He moved his hand down Tully's back, tried to pull her close. "What's wrong with bad?"

Before Tully could answer, someone called out her name and she spun around.

Chad was pushing through the gyrating, slam-dancing crowd. With his long hair and ragged Springsteen T-shirt, he looked like a hard rock guy in a new wave world.

Tully ran for him. They kissed as if they were alone in the room, then Kate heard her friend say, "Take me to bed, old man."

Without a wave or a goodbye or a hello, they were gone. Kate stood there, still in Johnny's arms. He was staring at the door as if he expected Tully to return, to shout out April Fools and start dancing with them again.

"She won't be coming back," Kate said.

Johnny snapped out of it. Letting go of her, he went back to the table and ordered two drinks. In the silence that followed, she stared at him, thinking: *Look at me.*

"That was Chad Wiley," he said.

Kate nodded.

"No wonder . . ." He stared at the blank hallway on the other side of the dance floor.

"They've been together a long time." She studied his profile. For a crazy second, she thought about making a move, reaching for him. Maybe she could get him to forget about Tully or change his mind; maybe tonight she didn't care if she would be his second choice, or if it would be because of the booze. Love could grow from drunken passion, couldn't it? "You thought you and Tully might—"

He nodded before she could finish and said, "Come on, Mularkey. I'll walk you home."

All the way back to her apartment, she told herself it was for the best.

"Well, goodnight, Johnny," she said at her front door.

"Goodnight." He started for the elevator. Halfway there, he stopped and turned to her. "Mularkey?"

She paused, glanced back. "Yeah?"

"You were really good today. Did I tell you that? You're one of the most talented writers I've ever seen."

"Thanks."

Later, lying in her bed, staring into the darkness, she remembered his words, and how he'd looked when he'd said them.

In some small way, he'd noticed her today.

Maybe it wasn't as hopeless as she'd thought.

CHAPTER THIRTEEN

From the moment Tully did her first on-air broadcast, everything changed. They became the fearsome foursome; Kate and Tully and Mutt and Johnny. For two years they were together constantly, huddled together in the office, working on stories, going from place to place like gypsies. The second story that Tully covered was about a snowy owl who'd taken up residence on a streetlamp in Capitol Hill. Next, she followed the gubernatorial campaign of Booth Gardner, and though she was one of dozens of reporters on the case, it seemed that Gardner often answered her questions first. By the time the first Microsoft millionaires began driving through downtown in their mint-new Ferraris, listening to geek music on supersized headphones, everyone at KCPO knew that Tully wouldn't last on the smallest local channel for long.

They all knew it, but perhaps Johnny most of all. So, although the three of them didn't talk about the future, they felt its shadowy presence constantly, and somehow that made their time together sweeter and more intense. On the rare night when they weren't working on a story,

Johnny, Tully, and Kate met at Goldies to play pool and drink beer. By the end of their second year together, they knew all there was to know about each other; at least, all that each was willing to share.

Except the stuff that truly mattered. Kate often thought it ironic that three people who searched through the rubble of life to find pebbles of truth could be so stubbornly blind about their own lives.

Tully had no idea that Johnny wanted her, and he was completely unaware that Kate wanted him.

So their weird, silent triangle went on, day after day, night after night. Tully always asked Kate why she didn't date. She longed to come clean, tell Tully the truth, but every time she started to confess, she backed out. How could she tell the truth about Johnny, after the crap she'd given Tully about Chad? Your boss, after all, was worse than your professor.

And besides, what did Tully know about unrequited love? Her friend would just start pushing Kate to ask Johnny out. What would Kate say then? *I can't. He's in love with you.* Deeper down, in a dark place she rarely acknowledged, there was another fear, one she only recognized in her dreams and nightmares. In the cold light of day, she didn't believe it, but at night, alone, she worried that if Tully found out about Kate's love, it might actually make Johnny more attractive to Tully. That was the thing about her best friend; it wasn't that she wanted what she couldn't have. It was that she wanted everything, and sooner or later, Tully got what she wanted. Kate couldn't risk it. Not having Johnny she could live with. Losing him to Tully would be unbearable.

So Kate kept her head down, her hands busy, and her dreams of love hidden away. She smiled easily when Mom or Dad or Tully teased her about her social life, joked that her standards were higher than some people she could name, an answer which was always good for a laugh.

She tried not to be alone with Johnny too much, either, just to stay on the safe side. Although she no longer fumbled things or got tongue-tied around him, she always sensed that he was quite perceptive, and that, given too many opportunities, he might sense that which she worked so hard to hide.

Her plan went pretty well, all things considered, until a cold November day in 1984 when Johnny called her into his office.

They were alone again, that day. Tully and Mutt were tracking down a Sasquatch sighting in the Olympic rain forest.

Kate smoothed her angora sweater and schooled her face into an impersonal smile as she went into his office and found him standing at the dirty window. "What is it, Johnny?"

He looked terrible. Haggard. "Remember when I told you about El Salvador?"

"Sure."

"Well, I still have friends down there. One of them, Father Ramón, is missing. His sister thinks they've taken him somewhere for torture, or that they've killed him. She wants me to come down and see if I can help."

"But it's dangerous—"

"Danger is my middle name." He smiled, but it was like a reflection on water, distorted and unreal.

"This isn't something to joke about. You could be killed. Or disappear like that journalist in Chile during the coup. He was never seen again."

"Believe me," he said, "I'm not joking. I've been there, remember? I know what it's like to be blindfolded and shot at." He turned his head. His eyes took on a vague, unfocused look, and she wondered what he was remembering. "I can't turn my back on the people who protected me down there. Could you turn away from Tully if she begged you for help?"

"I would help her, as you well know. Although I don't expect to see her in a war zone, unless you count the anniversary sale at Nordstrom."

"I knew you were my girl. So you'll keep this place running while I'm gone?"

"Me?"

"Like I said once, you're a responsible girl."

She couldn't help herself; she moved toward him, looked up. He was leaving, could be hurt down there, or worse. "Woman," she said.

He stared down at her, unsmiling. She felt the mere inches between them. It would take nothing, barely a movement to touch.

"Woman," he said.

Then he left her there, standing alone, surrounded by word ghosts; things she could have said.

When Johnny was gone, Kate learned how elastic time was, how it could stretch out until minutes felt like hours. All it would take was a phone call, though, an official saying he was sorry, to make it snap like a rubber band. Every time the phone rang, she tensed. By the end of the first day, she had a pounding headache.

She learned another lesson that first week, too. Life went on. The head honchos in Tacoma still called, and a producer was assigned to oversee the assignments the team was given, but in truth, the way it worked out, Kate began to take over some of the producing responsibilities. Mutt and Tully trusted her, and she knew how to make things work on the shoestring budget they'd been given. All that longing of hers had paid off; it seemed she'd watched Johnny closely enough that she knew how to do his job. She was a seamstress to his couturier, of course, but still, she was competent. By Thursday of the first week, the out-of-town producer had thrown up his hands, said he had better things to do than follow crazy people around all day, and returned to Tacoma.

On Friday, Kate produced her first segment. It was soft and unimportant—an update on former children's TV star Brakeman Bill—but still it was hers, and it hit the air.

What an adrenaline rush it had been to see her work on-screen, even if it was Tully's face and voice that everyone remembered. She'd called her parents and they drove down to watch the broadcast with Kate and Tully. Afterward, they'd toasted to "the dream" and agreed that it was that much closer to coming true.

"I always thought Katie and I would be on air together, an anchoring team, but I guess I was wrong," Tully had said. "She'll be the producer of my show someday instead. And when Barbara Walters interviews me, I'll say I couldn't have done it without her."

Kate had toasted when it was expected of her, smiling purposely and reliving every moment through Tully's chatter. She'd been proud of herself, truly she had, and she'd loved doing the piece and celebrating with her parents. It had been especially poignant when Mom took her aside and said, "I'm proud of you, Katie. You're on your way now. Aren't you glad you didn't give up?"

But all the while, a part of her was watching the clock, thinking how slowly time was moving.

"You look terrible," Tully said the next day, dropping a stack of tapes on Kate's desk.

The clattering sound startled Kate. She realized she'd been staring at the clock again. "Yeah, well, your singing sucks."

Tully laughed at that. "Everyone has something they can't do." She put her palms on Kate's desk and leaned forward. "Chad and I are going to the Backstage tonight. Junior Cadillac is playing. You want to come?"

"Not tonight."

Tully eyed her. "What in the hell is wrong with you? You've been moping around for more than a week. I know you're not sleeping—I hear you up walking around in the middle of the night—and you won't go anywhere. It's like living with the Elephant Man."

Kate couldn't help glancing at Johnny's door and then up at her friend. Longing welled up inside her, sharp and strong; if only she could tell Tully the truth: that she'd accidentally fallen in love with Johnny and now she was worried about him. It would take such a load off of her. In ten years, this was the first thing she'd ever hidden from Tully, and it physically hurt to conceal it.

But her feelings for Johnny were so fragile; she knew that Tropical Storm Tully would rain all over them, ruin them.

"I'm just tired," she said. "This producing is hard work. That's all."

"But you love it, don't you?"

"Sure. It's great. Now go on, meet Chad. I'll close up." After Tully left, Kate lingered in the dark, quiet office. The strange thing was, she liked being here; she felt close to him.

"You're an idiot," she said aloud. Truthfully, she said it to herself at least twice a day lately. She was acting like—felt like—a left-behind lover, but it was all in her imagination. At least she wasn't so far gone that she'd forgotten that.

She went home by herself. The bus dropped her off at the corner of Pike and Pine. Amid the colorful crowd of tourists and weirdos and hippies, she picked up some food for dinner. Back in her apartment, she curled up on the couch, ate her dinner out of white cardboard containers, and watched the nightly news. Afterward, she made some notes on story ideas, called her mom, then turned the channel to NBC for *Dynasty* and *St. Elsewhere*.

Halfway through the medical drama, the doorbell rang.

Frowning, she went to the door. "Who is it?"

"Johnny Ryan."

The jolt Kate felt almost knocked her off her feet. Relief. Joy. Fear. She experienced all three emotions in a heartbeat of time.

She glanced in the mirror hanging on the wall beside her and gasped. She looked like a fashion magazine "before" photo—limp hair, no makeup, eyebrows untrimmed.

He pounded on the door again.

She opened it.

He stood there, leaning heavily against the doorframe, wearing dirty Levi's and a torn BORN IN THE USA tour T-shirt. His hair was long and uncombed, and though he was tanned, his face looked worn, older. She could smell alcohol, too.

"Hey," he said, opening his fingers from along the doorframe in greeting. At the movement he lost his balance and almost fell.

Kate moved toward him. Holding him up, she guided him into the apartment, kicked the door shut, and led him to the sofa, where he half stumbled to a sit.

"I've been sitting over in the Athenian," he said, "trying to get up the nerve t' come over here." He glanced blearily around the place. "Where's Tully?"

"She's not here," Kate said, feeling a clutch in her heart.

"Oh."

She sat down beside him. "How did it go in El Salvador?"

When he turned to her, the look in his eyes was so devastating that she reached out, put her arm around him, and drew him close.

"He was dead," he said after a long silence. "Before I even got there, he was dead. But I had to find him . . ." He pulled a flask out of his back pocket and took a long drink. "Y' want some?"

She took a sip, felt it burn all the way down her throat and settle like a hot coal in the pit of her stomach.

"It's damned heartbreaking wha's going on. And not enough is getting on air. No one cares."

"You could go on assignment," she said, even though she hated the idea.

"I wish I could . . ." His voice faded away, then turned sharp. "Old news." He took another drink.

"Maybe you should slow down a little." She tried to take the flask from him. Instead, he grabbed her wrist and pulled her onto his lap. He touched her face with his other hand, caressing her cheek as if he were blind and trying to come up with an image of what she looked like.

"You're beautiful," he whispered.

"You're drunk."

"You're still beautiful." He slid one hand up her arm and the other down her throat until he was holding her in his arms. She knew he was going to kiss her, felt the knowledge in every nerve ending in her body, just as she knew she should stop him.

He pulled her closer and all her good intentions disappeared. She gave herself over to the pressure of his hands, let herself be guided down, down toward his mouth.

The kiss was like nothing she'd ever experienced

before: tender and sweet at first, then searching, demanding.

She surrendered to him as completely as she'd dreamed of doing. His tongue electrified her, sparked a new and painful desire. She became greedy for him, desperate. Without thinking, she shoved her hands up under his T-shirt, feeling his warm skin, needing to be closer . . .

Her hands were at his collarbone, pushing the soft warm cotton upward, when she realized he'd gone still.

Her senses were so scrambled it took her a moment to clear her head. Breathing hard, aching with this new need, she drew back enough to look at him.

He lay back against the sofa, his eyes at half mast. He lifted his hand slowly, jerkily, almost as if he weren't quite controlling his own movements, and touched her lips, tracing their contour with his fingertip. "Tully," he whispered. "I knew you'd taste good."

And with that blow to the heart, he fell asleep.

Kate wasn't sure how long she sat on his lap, staring down at his sleeping face. Once again, time seemed elastic between them. It felt as if she were bleeding—but it wasn't blood that leaked out of her, not something that could be so easily transfused. Instead, she was losing her dreams. The fantasy flower of love she'd planted all by herself and tended so carefully.

She climbed off him and settled him onto the sofa, taking off his shoes and covering him with a blanket.

In her own bed, with a door closed between them, she lay awake for a long time, trying not to replay it over and over in her mind, but it was impossible. She kept tasting his lips, feeling his tongue against hers, and hearing him whisper, *Tully.*

When she finally fell asleep, it was already well past midnight and morning came much too quickly. At six o'clock, she slammed the silencer on her alarm, brushed her teeth and hair, put on a robe, and hurried into the living room.

Johnny was up, sitting at the kitchen table, drinking coffee. At her entrance, he put the cup down and got up. "Hey," he said, shoving his fingers through his hair.

"Hey."

They stared at each other. She tightened the belt on her terrycloth robe.

He glanced at Tully's door.

"She's not here," Kate said. "She spent last night at Chad's."

"So you put me to bed on the couch and covered me."

"Yep."

He moved toward her. "I was pretty baked last night. I'm sorry. I shouldn't have come by."

She wasn't sure what to say.

"Mularkey," he finally said, "I know I was out of it . . ."

"Yes, you were."

"Did . . . anything happen? I mean, I'd hate to think—"

"Between us? How could it?" she said before he could finish saying how much he would regret a liaison between them. "Don't worry. Nothing happened."

The smile he gave her was so relieved she wanted to cry. "Then I guess I'll see you at work today, huh? And thanks for taking care of me."

"Sure." She crossed her arms. "What are friends for?"

CHAPTER
FOURTEEN

L ate in 1985, Tully got her big break. Assigned to do a live broadcast from Beacon Hill, she was surprised by the flurry of nerves that made her fingers tremble and her voice break, but when it was over, she felt invincible.

She'd been good. Maybe even amazing.

Now she sat upright in the passenger seat of the live truck, a van specifically designed for the technical requirements of a live broadcast, bouncing slightly with enthusiasm. When she closed her eyes, she relived every second of it: the way she'd pushed into the front of the crowd and asked her questions, her flawless wrap-up at the end, shot in front of the well-lit bank, with the red and yellow police lights cutting through the darkening night. Afterward, it had taken forever to load up all the gear and get back on the road, but she didn't care. The longer this night lasted, the better. She hadn't even taken off her earpiece, battery pack, wireless microphone, or walkie-talkie. They were badges of honor.

"Pull over at that 7-Eleven," Johnny said from the back of the van. "I'm thirsty. Mutt, jump out and get a few establishing shots while we're here. It's your turn to make the drink dash, Tully."

Mutt drove into the parking lot. "Cool."

When they parked, Tully collected their money, then got out of the van and headed for the brightly lit mini-mart.

"None of that New Coke for me," Johnny said into her earpiece.

She pulled the walkie-talkie off her belt, switched it on, and said, "You say that to me every time. I'm not an idiot."

Inside the brightly lit store, she looked around for the cooler case, found it, and walked down the medicine aisle.

"Hey, look," she said, talking into the walkie-talkie, "they have Geritol. You need some, Johnny?"

"Smartass," he answered in her earpiece.

Laughing, she reached for the cooler case's handle when she noticed a shadow move across the glass. Turning, she saw a man in a gray ski mask point a gun at the cashier.

"Oh, my God."

"Are you talking about me?" Johnny said. "Because it's about time—"

She fumbled for the volume on the walkie-talkie and switched it off before the robber heard something. She clipped it to her belt and pulled her jacket over it, hiding her battery pack at the same time.

At the register, the robber swung to face her.

"You! Get on the floor." The masked man pointed his gun at the ceiling and pulled the trigger to make his point.

"Tully? What the *hell* is going on?" came Johnny's voice through the earpiece.

Tully fumbled with the earpiece cord, trying to conceal it under her jacket. Then she turned up the volume on the walkie-talkie's outgoing message, hoping like hell Johnny would be able to pick up some sound. "Someone's robbing the store," she whispered as loudly as she dared, depressing the outgoing button.

In her earpiece, she heard Johnny say, "Holy shit. Mutt, call 911 and then start shooting. Tully, keep calm and get the hell to the floor. We can go live with this. Turn on your mic. I'm getting hold of the station. They're on air now. Stan, can you hear me?"

A few seconds later, Johnny said, "Okay, Tully. We're putting this through to Mike. He's on air now with the ten o'clock news. Your audio is going on live. You won't be able to hear him, but he'll hear you."

Tully turned on her mic, whispered into it, "I don't know, Johnny. How do—"

"Your mic is hot, Tully," he said urgently. "You're on live. Go."

The masked man must have heard something; he suddenly swung toward her again, pointing his gun at her. "I told you to get down, damn it."

She just had time to process "I've had enough o' this shit" when he pulled the trigger.

There was a loud crack of sound. Tully barely had time to scream before the bullet hit her in the shoulder and knocked her off her feet. She crashed into the shelves beside her, was vaguely aware of colored boxes crumbling and falling around her. Her head hit the linoleum floor hard.

For a moment, she lay there, gasping, staring up at a wiggling snake of fluorescent lighting.

"Tully?"

It was Johnny's voice, in her ear. She eased slowly—slowly—onto her side. Her shoulder throbbed with pain, but she gritted her teeth and kept moving. Keeping low, she crawled to the end of the aisle, ripped open a box of Kotex, and shoved a pad over her wound, holding it in place. The pressure hurt like hell and made her dizzy.

"Tully? What happened? Talk to me. Are you okay?"

"I'm here," she said. "I just put . . . a dressing on my wound. I think I'm fine."

"Thank God," Johnny said. "You want to turn off your mic?"

"No way."

"Okay. You're live, remember? Keep talking. They can't hear me, but they can hear you. This is your big break, kiddo, and I'm right here to help you. Can you describe the scene?"

She got to a crouch, wincing at the pain, and moved forward slowly, trying to gauge when she could actually look up. "Moments ago, a masked man came into this mini-mart on Beacon Hill, wielding a handgun and demanding money from the clerk. He fired once into the air to make his point and once into me." Her voice was as loud a whisper as she dared.

She heard a noise; it sounded like crying. Keeping low, she came around the corner and found a little boy, huddled against the neon candy aisle.

"Hey," she said, holding out her hand. He took it greedily, squeezing so tightly she couldn't pull away. "Who are you?"

"Gabe. I'm here with my grandpa. Did you see that guy shoot his gun?"

"I did. I'm going to go find your grandpa to make sure he's okay. You stay here. What's your last name, Gabe, and how old are you?"

"Linklater. I'm gonna be seven in July."

"Okay, Gabe Linklater. You stay low and keep quiet. No more crying, okay? Be a big boy."

"I'll try."

She tucked her chin toward her chest and talked quietly into the mic. She wasn't sure what the station could hear, but she just kept talking. "I found seven-year-old Gabe Linklater in the candy aisle. He came in with his grandfather, who I'm looking for now. I can hear the gunman over at the register, threatening the cashier. Tell the police there's only one robber." She turned the corner.

There she found an old man, sitting cross-legged on the floor, holding a box of Purina Dog Chow. "Are you Gabe's grandfather?" she whispered.

"Is he okay?"

"A little scared, but fine. He's in the candy aisle. What did you see?"

"The robber drove up in a blue car. I saw him through the window." He looked at her shoulder. "Maybe you should—"

"I'm going to move in closer." She compressed the pad against her wound again, winced at the pain, and waited for the nausea to pass. This time, her hand came away bloody. Ignoring it, she reported in again to the anchor she couldn't hear. "Apparently, Mike, the lone gunman arrived in a blue car, which should be parked outside in front of one of the windows. I'm happy to say that Gabe's grandfather is also alive and unharmed. Now I'm working my way toward the register. I can hear the gunman yelling that there has to be more money and the cashier saying that he can't open the safe. I can see the flash of lights outside. So the police have arrived. They're shining the lights into the store, telling him to come out with his hands up." She scuttled out in the open for just a second and then crouched behind a life-sized standee of Mary Lou Retton eating Wheaties. "Tell the police he's taken off his mask, Mike. He's blond-haired, with a snake tattoo that wraps around his neck. The gunman is extremely agitated. He's screaming obscenities and waving his gun around. I think—"

Another gunshot rang out. Glass shattered. Seconds later a SWAT team stormed through the glass doors.

"Tully!" It was Johnny, calling out for her.

"I'm okay." She stood up slowly, feeling a wave of pain and nausea at the movement. She saw the live truck through the broken window. Mutt was there with the camera, shooting all of it, but she couldn't see Johnny. "Seattle SWAT has just shot the glass out of the window and come in. They have the robber on the ground. I'll see if I can get close enough to ask them some questions."

She eased around the standee and moved slowly forward. She was near the cereal aisle now, and for a split second she thought about Saturday morning breakfasts at the Mularkeys'. Mrs. M. used to let her have Quisp. Only on the weekends, though.

That was her last conscious thought before she passed out.

The drive to the hospital seemed to last forever. All the way there, through the stop-and-go city traffic, Kate sat in the backseat of the smelly cab and prayed that Tully would be okay. Finally, at just past eleven o'clock, they pulled up out front. She paid the driver and ran into the brightly lit lobby.

Johnny and Mutt were already there, slumped in uncomfortable plastic chairs, looking haggard. At her entrance, Johnny stood.

She ran to him. "I saw the news. What happened?"

"A man shot her in the shoulder and she kept on broadcasting. You should have seen her, Mularkey, she was brilliant. Fearless."

Kate heard the admiration in his voice, saw it in his eyes. Any other time it might have wounded her, that obvious pride; now it pissed her off. "That's why you're in love with her, isn't it? Because she has the guts you don't. So you put her in harm's way and get her shot and you're proud of her *passion*." Her shaking voice drew the last word out like a piece of poisoned taffy. "Screw the heroics. I wasn't talking about the news. I was asking about her life. Have you even asked how she is?"

He looked startled by her outburst. "She's in surgery. She—"

"Katie!"

She heard Chad call out her name and she turned, seeing him run into the lobby. They came together as naturally as wind and rain, clinging to each other.

"How is she?" he whispered against her ear, his voice as fragile as she felt.

She drew back. "In surgery. That's all I know. But she'll be fine. Bullets can't stop a storm."

"She's not as tough as she pretends to be. We both know that, don't we, Kate?"

She swallowed, nodded. In an awkward silence they stood together, bound by the invisible threads of their mutual concern. She saw it in his eyes, as clear as day; he *did* love Tully, and he was scared. "I better go call my mom and dad. They'll want to be here."

She waited for him to respond, but he just remained there, glassy-eyed, his hands flexing into fists at his sides like a gunslinger who might soon have to draw his weapon. With a tired smile, she walked away. As she passed Johnny, she couldn't help but say, "That's how real people help each other through hard times."

At the bank of pay phones, she put in four quarters and dialed home. When her dad answered—thank God it wasn't her mother; Kate would have lost it then—she gave him the news and hung up.

She turned around and Johnny was there, waiting for her. "I'm sorry."

"You should be."

"One of the things about this business, Katie, is that you learn to compartmentalize, to put the story first. It's a hazard of the trade."

"It's always about the story with people like you and Tully." She left him standing there and went to the sofa, where she sat down. Bowing her head, she prayed again.

After a moment she felt him come up beside her. When he didn't say anything, she looked up.

He didn't move, didn't even blink, but she could see how tense he was. He seemed to be holding on to his composure by a rapidly fraying thread. "You're tougher than you look, Mularkey."

"Sometimes." She wanted to say that love gave her strength, especially during a time like this, but she was afraid to even say the word while she was looking at him.

He sat down slowly beside her. "When did you get to know me so well?"

"It's a small office."

"That's not it. No one else knows me like you do." He sighed and leaned back. "I did put her in danger."

"She wouldn't have it any other way," she conceded. "We both know that."

"I know, but . . ."

When he let his sentence trail off, she looked at him. "Do you love her?"

He didn't respond at all, just sat there, leaning back, with his eyes closed.

She couldn't stand it. Now that she'd finally dared to ask the question, she wanted it answered. "Johnny?"

He reached over for her, put an arm around her shoulder, and drew her to him. She sank into the comfort he offered. It felt as natural as breathing being beside him like this, though she knew how dangerous that feeling was.

There, saying nothing more, they sat together through the long, empty hours of the night. Waiting.

Tully came awake slowly, taking stock of her surroundings: white acoustic-tile ceiling, bars of fluorescent lighting, silver rails on her bed, and a tray beside her.

Memories trickled into her consciousness: Beacon Hill. The mini-mart. She remembered the gun being pointed at her. And the pain.

"You'll do anything to get attention, won't you?" Kate stood by the door, wearing a pair of baggy UW sweatpants and an old Greek Week T-shirt. As she approached the bed, tears filled her eyes. She wiped them away impatiently. "Damn. I swore I wouldn't cry."

"Thank God you're here." Tully hit the button on her bed control until she was sitting up.

"Of course I'm here, you idiot. Everyone is here. Chad, Mutt, Mom, Dad. Johnny. He and my dad have been playing cards for hours and talking about the news. Mom has made at least two new afghans. We've been so worried."

"Was I good?"

Kate laughed at that even as tears spilled down her cheeks. "That would be your first question. Johnny said you kicked Jessica Savitch's ass."

"I wonder if *60 Minutes* will want to interview me."

Kate closed the distance between them. "Don't scare me like that again, okay?"

"I'll try not to."

Before Kate could say anything, the door opened and Chad stood in the doorway, holding a pair of Styrofoam coffee cups. "She's awake," he said quietly, putting the cups down on the table beside him.

"She just opened her eyes. Of course, she's more interested in her chances of winning an Emmy than in her recovery." Kate looked down at her friend. "I'll leave you two alone for a minute."

"You won't leave, though?" Tully said.

"I'll come back later, when everyone else has gone home."

"Good," Tully said. "'Cause I need you."

As soon as Kate was gone, Chad moved closer. "I thought I'd lost you."

"I'm fine," she said impatiently. "Did you see the broadcast? What do you think?"

"I think you're not fine, Tully," he said softly. "You're farther from fine than anyone I know, but I love you. And all night I've been thinking about what my life would be without you and I don't like what I see."

"Why would you lose me? I'm right here."

"Marry me, Tully."

She almost laughed, thinking it was a joke; then she saw the fear in his eyes. He really was afraid of losing her. "You mean it," she said, frowning.

"I got offered a job at Vanderbilt in Tennessee. I want you to come with me. You love me, Tully, even if you don't know it. And you need me."

"Of course I need you. Is Tennessee a top forty market?"

His rough face crumpled at that; his smile faded. "I love you," he said again, softly this time and without the kiss to seal the words and give them weight.

The door behind him opened. Mrs. Mularkey stood there, arms akimbo, wearing a cheap jean skirt and a plaid blouse with a Peter Pan collar. She looked like an extra from *Footloose*. "The nurse said five more minutes with visitors and then they're throwing us all out."

Chad bent down and kissed her. It was a beautiful, haunting kiss that somehow managed both to bring them together and highlight how far apart they could be. "I loved you, Tully," he whispered.

Loved? Had he said *loved*? As in past tense? "Chad—"

He turned away from the bed. "She's all yours, Margie."

"Sorry to kick you out," Mrs. Mularkey said.

"Don't worry about it. I think my time was up. Goodbye, Tully." He walked past her and left the room, letting the door bang shut behind him.

"Hey, little girl," Mrs. Mularkey said.

Tully surprised herself by bursting into tears.

Mrs. Mularkey just stroked her hair and let her cry.

"I guess I was really scared."

"Shhh," Mrs. Mularkey said soothingly, drying her tears with a Kleenex. "Of course you were, but we're here now. You're not alone."

Tully cried until the pressure in her chest eased and the tears dried up. Finally, feeling better, she wiped her eyes and tried to smile. "Okay. I'm ready for my lecture now."

Mrs. Mularkey gave her The Look. "Your professor, Tallulah?"

"Ex-professor. That's why I never told you. And you'd say he was too old for me."

"Do you love him?"

"How would I know?"

"You'd know."

Tully stared up at Mrs. M. For once, she felt like the older of them, the one with more experience. The Mularkeys all saw love as a durable, reliable thing, easy to recognize. Tully might be young, but she knew they were wrong. Love could be more fragile than a sparrow's bone. But she wouldn't say it out loud. Instead, all she said was, "Maybe."

Overnight, Tully became a media sensation in Seattle. Newspaperman Emmett Watson took a break from ranting about the Californication of Washington State to write a column about courage under fire and how proud we should be of Tallulah Hart's commitment to the news. Radio station KJR dedicated a whole day of rock 'n' roll songs to the "news chick who used a microphone to stop a robbery," and even *Almost Live,* the local comedy show, aired a segment that made fun of the bumbling robber and showed Tully in a Wonder Woman outfit.

Flowers and balloons poured into her hospital room, many of them signed by people who normally made the news themselves. By Wednesday, she'd had to start donating the beautiful bouquets and arrangements to other patients. The nurses in charge of her learned how to be bodyguards and bouncers in addition to their normal jobs.

"So, you're the genius here. What do I do?" She sat up in bed, going through the pile of pink While You Were Out messages that Kate had brought with her from the office. It was an impressive list of names, but she was having trouble concentrating. Her arm hurt and the sling made even little tasks difficult. Worst of all, she couldn't stop thinking about Chad's out-of-left-field proposal. "I mean: Tennessee. I might as well be in Nebraska."

"For sure."

"How can I get to the top in a place like that? Or maybe that's exactly where I could get to the top fast and get noticed by the networks."

Kate sat at the other end of the bed, her legs stretched out alongside Tully's. "Look. We've been talking about this for, like, an hour. Maybe I'm not the best person to ask, but it seems to me that at some point you've got to at least mention love."

"Your mom said I'd know if I loved him." She looked down at her bare left hand, trying to imagine a diamond ring.

"You said I was supposed to shoot you if you even thought about marriage before thirty." Kate grinned. "You want to amend that?"

"Very funny."

The bedside phone rang. Still staring at her hand, she picked it up quickly, hoping it was Chad. "Hello?"

"Tallulah Hart?"

She sighed, disappointed. "This is she."

"I'm Fred Rorbach. You may remember me . . ."

"Of course I remember you. KILO-TV. I sent you a résumé every week for my entire senior year of high school, and then I sent you tapes in college. How are you?"

"I'm fine, thanks, but I'm at KLUE-TV now, not KILO. I'm running the evening news."

"Congratulations."

"Actually, that's why I'm calling. We're probably not the first station to call you, but we feel certain we'll make the best offer."

He had her full attention now. "Oh, really?"

Kate slid off the bed and stood next to Tully, mouthing: *What's the buzz?*

Tully waved her off. "Tell me about it."

"We want to do whatever it takes to make you part of the KLUE news family. When can you come in to talk to me about this?"

"I'm being discharged right now. How about tomorrow? Ten A.M."

"We'll see you then."

Tully hung up the phone and shrieked. "That was KLUE-TV. They want to hire me!"

"Oh, my gosh," Kate said, jumping up and down. "You're going to be a star. I knew it. I can't wait to—" She stopped in the middle of her sentence; her smile fell.

"What?"

"Chad."

Tully felt something twist deep inside her. She wanted to pretend there was something to think about, a decision to be made, but she knew the truth, and so did Kate.

"You're going to be a huge star," Kate said firmly. "He'll understand."

CHAPTER
FIFTEEN

Kate pretended to focus all of her attention on driving Tully's car, but it wasn't easy. Ever since she'd picked her up from the interview, Tully hadn't stopped talking, spinning out the old little-girl dreams. *We're on our way, Kate. As soon as I get an anchor spot, I'll make sure they hire you as a reporter.*

Kate knew she should put the brakes—finally—on this dual future of theirs. She was tired of following Tully, and besides, she didn't want to quit her job. She had a reason, finally, to stay where she was.

Johnny.

How pathetic was that? He didn't love her, but she couldn't help thinking that maybe with Tully gone, she'd have a chance.

It was ridiculous, and embarrassing, but her dreams centered more on him and less on broadcasting. Not that she could admit that to anyone. Twenty-five-year-old college-educated women were expected to dream of more money and higher positions on the corporate ladder and running the very companies that had refused to hire their mothers. Husbands were to be avoided in the pre-thirty years. There was always time for marriage and children; that was the common refrain. You couldn't give up *you* for *them*.

But what if you wanted *them* more than you wanted a singular, powerful you? No one ever talked about that. Kate knew that Tully would laugh at such thoughts, say Kate was stuck in the fifties. Even her mother would say she was wrong and bring up that weighted word: *regret*. She'd parrot the words that filled the pages of *Ms.* magazine—that being *just* a mother was a waste of talent. Her mother wouldn't even notice how sad she looked as she spoke, as if the life she'd chosen had been for nothing.

"Hey, you missed the turn."

"Oh. Sorry." Kate turned at the next block and circled back, pulling up in front of Chad's house. "I'll wait here. I've got *The Talisman* to finish."

Tully didn't open her door. "He'll understand why I can't marry him yet. He knows how much this means to me."

"He certainly knows," Kate agreed.

"Wish me luck."

"Don't I always?"

Tully got out and walked up to the front door.

Kate opened her paperback and dove into the story. It wasn't until much later that she looked up, noticing it had begun to rain.

Tully should have come back by now, told her to drive on home, that she'd be spending the night with Chad. Kate closed the book and got out of the car. As she walked up the cement path, she had a bad feeling that something was wrong.

She knocked twice, then opened the door.

Tully was in an empty living room, kneeling in front of the fireplace, crying.

Tully handed her a piece of paper that was splotched with tears. "Read it."

Kate sat back on her heels and looked down at the bold black handwriting.

Dear Tully,

I was the one who recommended you to KLUE, so I know all about the job you've come to tell me about, and I'm proud of you, baby. I knew you could do it.

When I took the job at Vanderbilt I knew what it meant for us.

I hoped . . . but I knew.

You want a lot from this world, Tully. Me, I just want you.

It ain't exactly lock-and-key perfect, is it?

Here's what matters: I'll always love you.

Light the world on fire.

It was signed simply, *C.*

"I thought he loved me," Tully said when Kate handed her back the letter.

"It sounds like he does."

"Then why would he leave me?"

Kate looked at her friend, hearing the distant echo of all the times Tully had been abandoned by her mother. "Did you ever tell him you loved him?"

"I couldn't."

"Maybe you don't love him, then."

"Or maybe I do," Tully said, sighing. "It's just so damned hard to believe in."

That was the fundamental difference between them. Kate believed in love with all her heart; unfortunately, she'd fallen in love with a man who didn't know she existed. "What matters now is your career, anyway. There's always time for love and marriage."

"Yeah. When I've made it."

"Yeah."

"Someone will definitely love me then."

"The whole world will love you."

But later, long after Tully had said, "Screw him anyway," and laughed a little desperately, Kate couldn't expel those last words from her mind. Suddenly she was worried.

What if someday the whole world loved Tully and it still wasn't enough?

Tully had forgotten how long and lonely a night could be. For so many years, Chad had been her protection, her port. With him, she'd learned to sleep through the night, breathing peacefully, dreaming only of her bright future, and because he'd loved her, she'd slept well in her own bed, too, on their nights apart, comforted by the knowledge that she could go to him anytime.

She threw the covers back and got out of bed. A quick glance at the alarm clock on her nightstand revealed that it was just past two o'clock in the morning.

As she'd thought: long and lonely.

In the kitchen, she put a pot of water on the stove and stood there, waiting for it to boil.

Maybe she'd made a mistake. Maybe this emptiness she felt right now was love. With the life she'd led it made sense that she would notice the negative of an emotion rather than the positive. But if she did love him, what difference did it make? What would she do? Follow him to Tennessee and settle in university housing and become Mrs. Wiley? How would she be the next Jean Enersen or Jessica Savitch then?

She got a big KVTS cup out of the cupboard and poured her tea, then went to the living room, where she sat on the couch, tucking her feet beneath her, warming her cold hands on the porcelain. Fragrant steam floated upward. She closed her eyes and tried to let her mind clear.

"Can't sleep?"

She glanced up and saw Kate, who stood in front of her bedroom door, wearing the same flannel nightgown she'd worn for years. Tully usually teased her that she looked like one of the Waltons, but tonight she appreciated the familiarity. It was funny how a single garment could remind you of years together—slumber parties and makeovers and breakfasts spent watching Saturday morning cartoons. "I'm sorry if I woke you."

"You walk like an elephant. Is there more tea water?"

"The pot is on the stove."

Kate went into the kitchen and came back with a cup of tea and a box of Screaming Yellow Zonkers. Tossing the box between them, she sat down facing Tully, leaning against the arm of the sofa. "You okay?"

"My shoulder hurts like hell."

"When did you take your last pain pill?"

"I'm overdue."

Kate put down her cup, went into the bathroom, and came out with a Percodan and a glass of water.

Tully took the pill and washed it down.

"Now," Kate said, retaking her seat. "You want to talk about what's really wrong?"

"No."

"Come on, Tully. I know you're thinking about Chad, wondering if you did the right thing."

"This is the problem with forever friends. They know too much."

"Maybe."

"And what do you and I know about love anyway?"

Kate's face took on that sad, semi-judgmental look that Tully hated. It was almost a poor-Tully look. "I know about love," she said quietly. "Maybe not being in love or being loved, but I know about loving someone and how much it can hurt. I think if you really loved Chad, you'd know it, and you'd be in Tennessee right now. At least, if I loved someone, I'd know it."

"Everything is always black and white with you. How do you always know what you want?"

"You know what you want, Tully. You always have."

"So I don't get to fall in love? That's my price for fame and success? Always being alone?"

"Of course you can fall in love. You just have to let yourself. They don't call it falling for nothing."

The words should have comforted Tully; they were intended to be hopeful, she knew that, but just then, she couldn't feel that optimism. Rather, she felt colder and emptier having heard them from Kate. "There's something missing in me," she said quietly. "First my dad saw it. Whoever the hell he is; he must have taken one look at me and run. And let's not even discuss my loving mother. I'm . . . easy to leave. Why is that?"

Kate scooted down the couch, leaned against Tully just the way they used to, all those years ago on the banks of the Pilchuck. The snack box poked into her back and she pulled it out from behind her and tossed it onto the messy, newspaper-strewn coffee table. "There's nothing missing in you, Tully. It's the opposite, in fact. You're *more* than most people. You are really, really special, and if Chad didn't see that—or couldn't wait for you to be ready for him—then he wasn't the guy for you. Maybe that's a normal problem when you're with an older guy. He's ready to land when you're just taking off."

"That's true. I am young. I forgot about that. He should have understood that and waited for me. I mean, if he really loved me, how could he have left me? Could you leave someone you loved?"

"It depends."

"On what?"

"If I thought he was ever going to love me back."

"How long would you wait?"

"A long time."

That made Tully feel better for the first time since she'd read the note from Chad. "You're right. I loved him, but I guess he didn't love me. Not enough anyway."

Kate frowned. "That's not exactly what I said."

"Close enough. We're way too young to get tied down by love. How could I have forgotten that?" She gave Kate a hug. "What would I do without you?"

It wasn't until much later, after a long and sleepless night, as Tully lay in bed watching another day dawn through the window, that her own words came back to her, haunting in their intensity. *Easy to leave.*

CHAPTER
SIXTEEN

From the moment Tully took the new job, Kate found herself watching her friend's life from a distance. Month after month passed with them living separate lives, connected only by place. By the following summer's end, their tiny apartment, once the container of their lives, had become something of a way station. Tully spent twelve hours a day, seven days a week, working. When she wasn't technically at work, she was chasing down leads and following stories, trying like hell to do something—anything—that would put her in front of the camera.

Without Tully, Kate's life lost its shape, and like some overwashed sweater, no amount of positioning or folding could make it right again. Her mother told her repeatedly to snap out of her funk and start dating, have some fun, but how could she date when she had no interest in the guys who had interest in her?

Tully did not suffer from the same malaise. While she still cried about Chad when they were drinking late at night, she had no problem meeting guys and bringing them home. Kate had yet to see the same guy come out of Tully's bedroom twice. According to Tully, that was the plan. She had, or so she said, no intention of falling in love. In retrospect, of course, Tully came to believe that she'd loved Chad desperately, so much so that no other man could measure up. But not enough, as Kate repeatedly pointed out, to call him or move to Tennessee.

To be honest, Kate was growing tired of her friend's drunken reminiscences about the epic love she'd had for Chad.

Kate knew what love was, how it could turn you inside out and dry up your heart. An unreturned love was a bleak and terrible thing. All day long, every day, she moved like a lesser planet in Johnny's orbit, watching him, wanting him, aching for him in lonely silence.

After that long night spent together in the hospital waiting room, Kate had thought there might actually be some hope. She'd felt that a door had opened between them; they'd talked easily, and about important things. But whatever inroads had been made in the bright light of the waiting room had faded with the dawn. She'd never forget the look on his face when he learned that Tully would be fine. It was more than relief.

That was when he'd pulled away from her.

Now finally it was time for her to pull away from him. Time to leave her little-girl fantasies in the sandbox along with other forgotten toys and move on. He didn't love her. Any dreams to the contrary were simply that.

It couldn't go on anymore. That was the decision she'd made at work today, while she stood in the doorway to his office, waiting for him to notice she was there.

As soon as her workday had ended, she'd gone to the newsstand in the Public Market and purchased all the local papers. While Tully was out bar-hopping with her guy du jour, or working late, Kate intended to rechart the course of her life.

Sitting at the kitchen table, with her half-eaten dinner still in cartons around her, she opened the *Seattle Times* and turned to the classified section. There, she saw several interesting choices. Reaching for a pen, she was about to circle one when the door behind her opened.

She turned around and saw Tully in the doorway; her friend wore her dating clothes—an artfully torn sweatshirt that exposed one bare shoulder, jeans tucked into slouchy ankle boots, and a big low-slung belt. Her hair had been puffed up around her face and pulled into a bright banana clip over her left ear. An ornate set of crucifixes hung from around her neck.

Of course she had a guy with her; she was draped all over him.

"Hey, Katie," she said in a slurred I've-already-had-three-margaritas voice. "Look who I ran into."

The guy stepped out from behind the door.

Johnny.

"Hey, Mularkey," he said, smiling. "Tully wants you to come dancing with us."

She closed the newspaper with exaggerated care. "No, thanks."

"Come on, Katie. It'll be like old times," Tully said. "The Three Musketeers."

"I don't think so."

Tully let go of Johnny's hand and half stumbled, half lunged toward her. "Please," she said. "I had a bad day today. I need you."

"Don't," Kate started, but Tully wasn't listening.

"We'll go to Kells."

"Come on, Mularkey," Johnny said, moving toward her. "It'll be fun."

The way he smiled made it impossible to say no, even though she knew it was a bad idea to join them.

"Okay," she said. "I'll get dressed."

She went into her bedroom and put on a sparkly blue dress with shoulder pads and a cinch belt. By the time she came back out of her room, Johnny had Tully pressed up against the wall, with her hands over her head and his hands covering hers, and was kissing her.

"I'm ready," Kate said dully.

Tully wiggled out from underneath Johnny and grinned at her. "Excellent. Let's rock 'n' roll."

Three abreast, their arms linked, they walked out of the apartment and down the empty cobblestone street. At Kells Irish Pub, they found a small empty table close to the dance floor.

The minute Johnny left to get them drinks, Kate looked across the table. "What are you doing with him?"

Tully laughed. "What can I say? We ran into each other after work and had a few drinks. One thing led to another, and . . ." She looked sharply at Kate. "Do you *care* if I sleep with him?"

There it was. The question that mattered. Kate had no doubt that if she bared her soul and told the truth, this horrible night would be over. Tully would shut Johnny down faster than a storm door in a tornado, and she wouldn't tell Johnny why.

But what good would come of that? Kate knew how Johnny felt about Tully, how he'd always felt. He wanted a woman with passion and fire; losing Tully wouldn't make him turn to Kate. And maybe it was time for drastic measures, finally. Kate's hope had endured so much, but this—him sleeping with Tully—would be the end of it.

She lifted her gaze, praying her eyes were dry. "Come on, Tully, you know better than that."

"Are you sure? Do you want—"

"No. But . . . he cares about you, you do know that, right? You could break his heart."

Tully laughed at that. "You Catholic girls worry about everyone, don't you?"

Before Kate could answer, Johnny returned to the table with two margaritas and a bottle of beer. Setting them down, he took Tully's hand and dragged her onto the floor. There, they melted into the crowd, where he took her into his arms and kissed her.

Kate reached for her drink. She had no idea what that kiss meant to Tully, but she knew what it meant to Johnny, and the knowledge seeped through her like some kind of poison.

For the next two hours, she sat with them, drinking heavily, pretending she was having fun. All the while something inside of her was slowly dying.

At some point during the endless, excruciating evening, Tully went to the bathroom and left Johnny and Kate alone. She tried to think of something to say to him, but frankly, she didn't dare make eye contact. With his damp, curling hair and flushed cheeks, he looked so damned sexy it made her chest ache.

"She's really something," he said. Behind him, the band finished their song and turned to their sheet music for inspiration. "I was starting to think it would never happen . . . her and me," he said, sipping his beer, gazing back toward the bathroom, as if he could draw her back by will alone.

"You should be careful," Kate said almost too quietly to be heard. She knew the words, and the warning, would reveal something of her heart, but she couldn't help herself. Johnny might wear the suit of a cynic at work, but at the hospital she'd learned the truth. Inside, where it mattered, he was an idealist. No one bruised as easily as a believer. She should know.

Johnny leaned toward her. "What was that, Mular-key?"

She shook her head. There was no way she could say it again, and besides, Tully was back.

Much later, when she lay in her lonely bedroom, listening to the sound of lovemaking coming from another room, she finally cried.

In the months since their party night at Kells Pub, Kate was not the only one to notice the change in Johnny. As autumn settled into the city and stripped it of color, the mood in the office became sullen and quiet. Mutt kept completely to himself, cleaning and rearranging his equipment, filing negatives in notebooks. Carol, who had been cajoled back to work after Tully's departure, stayed in her own office, with the door shut, barely saying a word to everyone, even when she got her coffee.

No one said a word about Johnny's appearance, but everyone saw that he seemed lately to be simply rolling out of bed and coming to work. His hair was too long and beginning to curl in all kinds of weird ways. He hadn't shaved in days; his beard grew in dark, shadowed patches on his hollowed cheeks, and his clothes often didn't match.

The first few times he'd come to work this way, they'd rallied around him like geese, clucking their worry. Quietly but firmly he'd shut the door to his office, saying he was fine. Mutt had mounted an offensive that began with an offer of pot and ended with, "Whatever, man. I'm here if you wanna talk."

Carol had tried in her own way to swim the invisible moat Johnny had ringed around himself; her attempts failed as utterly as Mutt's.

The only one who didn't try to reach Johnny was

Kate, and she was the only one who knew what the problem was.

Tully.

Just that morning, as they'd been having breakfast, Tully had said, "Johnny keeps calling me. Should I go out with him again?"

Fortunately for Kate, it had turned out to be a rhetorical question.

Tully answered it herself. "No way. I want a relationship like I want a lethal injection. I thought he knew that."

Now Kate sat at her desk, supposedly filing their new insurance information.

She and Johnny were alone in the office for the first time in days. Carol and Mutt were out on assignment.

She got up slowly, walked to his closed office door. It made no sense for her to go to him; certainly if the tables were turned he wouldn't have gone to her, but he was hurting right now, and she couldn't stand that. After a long minute, she knocked.

"Come in."

She opened the door.

He was at his desk, hunched over, writing furiously on a yellow legal pad. Hair fell across his profile; he impatiently tucked it behind his ear and looked up at her. "Yeah, Mularkey?"

She went to the fridge in the corner of his office and got two Henry Weinhard's beers. Opening them, she handed one to him, then sat down on the edge of his cluttered desk. "You look like a man who is drowning," she said simply.

He took the beer. "It shows, huh?"

"It shows."

He glanced at the door. "Are we alone?"

"Mutt and Carol left about ten minutes ago."

Johnny took a long drink of his beer and leaned back in his chair. "She won't return my phone calls."

"I know."

"I don't get it. That night—our night together, I mean—I thought . . ."

"Do you want the truth?"

"I know the truth."

They sat there in silence for a long time, each sipping beer.

"It's fucking awful to want someone you can't have."

And with those few words, Kate knew: she had never had a chance with him. "Yeah, it is." She paused, looking down at him. It was time—past time, really—for her to let go of this dream and move on. "I'm sorry, Johnny," she finally said, getting up from the edge of his desk.

"What are you sorry about?"

She wished she had the nerve to answer him, to tell him how she felt, but some things were better left unspoken.

Seated in an uncomfortable chair in an unfamiliar office, Kate stared out the window at a bare, leafless tree and the gray sky behind it. She wondered idly when the last tangerine-colored leaves had fallen away.

"Well, Ms. Mularkey, you have a very impressive résumé for someone your age. May I ask why you're considering a career change to advertising?"

Kate tried to look relaxed. She'd dressed carefully for today in a plain black wool gabardine suit, with a white blouse and a silk paisley tie tamed into a floppy bow at her throat. She hoped it was a look that said professional through and through. "In my years in TV news I've learned a few things about myself and a few things about the world. The news, as you know, is go-go-go. We're always moving at top speed, just getting the facts and then moving on. I often find myself more interested in what comes after the story than the story itself. I'm better, I believe, at long-range thinking and planning. Details, rather than broad strokes. And I'm a good writer. I'd like to learn more about that, but I won't do it in ten-second sound bites."

"You've given this a lot of thought."

"I have."

The woman across the desk leaned back, studying Kate through a pair of trendy, bead-encrusted glasses. She seemed to like what she saw. "Okay, Ms. Mularkey. I'll discuss this with my partners and we'll get back to you. Just so I know, when could you start work?"

"I'd need to give two-weeks notice and then I'd be ready to go."

"Excellent." The woman stood. "Do you need a parking voucher?"

"No, thank you." Kate shook the woman's hand firmly and left the office.

Outside, Pioneer Square huddled beneath a stern charcoal-hued sky. Cars clogged the narrow, old-fashioned streets, but very few pedestrians walked past the brick-faced buildings. Even the homeless people who usually slept on these park benches and bummed smokes and money from passersby were somewhere else on this cold afternoon.

Kate walked briskly along First Avenue, buttoning up her old college coat as she went. She caught the uptown bus and got off at the stop in front of the office at exactly 3:57.

Surprisingly, the main office room was empty. Kate hung up her coat and tossed her purse and briefcase under her desk, then went around the corner to Johnny's office. "I'm back."

He was on the phone, but he motioned for her to come in. "Come on," he was saying in an exasperated voice, "how am I supposed to help you with that?" He was silent for a moment, frowning. Then, "Fine. But you owe me one." He hung up the phone and smiled at Kate, but it wasn't the old smile, the one that had taken her breath away. She hadn't seen that one since the night with Tully.

"You're wearing a suit," he said. "Don't think I haven't noticed. Around here, that means only two things, and since I know you aren't anchoring the news . . ."

"Mogelgaard and Associates."

"The ad agency? What position did you apply for?"

"Account executive."

"You'd be good at that."

"Thanks, but I don't have the job yet."

"You will."

She waited for him to say more, but he just stared at her, as if something troubled him. No doubt she reminded him of the night with Tully. "Well, I better get back to work."

"Wait. I'm working on this story for Mike Hurtt. I could use some help."

"Sure."

For the next few hours, they sat huddled together at his desk, working and reworking the problematic script. Kate tried to keep her distance from him and told herself never to make eye contact. Both resolutions failed. By the time they finished work, night had fallen outside; the quiet outer offices were banked in shadows.

"I owe you dinner," Johnny said, putting his papers away. "It's almost eight."

"You don't owe me anything," she answered. "I was just doing my job."

He looked at her. "How will I get along without you?"

Months ago, when there was still hope, she would have blushed at a moment like this. Maybe even a week ago she would have. "I'll help you hire someone."

"You think replacing you will be easy?"

She had no answer for that. "I'm going now—"

"I owe you dinner. That's all there is to it. Now get your coat. Please."

"Okay."

They went downstairs and got into his car. In minutes, they were pulling up to a beautiful cedar-shaked houseboat on Lake Union.

"Where are we?" Kate asked.

"My house. Don't worry, I'm not going to make you dinner. I just want to change my clothes. You're all dressed up."

Kate steeled herself against the emotion knocking on her heart. She would not let it in. For too long she'd let herself be pulverized by dreams of a happy ending that wasn't to be. She followed him down the dock and into a house that was surprisingly spacious.

Johnny immediately went to the fireplace, where a fire was already set. He bent down, lighting the newspapers and kindling, and the fire roared to life. Then he turned to her. "Would you like a drink?"

"Rum and Coke?"

"Perfect." He went to the kitchen, poured two drinks, and returned. "Here you go. I'll be right back."

She stood there a moment, uncertain of what to do. She glanced around the living room, noticing how few photographs he had. On the television cabinet there was a single picture of a middle-aged couple, dressed in brightly colored clothing, squatting together in a jungle-looking setting with children clustered around them.

"My parents," Johnny said, coming up behind her. "Myrna and William."

She spun around, feeling as if she'd been caught snooping. "Where do they live?" she said, going to the couch, sitting down. She needed distance between them.

"They were missionaries. They were killed in Uganda by Amin's death squads."

"Where were you?"

"When I was sixteen, they sent me to school in New York. That was the last time I saw them."

"So they were idealists, too."

"What do you mean, 'too'?"

She saw no reason to put it into words, this knowledge she'd gleaned over the years, cobbled together into an image of his life. "It doesn't matter. You were lucky to be raised by people who believed in something."

He stared at her, frowning.

"Is that why you became a war correspondent? To fight in your own way?"

He sighed and shook his head, then walked over to the sofa and sat down beside her. The way he looked at her, as if she were somehow watery or out of focus, made her heartbeat speed up. "How do you do that?"

"What?"

"Know me?"

She smiled, hoping it didn't look as brittle as it felt. "We've worked together a long time."

It was a long moment before he said, "Why are you really quitting, Mularkey?"

She leaned back a little. "Remember when you said it was awful to want something you can't have? I'm never going to be a kick-ass reporter or a first-rate producer. I don't live and breathe the news. I'm tired of not being good enough."

"I said, it was awful to want some*one* you couldn't have."

"Well . . . it's all the same."

"Is it?" He put his drink on the coffee table.

She shifted her weight to face him, pulled her legs up underneath her. "I know about wanting someone."

He looked skeptical. No doubt he was thinking about the times Tully teased her about never dating. "Who?"

She knew she should lie, gloss over the question, but just now, with him so close, she felt a wave of longing that nearly overwhelmed her. God help her, but that door seemed opened again. Though she knew it wasn't, knew it was an illusion, she walked through it anyway. "You."

He drew back; it was obvious that he'd never imagined this. "You never . . ."

"How could I? I know how you feel about Tully."

She waited for him to say something, but he just looked at her. In the silence, she could make up anything. He hadn't said no, hadn't laughed. Maybe that meant something.

For years, she'd expended effort to keep the faucet of her longing for him turned off, but now that he so close, there was no holding back. This was her last chance. "Kiss me, Johnny. Show me I'm wrong to want you."

"I wouldn't want to hurt you. You're a nice girl, and I'm not looking for—"

"What if not kissing you hurts me?"

"Katie . . ."

For once, she wasn't Mularkey. She leaned closer. "Now who's afraid? Kiss me, Johnny."

Just before her lips touched his, she thought she heard him say, "This is a bad idea," but before she could reassure him, he was kissing her back.

It wasn't the first time Kate had been kissed; it wasn't even the first time she'd been kissed by a man she cared about, and yet, absurdly, she started to cry.

He tried to pull away when he noticed her tears, but she wouldn't let him. One moment they were on the sofa, making out like teenagers; the next thing she knew, she was on the floor in front of the fire, naked.

He knelt beside her, still clothed. Shadows concealed

half his body and highlighted the sharp angles and hollows of his face. "Are you sure?"

"That would have been a good question *before* my clothes came off." Smiling, she angled up and began unbuttoning his shirt.

He made a sound that was part desperation, part surrender, and let her undress him. Then he took her in his arms again.

His kisses were different now, harsher, deeper, more erotic. She felt her body responding in a way it never had before; it was as if she became nothing and everything, just a ragged collection of nerve endings. His touch was her torture, her salvation.

Sensations became everything, all that she was, all that she cared about; pain, pleasure, frustration. Even her breathing wasn't her own. She was gasping, choking, crying out for him to stop, and not to stop, and to make it go on and make it go away.

She felt her body arching up, as if the whole of her were reaching for something, needing it with a desperation that made her ache, but she didn't even know what it was.

And then he was inside her, hurting her. She gasped at the suddenness of the pain but made no sound. Instead, she clung to him, kissing him and moving with him until the pain dissolved and there was none of her left; there was only this, the feelings of them where they came together, the sharp, aching need for something more . . .

I love you, she thought, holding him, rising to meet him. The withheld words filled her head, became a soundtrack to the rhythm of their bodies.

"Katie," he cried out, thrusting deep inside her.

Her body exploded, like some star in space, breaking apart, floating away. Time stopped for a moment, then settled slowly back in place.

"Wow," she said, flopping back onto the warm carpet. For the first time in her life, she got what all the hype was about.

He stretched out beside her, his sweat-dampened body tucked in close to hers. Keeping one arm around her, he stared up at the ceiling. Like hers, his breathing was ragged.

"You were a virgin," he said, sounding frighteningly far away.

"Yes," was all she could say.

She rolled onto her side, slid her naked leg over him. "Is it always like that?"

When he turned to her, she saw something in his blue eyes that confused her: fear.

"No, Katie," he said after a long time. "It's not."

Kate woke in Johnny's arms. They both lay on their backs, with the sheets puddled around their hips. She stared up at the planked ceiling, feeling the heavy, unfamiliar weight of his hand between her naked breasts.

Dawn's pale glow slanted through the open window, collecting in a buttery smear on the hardwood floor. The endless slapping of waves against the pilings echoed the slow and steady beat of her heart.

She didn't know what she was supposed to do now, how she was supposed to act. From their first kiss, this had been a magical and unexpected gift. They'd made love three times during the night, the last time only a few hours ago. They'd kissed, they'd made omelettes and eaten in front of the fire, they'd talked about their families and their job and their dreams. Johnny had even told a series of extremely stupid jokes.

What they hadn't talked about was tomorrow, and it was here now, as much a presence between them as the soft sheets and the sound of their breathing.

She was glad she'd waited to make love, even though waiting for the right guy was unfashionable these days. Everything about last night had rocked her world, just as the poets predicted.

But what if Johnny didn't think she was the right girl? He hadn't said he loved her—of course he hadn't—and without those words, how was a woman to put passion in context?

Was she supposed to get dressed and sneak out and pretend it never happened? Or should she go downstairs and make breakfast and pray to God that last night was a beginning and not an ending?

When she felt him stir beside her, she tensed up.

"Morning," he said in a gravelly voice.

She didn't know how to play coy or act indifferent. She'd loved him too long to pretend otherwise. What mattered now was that they didn't just get up and go their separate ways. "Tell me something I don't know about you."

He stroked her upper arm. "Hmmm. I used to be an altar boy."

It was surprisingly easy to picture him like that, a young, skinny boy, with his hair slicked back from his face with water, walking carefully up the aisle. The image made her giggle. "My mother would love you."

"Now tell me something about you."

"I'm a science fiction geekess. *Star Wars, Star Trek, Dune*. I love them all."

"I would have pegged you for a romance reader."

"That, too. Now tell me something that matters. Why did you quit reporting?"

"You always go right for deep water, don't you?" He sighed. "I think you've figured it out anyway. El Salvador. I went down there like some kind of white knight, ready to shine my light on the truth. And then I saw what was happening . . ."

She said nothing, just kissed the curl of his shoulder.

"My folks had hidden so much from me. I thought I was prepared, but you can't be. It's blood and death and body parts being blown off. It's dead kids in the street and boys with machine guns. I got captured . . ." His voice faded away; he cleared his throat and reinforced it. "I don't know why they let me live, but they did. Lucky me. I tucked my tail between my legs and ran home."

"You didn't do anything to be ashamed of."

"I ran like a coward. And I failed. So now you know it all, why I'm in Seattle."

"Do you think it changes how I feel about you?"

It was a moment before he said, "We need to take this slow, Katie."

"I know." She rolled over, so that she was pressed against him. She tried to memorize everything about his face and how he looked first thing in the morning. She saw the shadow of a beard that had grown in their sleeping hours and thought: *Already, changes.*

He tucked the hair behind her ear. "I don't want to hurt you."

She wanted to say simply, *Then don't,* but this wasn't a time for simple answers or pretense. Honesty mattered now. "I'll take the risk of getting hurt if you will," she said evenly.

A hint of a smile played at the edges of his mouth, but she didn't see it in his eyes. In fact, he looked more than a little worried. "I knew you'd be dangerous."

She didn't understand. "Me? You must be joking. No one has ever thought I was dangerous."

"I do."

"Why?"

He didn't answer; instead, he leaned forward just

enough to kiss her. She closed her eyes, waiting for it. She wasn't sure, but maybe, just before his lips touched hers, he said, "Because you're the kind of girl a guy could fall in love with."

He didn't sound particularly happy as he said it.

Outside her front door, Kate paused. Only moments before she'd been flying high, reveling in the night spent in Johnny's arms, but now she was back in the real world, where she'd just slept with a man her best friend had slept with first.

What would Tully say?

She opened the door and went inside. On this gray, rainy morning, the apartment was surprisingly quiet. She tossed her purse on the kitchen table and made herself a cup of tea.

"Where the hell have you been?"

She turned, flinched.

Tully stood there, her hair dripping wet, wearing nothing but a towel. "I almost called the cops last night. Where—You're wearing the suit from yesterday." A slow, knowing smile crept across her face. "Did you spend the night with someone? Oh, my *God,* you did. You're blushing." Tully laughed. "And I thought you were going to die a virgin." She grabbed Kate's arm and dragged her over to the sofa. "Talk."

Kate stared at her best friend, wishing she'd come home after Tully had left for work. This needed thought, planning. Tully could ruin it all with a word, a look. *He's mine,* her friend could say, and what would Kate do?

"Talk," Tully said again, bumping her.

Kate took a deep breath. "I'm in love."

"Whoa there, Penelope Pitstop. Love? After one night?"

It was now or never, and though never sounded good, there was no point in putting off the inevitable. "No," she said. "I've loved him for years."

"Who?"

"Johnny."

"*Our* Johnny?"

Kate refused to let the pronoun wound her. "Yes. Last night—"

"He slept with me, what? A few months ago, then wouldn't stop calling. He's on the rebound, Katie. He can't be in love with you."

Kate tried not to let the word *rebound* find purchase, but it did. "I knew you'd make it about you."

"But . . . he's your boss, for God's sake."

"I quit. I'm starting a job in advertising in two weeks."

"Oh, great. Now you're giving up your career for a guy."

"We both know I'm not good enough to make it at the networks. That's your dream, Tully. It always was." She could see that her friend wanted to argue the point; she saw, too, that any argument would be a lie. "I'm in love with him, Tully," she said finally. "I have been for years."

"Why didn't you tell me?"

"I was scared."

"Of what?"

Katie couldn't answer.

Tully stared at her. In those dark, expressive eyes, she saw everything: fear, worry, and jealousy. "This has disaster written all over it."

"I didn't trust Chad all those years ago, remember? But I put it aside because you needed me to."

"Speaking of love disasters."

"Can you be happy for me?"

Tully stared at her, and though she finally smiled, it wasn't the real thing and both of them knew it. "I'll try."

Rebound. The word, like the image it represented, kept springing into Kate's mind.

He slept with me, what? A few months ago . . .

. . . can't be in love with you . . .

As soon as Tully left the apartment, Kate called in sick to work and crawled into bed. She hadn't been there more than twenty minutes when a knock at the front door startled her out of her thoughts. "Damn it, Tully," she muttered, pulling on her pink velour robe and slipping into her bunny slippers. "Can't you ever remember your key?" She opened the door.

Johnny stood there. "You don't look sick."

"Liar. I look terrible."

He reached forward, untied the belt, and pushed the robe off her shoulders. It fell around her feet in a poufy pink puddle. "A flannel nightgown. How sexy." He closed the door behind them.

She tried not to think about her conversation with Tully—

rebound

can't love you

—but the words chased one another across her mind, tripping every now and then over his: *. . . don't want to hurt you.*

She saw now, suddenly, the danger she'd accepted so naïvely. He could shatter her heart and there was no way to protect herself.

"I thought you'd be happy to see me," he said.

"I told Tully about us."

"Oh. And was there a problem?"

"She thinks I'm a rebound girl."

"She does, does she?"

Kate swallowed hard. "Do you love her?"

"That's what this is about?" He swept her up into his arms, carrying her toward her bedroom as if she weighed nothing at all. Once they were in bed, he began unbuttoning her nightgown, planting kisses along the way. "It doesn't matter," he whispered against her bare skin. "She didn't love me."

She closed her eyes and let him rock her world again, but when it was over and she was curled against him again, the uncertainty returned. She might not be the most experienced girl in the world, but neither was she the most naïve, and there was one thing of which she was sure: it mattered whether Johnny had loved Tully.

It mattered very much.

CHAPTER
SEVENTEEN

Falling in love was everything Kate had dreamed it would be. By the time spring came again, painting the landscape with vibrant color, she and Johnny were an honest-to-God couple; they spent most of their weekends together and as many weeknights as possible. In March she'd brought him home to meet the parents and they'd been ecstatic. A nice Irish Catholic boy with a great career and a good sense of humor who liked to play board games and cards. Dad called him a "good egg" and Mom declared him to be perfect. "Definitely worth waiting for," she'd whispered at the end of the first meeting.

For his part, Johnny had fit into the Mularkey clan as if he'd been born into it. He'd never admitted it, but Kate was certain that he liked being part of a family again after so many solitary years. Although they didn't talk about the future, they enjoyed every minute of the present.

But that was all about to change.

Now she was in bed, staring up at the ceiling. Beside her, Johnny lay sleeping. It was just past four o'clock in the morning and already she'd thrown up twice. There was no point in putting off the inevitable any longer.

She peeled the covers back gently, careful not to wake him, and got out of bed. Barefoot, she crossed the thick pad of carpet and went into his bathroom, closing the door behind her.

Opening her purse, she dug through the clutter and withdrew the package she'd purchased yesterday. Then she opened the package and followed the directions.

Slightly less than two hours later, she had an answer: pink for pregnant.

She stared down at it. Her first ridiculous thought was that for a girl who'd dreamed of becoming a mother, she was damned close to crying.

Johnny wouldn't be happy about this. He was nowhere near ready for fatherhood. He hadn't even said he loved her yet.

She loved him so much, and everything had been so great for the past few months. Still, she couldn't shake the feeling that it was fragile, this relationship of theirs, that the balance was tenuous. A baby could ruin them.

She hid the package and indicator back in her purse—the extraordinary thing mixed in the ordinary debris of her life—and took a long hot shower. By the time she was dressed and ready for work, the alarm was going off. She went to the bed and sat beside him, stroking his hair as he woke up.

He smiled up at her, said, "Hey," sleepily.

She wanted to say simply, *I'm pregnant,* but the admission wouldn't come. Instead, she said, "I've got to go in early today. The Red Robin account."

He looped a hand around the back of her neck and pulled her down for a kiss. When it was over, she meant to ease away. "I love you," she whispered.

He kissed her again. "And that makes me the luckiest guy in the world."

She said goodbye as if this were just another in the string of mornings they'd woken up together, and went to work. In her office, she slammed her door shut and stood there, trying not to cry.

"I'm pregnant," she said to the ad-covered walls.

Now, if only she could say it to Johnny. She ought to be able to say anything to him, wasn't that how love was supposed to work? God knew she loved him enough, maybe even more than enough. She could no longer imagine a life without him. She loved the routine of their lives, the way they often had breakfast together in the kitchen of his houseboat, standing side by side in front of the sink, or the way they sat in bed at night, snuggled together, watching Arsenio Hall. When he kissed her, whether it was a quiet goodnight kiss or a passionate let's-start-something one, her heart always kicked into high gear. They talked all the time, about anything and everything; until today, she would have said there were no words she couldn't say to him.

For most of the day, she moved forward on autopilot, but somewhere around four o'clock, her will failed her. Picking up the phone, she dialed the familiar number and waited impatiently.

"Hello?" Tully said.

"It's me. I'm having a crisis."

"I'll be there in twenty," Tully said without hesitation.

For the first time all day, Kate smiled. Just being with Tully would help; it always had. Fifteen minutes later, she tidied up her already neat desk, grabbed her purse, and left her office.

Outside, the sun was a pale white ball in a washed-out blue sky. A few hardy tourists walked up and down Pioneer Square. Across the street, the homeless people who lived in Occidental Park lay sprawled out on the cobblestoned ground and the ironwork benches, huddled beneath filthy blankets and old sleeping bags. The trees around them were in full bloom.

Kate buttoned up her coat just as Tully pulled up in her brand-new metallic-blue Corvette convertible.

As always, the car made Kate both shake her head and smile. It was so damned . . . phallic, and yet somehow Tully fit it perfectly. Her wool pants and silk blouse were even the same color blue as the car.

Kate hurried around to the passenger side and got in.

"Where do you want to go?"

"Surprise me," Kate answered.

"You got it."

In no time at all, they'd snaked through the downtown traffic, rocketed over the West Seattle Bridge, and arrived at a restaurant on Alki Beach. On this faded spring day the place was empty, and they were seated instantly at a table overlooking the steely Sound.

"Thank God you called," Tully said. "This was the week from hell. They've had me traveling to every armpit town in the state. Last week I interviewed a guy in Cheney who's built a truck that runs on wood. I kid you not. He has a stove in the bed that's the size of an aircraft carrier and it takes a half a cord a week. I could barely see the damn truck through the black smoke it belched out, and he wanted me to report that he'd discovered the future. Tomorrow I'm supposed to go to Lynden to interview some Hutterite chick who won thirty-two blue ribbons at the fair. Yippee. Oh, and last week—"

"I'm pregnant."

Tully's mouth dropped open. "Are you kidding me?"

"Do I look like I'm kidding?"

"Holy shit . . ." Tully leaned back in her seat, looking stunned. "I thought you were on the pill."

"I am. And I've never missed one."

"Pregnant. Wow. What did Johnny say?"

"I haven't told him yet."

"What are you going to do?" The question was heavy, weighed down as it was by the unspoken option.

"I don't know." Kate looked up, met Tully's gaze. "But I know what I'm not going to do."

Tully stared at her for a long time, saying nothing. In those amazingly expressive dark eyes, Kate saw a parade of emotions—disbelief, fear, sadness, worry, and finally, love. "You'll be a great mother, Katie."

She felt the start of tears. It was what she wanted; now, here, for the first time she dared to admit it to herself. That was what a best friend did: hold up a mirror and show you your heart. "He's never said he loved me, Tully."

"Oh. Well . . . You know Johnny."

With that, Kate felt the past rear up between them. She knew Tully was feeling it, too, this thing they tried so hard to forget: their shared knowledge of John Ryan. "You're like him," she finally said. "How will he feel when he finds out?"

"Trapped."

It was exactly what Kate had told herself. "So what do I do?"

"You're asking me? The woman who can't keep a goldfish alive for more than a week?" Tully laughed; it sounded only the tiniest bit bitter. "You go home and tell the man you love that he's going to be a dad."

"You make it sound so easy."

Tully reached across the table, taking her hand. "Trust him, Katie."

She knew it was the best advice she could get. "Thanks."

"Now let's talk about the important shit, like names. You don't have to name her after me. Tallulah sort of sucks. No wonder dopehead picked it, but my middle name is Rose. That's not so bad . . ."

The rest of the afternoon passed in quiet conversation. They avoided talk of the baby and focused on inconsequential things. By the time they'd left the restaurant and driven back to town, Kate's desperation had eased. It wasn't gone, but having a plan of action helped.

When Tully parked behind the houseboat, Kate gave her friend a fierce hug and said goodbye.

Alone in Johnny's house, she changed into a pair of sweats and an old T-shirt, then went into the living room to wait for him.

As she sat there, knees pressed together (too late for that), her hands clasped, she listened to the ordinary sounds of this life she'd grown accustomed to—the slap of the waves on the pilings around her, the squawking of seagulls, the ever-present chug of a motorboat going past. It had never felt quite so fragile before, or so bittersweet. All her life she'd imagined love as a durable thing, a polyester emotion that could handle the wear and tear of everyday action, but now she saw how dangerous that perception was. It lulled you, put you at risk.

Across the room, the lock clicked and the door opened. Johnny smiled when he saw her. "Hey, there. I called you before I left the office. Where were you?"

"I played hooky with Tully."

"Happy hour, huh?" He pulled her up into his arms and kissed her.

She let herself melt against him. When she put her arms around him, she found that she couldn't let go.

She held on so tightly he had to actually pull her away. "Katie?" he said, stepping back enough to look down at her. "What's wrong?"

In the last hour she'd imagined a dozen different ways to tell him, to ease him into the news, but now, standing here in front of him, she saw what a waste all those plans were. This wasn't a gift that could be wrapped in pretty paper and she wasn't the kind of woman who could stay silent.

"I'm pregnant," she said in as firm a voice as she could manage.

He stared at her for an eternity, uncomprehending. "You're what? How did that happen?"

"The normal way, I'm pretty sure."

He let out a long, slow breath and sank to the sofa. "A baby."

"I didn't mean for it to happen." She sat down beside him. "I don't want you to feel trapped."

The smile he gave her was a stranger's, not the one she loved, that crinkled up his eyes and made her smile back. "You know how much I want to just pick up and leave when I'm finally ready. Follow a big story and redeem myself. It's been in my head for so long . . . ever since I screwed up in El Salvador."

She swallowed hard, nodded. Her eyes stung, but she refused to draw attention to her tears by wiping them away. "I know."

He reached out, touched her flat stomach. "But I couldn't just leave anymore, could I?"

"Because of the baby?"

"Because I love you," he said simply.

"I love you, too, but I don't want to—"

He slid off the couch, positioned himself on one knee, and she drew in a sharp breath. "Kathleen Scarlett Mularkey, will you marry me?"

She wanted to say yes, scream it, but she didn't dare. Fear was still too much a part of how she felt. So she had to say instead, "Are you sure, Johnny?"

And then, finally, she saw his smile. "I'm sure."

Kate had taken Tully's advice—of course—and gone for timeless elegance. Her wedding dress was an ivory silk gown with a heavily beaded bodice and an off-the-shoulder neckline. Her hair, carefully lightened in a trio of blonds, had been drawn back from her face and coiled into a Grace Kelly twist. The veil, when she put it on, would float over her face and fall down to her shoulders like a sparkling cloud. For the first time in her life she felt movie-star beautiful. Mom thought so, too; she took one look and started to cry. A few moments ago she had hugged Kate fiercely, kissed her cheek, and gone into the church, leaving Kate and Tully alone for the first time all day.

Now, standing in front of a full-length mirror that captured her fairy-tale reflection, Kate glanced over at Tully, who'd been uncharacteristically quiet on this grand poobah of hair and makeup days. Dressed in the pale pink strapless taffeta bridesmaid's gown, she looked vaguely out of place and fidgety.

"You look like you're gearing up for a funeral instead of a wedding."

Tully looked at her, trying to make a smile look real, but they'd been friends too long to pass each other such counterfeit emotions. "Are you sure about getting married? I mean really sure? There's no—"

"I'm sure."

Tully appeared unconvinced; more than that, she looked afraid. "Good," she said, biting her lower lip, nodding stiffly. "'Cause it's for*ever*."

"You know what else is forever?"

"Dirty diapers."

Kate reached out for Tully's hand, noticing how cold her friend's skin was. How could she convince Tully that this was the Y in their lives, the inevitable separation, but not an abandonment? "Us," she said pointedly. "We'll be friends through jobs and kids and marriages." She grinned. "I'm sure I'll outlast several of your husbands."

"Oh, that's nice." Tully laughed, bumping her shoulder into Kate's. "You think I won't be able to stay married."

Kate leaned against her friend. "I think you'll do whatever you want, Tully. You're such a bright light. Me, I just want Johnny. I love him so much it hurts sometimes."

"How can you say you only want Johnny? You have a great career. Someday you're going to be running that agency. This pregnancy won't throw you off course. These days women can have it all."

Kate smiled. "That's you, Tully. And I'm so proud of you that I can't stand it. Sometimes at Safeway I tell complete strangers that I'm your friend. But I need you to be proud of me, too. No matter what I do. Or don't do."

"I'm always there for you. You know that."

"I know."

They stared at each other, and in that moment, with both of them dressed up like princesses and standing in front of a mirror, they were fourteen years old again, planning the whole of their lives.

Tully finally smiled. This time it was the real thing. "When are you going to tell your mom about the baby?"

"After I'm married." Kate laughed. "I'll confess to God, but I'm not telling my mom till I'm Mrs. Ryan."

For a single, glorious moment, time simply stopped. They were TullyandKate again; girls sharing secrets.

Then the door opened.

"It's time," Dad said. "The church is full. Tully: you're up."

Tully gave Kate a big hug, then hurried out of the dressing room.

Kate stared at her dad in his rented tux, with his newly cut hair, and felt a rolling wave of love for him. Through the doors, they heard the music start up.

"You look beautiful," he said after a moment. His voice was uneven, not his usual sound at all.

She went to him, looked up, remembering a hundred moments in the space of a heartbeat. The way he read her bedtime stories when she was little and tucked spare money in her back pocket when she was older, the way he sang off-key at church.

He touched her chin, tilted her face up. That was when she saw the tears in his eyes. "You'll always be my little girl, Katie Scarlett. Don't you forget that."

"I could never forget it."

Inside, the music changed to "Here Comes the Bride." They linked arms and walked toward the church's double doors. One halting step after another, they made their way down the aisle.

Johnny stood at the altar, waiting for her. When he took her hand in his and smiled down at her, she felt that swelling in her chest again, the sweet knowing that this was the man for her. No matter what else would happen to her in this life, she knew that she was marrying her true love, and that made her one of the lucky ones.

From then on, the night took on the hazy, insubstantial edges of a dream. They stood at the end of the receiving line, kissing friends and relatives and collecting their well-wishes.

The world felt wide open. Anything was possible. Kate found that she couldn't stop smiling or crying.

When the music started—Madonna's "Crazy for You"—Johnny found her in the crowd and reached for her hand.

"Hey, Mrs. Ryan."

Touch me once and you'll know it's true . . .

She moved into the circle of his arms, loving the feel of him against her.

All around them, people stepped back, making room for the newlyweds to dance. She could feel them watching, smiling, saying how romantic the song was and how beautiful the bride looked.

It was the Cinderella-at-the-ball moment that Kate had dreamed of all her life. "I love you," she said.

"You'd better," he whispered, kissing her gently.

When the song ended, the audience burst into applause. Champagne glasses were raised alongside bottles of beer and cocktail glasses; guests shouted, "To the Ryans!"

It wasn't until the tail end of the most magical of nights that Kate's smile first left her. She was at the bar, getting another glass of sparkling cider and talking to her Aunt Georgia, when it happened.

Later, over the years that followed, especially in troubled times, she'd wonder why she looked up at precisely that instant, or why, with all the people in the room, dancing and talking and laughing, she'd had to look up at just that moment to see Johnny, standing all by himself, sipping a beer.

And looking at Tully.

CHAPTER
EIGHTEEN

I don't know who writes these directions, but I don't think the assholes speak English."

Kate smiled and stepped cautiously down the ladder. They were in the downstairs bedroom of the houseboat, readying the nursery. She could tell that Tully was about thirty seconds away from throwing the screwdriver at the freshly painted wall. "Let me look at the sheet."

From her place in the middle of the floor, surrounded by piles of white sticks and boards and groupings of screws and washers, Tully held up the long, wrinkled piece of paper. "Be my guest."

Kate studied the ridiculously complicated directions. "We start with that long flat piece. It dovetails into that piece, see? Then you screw that part on there . . ."

For the next two hours, they sat or stood, hunkered together and hunched over, putting together the most complicated crib of all time.

When it was done, and tucked in place against the

sunshine-yellow wall with the Winnie-the-Pooh border, they stood back and admired it. "What would I do without you, Tully?"

Tully put an arm around her. "Thankfully you'll never have to know. Come on, I'm making margaritas."

"I can't drink. You know that."

Tully grinned at her. "My deepest apologies for that, but you'll notice that I have no bun in the oven. I don't believe I'm within eight hundred miles of a bun, in fact. So, not only can I have a margarita, but after putting together that crib—a job which, I might add, is totally Johnny's and in fact required a scrotum to complete in less than a full day—I deserve a margarita. And you, O fattening one, can have a virgin drink. Ironic, don't you think?"

Arm in arm, they went to the kitchen and made the drinks. All the way there, and back to the living room, where they sat in front of the fire, they talked. About little things, mostly—the speeding ticket Tully got last week, Sean's new girlfriend, the class Mom was taking at the local community college.

"What's it like," Tully asked when Kate got up to put a log on the fire, "being married?"

"Well, it's only been three months, so I'm hardly an expert, but so far it's great." She sat back down and put her feet on the coffee table, resting her hand on the barely noticeable bump of her stomach. "You'll think I'm crazy, but I love the routine, the way we have breakfast together, each reading our own stuff; I love that he's the first person I see every morning and that he kisses me goodnight before I fall asleep." She smiled at Tully. "But I miss sharing a bathroom with you. He's constantly moving my stuff and putting it away—and then he forgets where he put it. How about you, Tully? How's life in our old apartment?"

"Lonely," Tully said, shrugging and smiling as if she didn't care. "I'm getting used to it again."

"You can call anytime, you know."

"And I do." Tully laughed and poured herself a second margarita. "Have you guys figured out the plan for life after my godchild's birth? Will they let you have a few weeks off?"

This was the subject Kate had tried to avoid. She'd known what she wanted to do from the moment Johnny had married her, but she hadn't had the courage to tell Tully. She took a deep breath. "I'm quitting."

"What? Why? They've got you on the best accounts, and you and Johnny are making good money. It's 1987 for crying out loud. You don't have to quit your job to be a mother. You can hire a nanny."

"I don't want someone else raising this baby. At least not until kindergarten."

That got Tully on her feet. "Kindergarten? What is that, eight years?"

Kate smiled at that. "Five."

"But—"

"No buts. It's important to me to be a good mother. You, of all people, should understand how much it matters to a kid."

Tully sat back down. They both knew there was nothing she could really say to that. Tully still bore the scars of a bad mother. "Women can do both, you know. This isn't the fifties."

"My mom went on every field trip I ever took. She was a helper in the classroom every year until I begged her to please stop coming. I didn't take the bus until I was in junior high and still remember talking to my mom on the ride home after school. I want my child to have all that. I can always go back to work later."

"And you think that will be enough for you—carpools and field trips and classroom-volunteering?"

"If it's not, I'll find something else. Come on, it's not like I'm an astronaut." She smiled. "So, tell me about your job. I'll live vicariously through you, so make the stories good."

Tully immediately launched into a hilarious story about her most recent assignment.

Kate leaned back and closed her eyes, listening.

"Kate? Kate?"

She was so lost in her thoughts it took her a moment to realize that Tully was talking to her. She laughed. "Sorry about that. What were you saying?"

"You fell asleep on me. I was telling you about this guy who asked me out and when I looked over, you were out like a light."

"I was not," Kate said quickly, but the truth was that she did feel drowsy, kind of light-headed, too. "I think I need a cup of tea." She stood up and swayed precariously, reaching out for the back of the couch. "Wow, that was—" In the middle of her sentence, she looked at Tully and frowned. "Tully?"

Tully got to her feet so quickly, she knocked over her margarita. She put an arm around Kate, steadying her. "I'm right here."

Something was wrong; a wave of dizziness struck her so hard and suddenly that she stumbled.

"Hold on, honey," Tully said, moving her gently toward the door. "We need to get to a phone."

A phone? Kate shook her head in confusion; her vision blurred. "I don't know what's happening," she mumbled. "Is this a surprise party for me? Is it my birthday?"

Then she looked down at the sofa where she'd been sitting.

A dark pool of blood stained the cushion and splattered the decking at her feet. "Oh, no," she whispered, touching her stomach. She wanted to say more, pray to

God for help, but while she was grasping for words, the world tilted sickeningly and she passed out.

Tully forced them to let her stay in the ambulance. She sat by Kate, saying, "I'm right here," over and over.

Kate was conscious, but barely so. Her skin was as pale as an old overwashed sheet; even her green eyes, usually so bright, were dull and glassy. Tears leaked down her temples.

The ambulance pulled up to the hospital. Tully was pushed aside in their haste to get Kate out of the van and into the bright lights of the hospital. She stood there in the open doorway, watching them take her best friend away. Suddenly she felt the full impact of what was happening.

Women having miscarriages could bleed to death.

"Please, God," she said, wishing for the first time in her life that she really knew how to pray, "don't let me lose her."

She knew it was the wrong prayer, not the one Kate would have wanted. "And take care of her baby."

It felt like throwing diamonds into a river, praying to this God that had never listened to her. "Katie goes to church every Sunday," she reminded Him, just in case.

In the small green hospital room that overlooked the parking lot, Kate lay sleeping. Beside her Mrs. M. sat in a molded plastic chair reading a paperback novel. As always, she moved her lips as she read.

Tully came up beside her, touched her shoulder. "I brought you some coffee." She let her hand rest on Mrs. M.'s shoulder. It had been almost two hours since Kate lost the baby and although Johnny had been called, he was on assignment in Spokane, on the other side of the state.

"I guess it's a blessing it happened early," Tully said.

"Four months isn't early, Tully," Mrs. Mularkey said quietly. "And people who haven't had a miscarriage always say that. It was what Bud said to me. Twice." She looked up. "It never felt like much of a blessing to me. It felt like losing someone I loved. You know about that, don't you?"

"Thanks," she said, squeezing Mrs. Mularkey's shoulder, and then moving closer to the bed. "Now I know what not to say. I just wish I knew what would help."

Kate opened her eyes and saw them.

Mrs. Mularkey stood up, moved next to the bed, standing shoulder to shoulder with Tully.

"Hey," Kate whispered. "How long until Johnny—" At her husband's name, her voice cracked like an egg and she started to shake.

"Did someone say my name?"

Tully spun around.

He stood in the open doorway, carrying a bouquet of flowers that wilted slightly to the left. Everything about him looked disheveled—his unshaven face was a contrasting palette of pale skin and stubbly black beard, his hair was a long, tangled black mess, and his eyes bespoke a bone-deep exhaustion. His Levi's were torn and dirty, his khaki shirt had more wrinkles than an unmade bed. "I hired a private plane. It's going to be a hell of a Visa bill."

He tossed the flowers on a chair and went to his wife. "Hey, baby," he whispered. "I'm sorry it took me so long."

"It was a boy," Katie said, bursting into tears, clinging to him.

Tully heard Johnny start to cry with Kate.

Mrs. Mularkey came up beside her, slipped an arm around her waist.

"He loves her," Tully said slowly. The memory of her night with Johnny had somehow blinded her, trapped her like an insect in the sap of a forgotten time. She'd imagined that Kate was his second choice somehow, his Miss Runner-Up to love.

But this . . . this was no second choice.

Mrs. Mularkey pulled her away from the bed. "Of course he loves her. Come on, let's leave them alone."

They took their coffees and went out into the hall-way, where Mr. M. was sitting on an uncomfortable chair. When he looked up, his eyes were bloodshot. "How is she?"

"Johnny's with her now," Mrs. M. said, touching his shoulder.

For the first time in years, Tully felt like an outsider in this family. "I should be with her."

"Don't you worry, Tully," Mrs. M. said, watching her closely. "She'll always need you."

"But things are different now."

"Of course they are. Katie's married. You girls are on separate paths, but you'll always be best friends."

Separate paths.

There it was; the thing she should have seen but somehow hadn't.

They took turns being with Kate during the next few days. On Thursday, it was Tully's time. She called in sick at work and spent the day with Kate. They played cards and watched television and talked. Most of the time, to be honest, Tully just listened. When it was her turn to answer, she tried to say the right thing, but she was pretty sure she failed more often than not. There was a sadness in her friend now, a graying around the edges that was so foreign Tully felt as if she'd stumbled upon some negative version of their friendship. Nothing she said was quite right.

Finally, around eight o'clock, Kate said, "I know

you'll think I'm crazy, but I'm going to bed. Johnny will
be home in an hour. You can go on home. Go have wild,
crazy sex with that new guy, Ted."

"Todd. And I'm not exactly in a make-out mood.
Then again . . ." Smiling, she helped Kate up the stairs
and got her settled in bed. Then she looked down at her.
"You don't know how much I want to say the right thing
to make you feel better."

"You do. Thanks." Kate closed her eyes.

Tully stood there a moment longer, feeling uncharacteristically impotent. With a sigh, she went back downstairs and started on the dishes. She was drying the last
glass when the door opened quietly, then clicked shut.

Johnny stood there, holding a bouquet of pink roses.
With his newly cropped hair and stonewashed jeans and
his white Adidas tennis shoes with the tongues hanging
out, he looked about twenty years old. In all the years
she'd known him, he'd never looked so sad and ruined.

"Hey," he said, putting the flowers on the coffee table.

"You look like you could use a drink."

"How about an IV drip?" He tried to smile. "She
asleep?"

"Yeah." Tully grabbed a bottle of scotch from the
counter and made him a stiff drink, then she poured
herself a glass of wine and went to him.

"Let's sit on the dock," he said, taking the glass from
her. "I don't want to wake her up."

Tully got her coat and followed him outside. They sat
side by side on the dock, as if they were kids, hanging
their legs out over the black waters of Lake Union.

It was still and peaceful out here. A full moon hung in
the sky, illuminating the rooflines and reflecting in various windows. The distant hum of cars on the bridge was
syncopated by the water slapping against the pilings.

"How are you doing, really?" Tully asked.

"It's Katie I'm worried about."

"I know," she answered, "but I asked about you."

"I've been better." He sipped his drink.

Tully leaned against him. "You're lucky," she said. "She loves you, and when a Mularkey falls in love, it's for life." The minute she said the words, she felt that strange sense of unraveling again. Of loneliness that was somehow just out of view, but moving toward her. For the first time, she wondered what her life could have been like if she'd been like Kate and chosen love. Would she then know how it felt to truly belong somewhere, with someone? She stared out across the water.

"What is it, Tully?"

"I guess I'm jealous of Kate and you."

"You don't want this life."

"What life do I want?"

He put an arm around her. "That's one thing you've always known. You want the networks."

"Does that make me shallow?"

He laughed. "I'm hardly the one to ask. I'll tell you what: I'll start making some calls. Sooner or later we'll find you a network job."

"You'd do that?"

"Of course. But you'll have to be patient. These things take time."

She twisted around and hugged him, whispering, "Thanks, Johnny." He knew her so well. Somehow he'd already known what she'd only just discovered: it was time for her to move on.

As tired as Kate was, she couldn't fall asleep. She lay in bed, staring up at the peaked ceiling, and waited for her husband.

It was in the very core of their relationship, this anxiety of hers. When things went bad, she remembered that she'd been his second choice, and no matter how often she told herself it wasn't true, there was a slim, shadowy version of herself that believed it, worried about it.

It was a destructive neurosis. Like water rising in the Pilchuck River, it eroded everything around it, sent big chunks of earth tumbling away.

Downstairs she heard a sound.

He was home.

"Thank God."

She eased painfully out of bed and went downstairs.

The lights were off. The fire was almost dead; only a faint orange glow remained. At first she thought she'd been wrong, that he wasn't home; then she noticed the shadows on the deck. Two people, sitting side by side, their shoulders touching. Moonlight revealed their shapes, turned them silver against the blackness of the water. She crossed the house quietly, opened the door, and stepped out into the night. A slight breeze ruffled her hair and nightgown.

Tully twisted around, hugged Johnny, whispered something in his ear. His response was muted by the sound of the water slapping the dock. He might have laughed; Kate couldn't be sure.

"You two having a party without me?" She heard the break in her voice and drew in a sharp breath to cover it. In her heart she knew that Johnny hadn't been turning to kiss Tully, but that shadow self of hers wasn't so sure. The ugly, toxic thought was smaller than a drop of blood, yet it poisoned the entire stream.

Johnny was at her side in an instant. He pulled her into his arms and kissed her. When he drew back, she looked around for Tully, but they were alone on the deck.

For the first time in her life, she wished she loved him less. It was dangerous to feel this way; she was like a naked infant exposed to the elements. Fragile and infinitely afraid. He could ruin her someday. Of that she had no doubt.

Tully tried, as the months passed and a new year began, to remain patient and believe in the best, but by the end of May, she'd almost given up hope. Nineteen eighty-eight was not shaping up to be a good year for her. It was early now, on a hot spring day, and she was working hard to enjoy her spot as the replacement anchor. At the end of the broadcast, she headed back to her office.

She was just sitting down at her desk when she heard: "Line two, Tully."

She picked up the phone, pushed the square white button for line two, which immediately lit up. "Tallulah Hart."

"Hello, Ms. Hart. Dick Emerson here. I'm the VP of programming for NBC in New York. I understand you're looking to move up to the networks."

Tully drew in a sharp breath. "I am."

"We have an opening on the early morning show for a general assignment reporter."

"Really?"

"I'll be seeing nearly fifty candidates next week. The competition will be fierce, Ms. Hart."

"So am I, Mr. Emerson."

"That's the kind of ambition I like to hear." She heard the ruffling of papers on a desk. "I'll have my secretary send you a ticket. She'll call to set you up with a place to stay in the city and the date of your interview. All that work for you?"

"Perfectly. Thank you, sir. You won't be disappointed in me."

"Good. I hate to waste my time." He paused. "And tell Johnny Ryan hi from me."

Tully hung up and dialed Kate and Johnny's number. Kate answered immediately. "Hello?"

"I'm in love with your husband."

There was a half second's pause. "Oh, really?"

"He got me an interview at NBC."

"Next week, right?"

"You knew?"

Kate laughed. "Of course I knew. He's been working on it for a long time. And yours truly mailed out the tapes."

"With everything that's on your mind, you were still thinking about me?" Tully said, awed.

"You and me against the world, Tully. Some things never change."

"This time I really am going to light the world on fire," she said, laughing. "I finally have a fucking match."

New York City was everything Tully had dreamed it would be. In her first week here, with her new NBC business cards clutched in her hand, she'd walked down these busy streets like Alice in Wonderland, her face perpetually tilted upward. The endless skyscrapers amazed her, as did the restaurants that never closed, the horse-drawn carriages lined up along the park, and the crowds of black-clad people who filled the streets.

She'd spent two weeks exploring the city, choosing a neighborhood, finding an apartment, learning to navigate the subways. It could have been a lonely time—after all, who wanted to see the sights of a magical city like New York alone? But the truth was, she was so excited about her new job that even being solitary didn't bother her. Besides, in the city that never slept, you were never really alone. There were always people in the streets, even in the darkest hours.

And then there was her job. From the moment she

first walked into the NBC building as a reporter, she was hooked. She woke every morning at two-thirty so that she could be at the studio by four o'clock. Although she didn't technically need to get there so early, she loved to hang around and help out. She studied Jane Pauley's every movement and mannerism.

Tully had been hired as a general assignment reporter, which meant that she was assigned bits and pieces on other people's stories. At some point, if she was lucky, she'd get to cover a story the big correspondents wouldn't touch with a ten-foot pole—the biggest pumpkin in the state of Indiana or something equally relevant. And she couldn't wait. When she'd paid her dues, she'd get a *real* story to cover, and when she finally got that break, she'd knock it out of the park. Truthfully, when she watched people like Pauley and Bryant Gumbel, she knew how far she had to go. They were gods in her eyes, and she spent every spare minute watching how they did their jobs. At home, she analyzed the broadcasts, recording each one on her videotapes and playing and replaying them.

By the fall of 1989, she'd found her groove and begun to feel less like a cub reporter and more like a young woman poised to make her mark. Last month she'd gotten her first honest-to-God assignment: she'd flown to Arkansas to report on a prize-winning hog. The story never actually made it on air, but she'd done her job and done it well, and she'd learned a lot that trip.

She would have learned more in the studio, she was certain, if the morning show hadn't been in such upheaval. There was a war going on on-set and the whole country knew about it. Last week they'd taken a new publicity photo and Deborah Norville, the host of the early, early show, had been on the couch with Jane and Bryant. That one picture sent shockwaves through the network and indeed the country. One article after another appeared; they all claimed that Norville was pushing Pauley out.

Tully kept her head down and stayed away from the gossip. No rumor mill was going to upset her chances for success. Instead, she kept the focus on her job. If she worked harder than anyone else, she might get a replacement shot on the early, early show, *NBC News at Sunrise*. From there, she was sure she'd someday get a crack at the *Today* news nook, and from there, the world would be her oyster.

Eighteen-hour workdays didn't leave her much time for a personal life but she still had Katie, even with all the miles between them. They spoke at least twice a week, and every Sunday Tully called Mrs. M. She told them both stories about work pressures and celebrity sightings and life in Manhattan; they responded with details about the new house Kate and Johnny had bought, the trip Mr. and Mrs. M. had planned for the spring, and—best of all—the news that Kate was pregnant again and it was going well.

The days passed like cards falling from a deck, so fast that sometimes they were just a blur of sound and color. But she was on her way. She knew that, and the knowledge kept her going.

Today, an icy cold late December one, just like each of the countless days that had come before it, she spent fourteen hours at the station, then headed tiredly home.

Down on the street, she was captivated by Rockefeller Center at the holidays. Even in the fading gray of an overcast evening, there were people everywhere, shopping, taking pictures of the giant Christmas tree, ice-skating in the seasonal rink.

She was about ready to start walking home when she saw the sign for the Rainbow Room and thought, *What the hell?* She'd been in New York for more than a year now, and although she had made a lot of acquaintances, she hadn't bothered with dating.

Maybe it was the Christmas decorations, or the way her boss had laughed at her when she asked for the holidays off; she wasn't sure. All she knew was that it was Friday night, only a few nights before Christmas, and she didn't feel like going to her quiet apartment. CNN could wait.

The view from the Rainbow Room was everything she'd heard and more. It was as if she were on the bridge of some great mothership from the future, hovering over the multicolored magnificence of Manhattan at night.

It was still early, so there was plenty of seating at the bar and at the tables. She chose a table by the window, sat down, and ordered a margarita.

She was just about to order another one when the bar started filling up. Men and women from Wall Street and Midtown congregated in groups alongside overdressed tourists, commandeering the tables and chairs, lining up three deep at the bar.

"Do you mind if I join you?"

Tully looked up.

A good-looking blond man in an expensive suit smiled down at her. "I'm tired of elbowing my way through the yuppies to get a drink."

An English accent. She was a sucker for that.

"I'd hate to think you were going thirsty." She kicked the chair across from her out just enough for him to sit down.

"Thank God." He flagged down a waiter, ordered a scotch on the rocks for himself and another margarita for her, then collapsed into the chair. "Bloody meat market in here, isn't it? I'm Grant, by the way."

She liked his smile and gave him one of hers. "Tully."

"No last names. Brilliant. That means we don't have to do that whole exchanging of our life stories. We can just have fun."

The waiter delivered the drinks and left them alone again.

"Cheers," he said, tipping his glass against hers. "The view in here is better than I'd been led to believe." He leaned toward her. "You're beautiful, but I expect you know that."

She'd heard those words all her life. Usually they meant nothing to her, bounced off her like raindrops on a metal roof, but for some reason, in this room, with the holidays approaching, the compliment was exactly what she needed to hear. "How long are you in town for?"

"A week or so. I work for Virgin Entertainment."

"Are you making that up?"

"No, really. It's one of Richard Branson's companies. We're scouting U.S. locations for a Virgin Megastore."

"I shudder to think what you sell."

"How naughty of you. It's a music store, for starters anyway."

She sipped her drink, eyeing him over the salted rim, smiling. Kate was always telling her to get out more, to meet people. Just now, it seemed like damned fine advice. "Is your hotel nearby?"

Part Three

THE NINETIES

I'm Every Woman

it's all in me

CHAPTER
NINETEEN

Just knock me out. I mean it. If they won't give me
drugs, get a baseball bat and hit me. This breathing
is bullsh—aagh!" Kate felt the pain twist through her
insides and tear her apart.

Beside her Johnny was saying "Come on . . . ha ha
ha . . . you can do it. Breathe ha . . . ha . . . like this. Remember our class? Focus. Visualize. D'you want that
statue we—"

She grabbed him by the collar and yanked him
close. "So help me God, if you mention breathing again
I'm going to take you down. I want drugs—"

And it was back, wrenching, cutting, twisting through
her until she cried out. For the first six hours she'd been
pretty good. She'd focused and breathed and kissed her
husband when he leaned down to her and thanked him
when he pressed a cool wet rag to her forehead. In the
second six hours she lost her natural sense of optimism.
The relentless, gnawing pain was like some horrible
creature biting away at her, leaving less and less.

By hour seventeen she was a flat-out, cast-iron bitch.
Even the nurse came and went like Speed Racer.

"Come on, baby, breathe. It's too late for drugs. You heard the doctor. It won't be much longer."

She noticed that even as he tried to soothe her, Johnny didn't get too close. He was like some terrorized soldier in a minefield who'd just seen his best friend blown up. He was afraid to move at all.

"Where's Mom?"

"I think she went down to call Tully again."

Kate tried to concentrate on her breathing, but it didn't help. The pain was rising again, cresting. She clung to the bedrails with sweaty hands. "Get . . . me . . . ice . . . chips!" She screamed the last word. It would have been funny, watching Johnny bolt for the door, if she hadn't felt like that girl swimming alone in *Jaws*.

The door to her private room banged open. "I hear someone is being a total bitch-o-rama in here."

Kate tried to smile, but another contraction was starting. "I don't . . . want . . . to . . . do this anymore."

"Changed your mind? Good timing." Tully moved to the side of the bed.

The pain hit again.

"Scream," Tully said, stroking her forehead.

"I'm . . . supposed to . . . breathe through it."

"Fuck that. Scream."

She did scream then, and it felt good. When the pain subsided again, she laughed weakly. "I take it you're against Lamaze."

"I wouldn't call myself a natural childbirth kind of gal." She looked at Kate's swollen belly and pale, sweaty face. "Of course, this is the best birth control commercial I've ever seen. From now on I'm using three condoms every time." Tully smiled, but her eyes were worried. "Are you okay, really? Should I get the doctor?"

Kate shook her head weakly. "Just talk to me. Distract me."

"I met a guy last month."

"What's his name?"

"That would be your first question. Grant. And before you barrel through some idiotic *Cosmo* girl list of how-well-do-you-know-your-man questions, let me say that I don't know squat about him except that he kisses like a god and screws like a devil."

Another contraction hit. Kate arched up and screamed again. As if from a distance she could hear Tully's voice, feel her stroking her forehead, but the pain was so overwhelming she couldn't do anything except gasp. "*Shit*," she said when it was over. "The next time Johnny comes near me I'm going to smack him."

"You were the one who wanted a baby."

"I'm getting a new best friend. I need someone with a shorter memory."

"I have a short memory. Did I tell you I'm seeing someone? He's perfect for me."

"Why?" Kate said, panting.

"He lives in London. We only see each other on the weekends. For totally rocking sex, I might add."

"Is that why you didn't answer when Mom called?"

"We were in the middle of it, but as soon as we finished, I started packing."

"I'm glad to see you have—oh, shit—priorities." Kate was in the middle of another contraction when the door to her room opened again. The nurse was first, followed by her mother and Johnny. Tully stood back, let everyone get in closer. At some point the nurse checked Kate's cervix and called the doctor in. He bustled into the room, smiling as if he'd run into her at the grocery store, and put on some gloves. Then the stirrups came out and it was time.

"Push," the doctor said in an entirely reasonable, pain-free voice that made Kate want to scratch his eyes out.

She screamed and pushed and cried until as quickly as it had begun, the agony was over.

"A perfect little girl," the doctor said. "Dad, do you want to cut the cord?"

Kate tried to lift herself up, but she was too weak. A few moments later, Johnny was beside her, offering her a tiny pink-wrapped bundle. She took her new daughter in her arms and stared down into her heart-shaped face. She had a wild shock of damp black curls and her mother's pale, pale skin, and the most perfect little lips and mouth Kate had ever seen. The love that burst open inside her was too big to describe. "Hey, Marah Rose," she whispered, taking hold of her daughter's grape-sized fist. "Welcome home, baby girl."

When she looked up at Johnny, he was crying. Leaning down, he kissed her with a butterfly softness. "I love you, Katie."

Never in her life had everything been so right in her world, and she knew that, whatever happened, whatever life had in store for her, she would always remember this single, shining moment as her touch of Heaven.

Tully begged for an additional two days off of work so that she could help Kate get settled in at home. When she'd made the call, it had seemed vital, unquestionably the thing to do.

But now, only a few hours after Kate and Marah had been discharged from the hospital, Tully saw the truth. She was about as useful as a dead microphone. Mrs. Mularkey was like a machine. She fed Kate before she even mentioned she was hungry; she changed the baby's handkerchief-sized diapers like a magician; and she taught Kate how to breast-feed her daughter. Apparently it was not as instinctual a thing as Tully would have thought.

And what was her contribution? When she was lucky, she made Kate laugh. More often than not, though, her best friend just sighed, looking both remarkably in love with her baby and profoundly worn out. Now Kate lay in bed, holding her baby in her arms. "Isn't she beautiful?"

Tully gazed down at the tiny, pink-swaddled bundle. "She sure is."

Kate stroked her daughter's tiny cheek, smiling down at her. "You should go home, Tully. Really. Come back when I'm up and around."

Tully tried not to let her relief show. "They *do* need me at the studio. Things are probably a real mess without me."

Kate smiled knowingly. "I couldn't have done it without you, you know."

"Really?"

"Really. Now kiss your goddaughter and get back to work."

"I'll be back for her baptism." Tully leaned down and kissed Marah's velvety cheek, and then Kate's forehead. By the time she whispered goodbye and made it to the door, Kate seemed to have forgotten all about her.

Downstairs she found Johnny slumped in a chair by the fireplace. His hair was a shaggy, tangled mess, his shirt was on backward, and his socks didn't match. He was drinking a beer at eleven o'clock in the morning.

"You look like hell," she said, sitting down beside him.

"She woke up every hour last night. I slept better in El Salvador." He took a sip. "But she's beautiful, isn't she?"

"Gorgeous."

"Katie wants to move to the suburbs now. She's just realized this house is surrounded by water, so it's off to some cul-de-sac where they have bake sales and play dates." He made a face. "Can you imagine me in Bellevue or Kirkland with all those yuppies?"

The funny thing was, she could. "What about work?"

"I'm going back to work at KILO. Producing political and international segments."

"That doesn't sound like you."

He seemed surprised by that. When he looked at her, she saw a flash of remembrance; she'd reminded him of their past. "I'm thirty-five years old, Tul. With a wife and daughter. Different things are going to have to make me happy now."

She couldn't help noticing that he'd said *going to.* "But you love gonzo journalism. Battlefields and mortar rounds and people shooting at you. We both know you can't give it up forever."

"You only think you know me, Tully. It isn't like we traded secrets."

She remembered suddenly, sharply, what she was supposed to forget. "You tried."

"I tried," he agreed.

"Katie would want you to be happy. You'd kick ass at CNN."

"In Atlanta?" He laughed. "Someday you'll understand."

"You mean when I'm married, with kids?"

"I mean when you fall in love. It changes you."

"Like it's changed you? Someday I'll have a kid and want to write for the *Queen Anne Bee* again, is that it?"

"You'd have to fall in love first, wouldn't you?" The look Johnny gave her then was so understanding, so knowing, she felt skewered by it. She wasn't the only one who was remembering the past.

She got to her feet. "I gotta get back to Manhattan. You know the news. It never sleeps."

Johnny put down his beer and got to his feet, moving toward her. "You do it for me, Tully. Cover the world."

It sounded sad, the way he said it; she didn't know if what she heard was regret for himself or sadness for her.

She forced herself to smile. "I will."

Two weeks after Tully got home from Seattle, a storm dumped snow on Manhattan, stopping the vibrant city in its tracks. For a few hours, at least. The ever-present traffic vanished almost immediately; pristine white snow blanketed the streets and sidewalks, turned Central Park into a winter wonderland.

Still Tully made it to work at four A.M. In her freezing walk-up apartment, with the radiator rattling and ice collecting on her paper-thin antique windows, she dressed in tights, black velour stirrup pants, snow boots, and two sweaters. Covering it all with a navy-blue wool coat and gray mittens, she braved the elements, angling her body against the wind as she made her way up the street. Snow obscured her vision and stung her cheeks. She didn't care; she loved her job so much she'd do anything to get there early.

Inside the lobby, she stamped the snow off her boots, signed in, and went upstairs. Almost instantly she could tell that much of the staff had called in sick. Only a skeleton crew remained.

At her desk, she immediately went to work on the story she'd been assigned yesterday. She was doing research on the spotted owl controversy in the Northwest. Determined to put a local's "spin" on the story, she was busily reading everything she could find— Senate subcommittee reports, environmental findings, economic statistics on logging, the fecundity of old growth forests.

"You're working hard."

Tully looked up sharply. She'd been so lost in her reading that she hadn't heard anyone approach her desk.

And this wasn't just anyone.

Edna Guber, dressed in her signature black gabardine pantsuit, stood there, one hip pushed slightly out, smoking a cigarette. Sharp gray eyes stared out from beneath an Anna Wintour razor cut of blueblack bangs. Edna was famous in the news business, one of those women who'd clawed her way to the top in a time when others of her sex hadn't been able to come in the front door unless they had secretarial skills. Edna—only the single name was ever used or needed—reportedly had a Rolodex filled with the home numbers of everyone from Fidel Castro to Clint Eastwood. There was no interview she couldn't get and nowhere on earth she wouldn't go to find what she wanted.

"Cat got your tongue?" she said, exhaling smoke.

Tully jumped to her feet. "I'm sorry, Edna. Ms. Guber. Ma'am."

"I hate it when people call me ma'am. It makes me feel old. Do you think I'm old?"

"No, m—"

"Good. How did you get here? The cabs and buses are for shit today."

"I walked."

"Name?"

"Tully Hart. Tallulah."

Edna's gaze narrowed. She looked Tully up and down steadily. "Follow me." She spun on her black boot heel and marched down the hallway, toward the office in the corner of the building.

Holy cow.

Tully's heart was pounding. She'd never been invited into this office, never even met Maury Stein, the big kahuna on the morning show.

The office was huge, with two walls of windows.

Falling snow turned everything outside gray and white and eerie. From this vantage point, it felt vaguely like standing inside a snow globe, looking out.

"This one will do," Edna said, cocking her head toward Tully.

Maury looked up from his work. He barely glanced at Tully, then nodded. "Fine."

Edna left the office.

Tully stood there, confused. Then she heard Edna say, "Are you epileptic? Comatose?"

Tully followed her out into the hallway.

"Do you have a pen and paper?"

"Yes."

"I don't need an answer, just do as I ask and do it quickly."

Tully fumbled into her pocket for a pen and found some paper on a nearby desk. "I'm ready."

"First off, I want a detailed report on the upcoming election in Nicaragua. You do know what's going on there?"

"Certainly," she lied.

"I want to know everything about the Sandinistas, Bush's Nicaraguan policy, the blockade, the people who live there. I want to know when Violeta Chamorro lost her virginity. And you've got twelve days to get it done."

"Yes—" She stopped herself from saying ma'am just in time.

Edna came to a stop at Tully's desk. "You've got a passport?"

"Yes. They made me apply for one when they hired me."

"Of course. We'll be leaving on the sixteenth. Before we go—"

"We?"

"Why the hell do you think I'm talking to you? Do you have a problem with this?"

"No. No problem. Thank you. I really—"

"We'll need immunizations; get a doctor here to take care of us and the crew. Then you can start setting up advance interview meetings. Got it?" She looked down at her watch. "It's one o'clock. Brief me on Friday morning at, say, five A.M.?"

"I'll get started right now. And thank you, Edna."

"Don't thank me, Hart. Just do your job—and do it better than anyone else could."

"I'm on it." Tully went to her desk and picked up the phone. Before she'd even finished punching in the number, Edna was gone.

"Hello?" Kate said groggily.

Tully looked at the clock. It was nine. That meant it was six in Seattle. "Oops. I did it again. Sorry."

"Your goddaughter doesn't sleep. She's a freak of nature. Can I call you back in a few hours?"

"Actually, I'm calling to talk to Johnny."

"Johnny?" In the silence that preceded the question, Tully heard a baby start to cry.

"Edna Guber is sending me to Nicaragua. I want to ask him some background questions."

"Just a second." Kate handed the phone off; there was a sound like wax paper being balled up and a flurry of whispers, then Johnny came on the line.

"Hey, Tully, good for you. Edna's a legend."

"This is my big break, Johnny, and I don't want to screw up. I thought I'd start by picking your brain."

"I haven't slept in a month, so I don't know how much good I'll be, but I'll do what I can." He paused. "You know it's dangerous down there. A real powder keg. People are dying."

"You sound worried about me."

"Of course I am. Now, let's start with the relevant

history. In 1960 or '61, the Sandinista National Liberation Front, or FSLN, was founded . . ."

Tully wrote as fast as she could.

For just under two weeks Tully worked her ass off. Eighteen, twenty hours a day she was reading, writing, making phone calls, setting up meetings. In the few rare hours when she wasn't working or trying to sleep, she went to the kind of stores she'd never frequented before—camping stores, military supply outlets, and the like. She bought pocketknives and netted safari hats and hiking boots. Everything and anything she could think of. If they were in the jungle and Edna wanted a damn fly swatter, Tully was going to produce it.

By the time they actually left, she was nervous. At the airport, Edna, wearing a pair of razor-pressed linen pants and a white cotton blouse, took one look at Tully's multipocketed khaki jungle attire and burst out laughing.

For the endless hours of their flights, through Dallas and Mexico City and finally onto a small plane in Managua, Edna fired questions at Tully.

The plane landed in what looked to Tully like a backyard. Men—boys, really—in camouflaged clothing stood on the perimeter, holding rifles. Children came out of the jungle to play in the air kicked up by the propellers. The dichotomy of the image was something Tully knew she'd always remember, but from the moment she got out of the plane until she reboarded the flight for home five days later, she had precious little time to think about imagery.

Edna was a mover.

They hiked through guerrilla-infested jungles, listening to the shrieking of howler monkeys, swatting mosquitoes, and floating up alligator-lined rivers. Sometimes they were blindfolded, sometimes they could see. Deep in the jungle, while Edna taped her interview with *el jefe,* the general in charge, Tully talked to the troops.

The trip opened her eyes to a world she'd never seen before; more than that, it showed her who she was. The fear, the adrenaline rush, the story; it turned her on like nothing ever had before.

Later, when the story was done and she and Edna were back in their hotel in Mexico City sitting on the balcony outside Edna's room, having straight shots of tequila, Tully said, "I can't thank you enough, Edna."

Edna took another straight shot and leaned back in her chair. The night was quiet. It was the first time they hadn't heard gunfire in days.

"You did well, kid."

Tully's pride welled to almost painful proportions. "Thank you. I learned more from you in the past few weeks than I learned in four years of college."

"So, maybe you want to go on my next assignment."

"Anywhere, anytime."

"I'm interviewing Nelson Mandela."

"Count me in."

Edna turned to her. The sticky-looking orange glow from the bare outdoor bulb highlighted her wrinkles, caused bags under her eyes. In this light she looked ten years older than usual, and tired; maybe a little drunk. "Have you got a boyfriend?"

"With my work schedule?" Tully laughed and poured herself another shot. "Hardly."

"Yeah," Edna said. "The story of my life."

"Do you regret it?" Tully asked. If they hadn't been drinking she never would have asked such a personal question, but tequila had blurred the lines between them for just this moment in time. Tully could pretend they were colleagues instead of icon/newbie. "Making this your life, I mean?"